IT SLEEPS IN ME

BY KATHLEEN O'NEAL GEAR AND W. MICHAEL GEAR
FROM TOM DOHERTY ASSOCIATES

THE ANASAZI MYSTERY SERIES

The Visitant

The Summoning God

Bone Walker

THE FIRST NORTH
AMERICANS SERIES

People of the Wolf

People of the Fire

People of the Earth

People of the River

People of the Sea

People of the Lakes

People of the Lightning

People of the Silence

People of the Mist

People of the Masks

People of the Owl

People of the Raven

People of the Moon*

People of the Weeping Eye*

BY KATHLEEN O'NEAL GEAR

Thin Moon and Cold Mist

Sand in the Wind

This Widowed Land

It Sleeps in Me

It Wakes in Me*

It Dreams in Me*

BY W. MICHAEL GEAR

Long Ride Home

Big Horn Legacy

The Morning River

Coyote Summer

The Athena Factor*

OTHER TITLES BY
KATHLEEN O'NEAL GEAR
AND W. MICHAEL GEAR

Dark Inheritance

Raising Abel

*Forthcoming
www.Gear-Gear.com

IT SLEEPS IN ME

Kathleen O'Neal Gear

A TOM DOHERTY ASSOCIATES BOOK

New York

This is a work of fiction. All the characters and events portrayed in this novel are either fictitious or are used fictitiously.

IT SLEEPS IN ME

Map and chapter ornaments by Ellisa Mitchell

A Forge Book
Published by Tom Doherty Associates, LLC
175 Fifth Avenue
New York, NY 10010

www.tor.com

Forge® is a registered trademark of Tom Doherty Associates, LLC.

ISBN 0-765-31415-0
EAN 978-0765-31415-4

First Edition: May 2005

Printed in the United States of America

0 9 8 7 6 5 4 3 2 1

DEDICATION

To Father Gabriel Sagard, a member of the Recollect Order, who arrived in New France in June 1623. Without his detailed descriptions of the erotic healing rituals practiced by the Huron tribe, our understanding of their culture would be greatly diminished. His book, *The Long Journey to the Country of the Hurons,* published in 1632, is still indispensable to any serious study of the aboriginal peoples of North America.

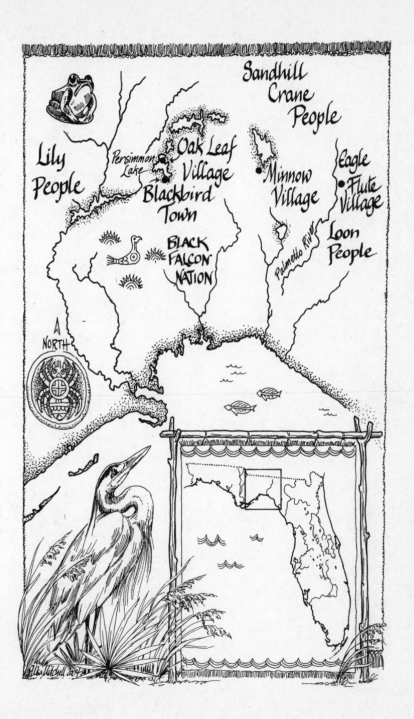

IT SLEEPS IN ME

"*OF COURSE, YOU DON'T UNDERSTAND. HOW COULD ANY SANE person believe that he is still alive inside me? He's my heartbeat, my breathing. He's always there looking out through my eyes. It doesn't matter that he's been dead for . . .*

"*Yes, of course, I know how crazy that sounds. But this obsession isn't recent. It started the moment I met Flint. That first moon was one breathless secret rendezvous after another. His best friend, Skinner; or a slave; or a Trader—anyone who wished to help the young lovers—would bring me a message: 'He's in the charnel house' or 'You'll find him at the canoe landing.' Often it was 'Go to him in the forest near the giant redbay tree . . . the dead oak covered with moss . . . the shell midden near the lake . . .'*

"*I had seen fourteen winters. I loved him desperately. Despite my mother's orders to stay away from Flint, I'd excuse myself from whatever meeting I was attending and run all the way to meet him.*

"*We loved each other in caves and moss-shrouded meadows, even treetops. The massive oak branches provided perfect hideaways where we would lie together for half the day, each exploring the other's body, listening to the oblivious people who walked the trails below. The sensations he brought forth during those lazy days of touching left me feeling as though the gods themselves had taught me what it meant to be human.*

"But it was really Flint who taught me. He . . .

"What? I'm sorry, Strongheart, what did you ask?

". . . No. No, it happened in the first half-moon. He talked me into wearing loose-fitting clothing so that no matter where we happened to be, I could just spread my legs and allow him to enter me.

"Even in the dark moments when his needs shocked me, he managed to make me relax enough that I didn't resist.

"I remember once, ten days after we met, my mother ordered me to attend a council meeting with her. She was grooming me for my eventual rise to the position of high chieftess of the Black Falcon Nation. Just before the meeting, I met Flint in the forest and he tucked an oiled wooden ball inside me, which he tied in place with a strip of woven hanging-moss cloth expertly passed between my legs and knotted around my waist beneath my dress. Throughout the meeting, whenever I moved, it caressed me. By the time the meeting was over, all he had to do was touch me for waves of joy to explode in my body.

"From that day onward, the carefully selected objects he brought into our life evoked a searing sweetness. It didn't take long before I couldn't even use a stone to pound dirty clothing in the lake without thinking of what Flint might . . .

"No. Just the opposite. The euphoria intensified over the fourteen winters we were married, probably because our couplings grew progressively more dangerous. He took me wherever and whenever he pleased. During a midnight ceremonial when hundreds of people filled the plaza, he would push me against a dark wall and take me standing up. Or he'd slip a marble owl inside me before I had to discuss a critical Trade agreement; then he would watch my eyes during the negotiations. More than the owl, it was his expectant gaze that brought me pleasure.

"Don't look at me like that. I'm trying to explain why I had no choice but to kill . . .

"No, I couldn't run away! He would have followed me. He would not leave me alone! And I could not stay away from him.

"I wanted Flint inside me."

SPIDERWEBS, BLOWN FREE BY THE SPRING WIND, DRIFTED across Persimmon Lake and strung glittering filaments on the sunlit oaks that ringed the seven pyramid-shaped mounds of Blackbird Town, but the people who stood in the broad plaza barely noticed. They had their gazes on the field, watching the game play out.

As Chieftess Sora ran down the field after the chunkey stone, she didn't recognize War Chief Skinner, not at first. All she saw was a muscular man brushing webs from his long black hair as he walked through the shadows of the mounds. A massive chert war club hung from his belt, and he had a bow and quiver over his left shoulder. He used his spear as a walking stick.

Warriors unconsciously placed their hands on belted stilettos as Skinner passed by, while women turned to stare admiringly at the stranger dressed in a war chief's raiding garb. His knee-length buckskin shirt was plain, except for the shark's teeth sewn across the front and the red buffalo-wool sash that belted his trim waist.

As she neared the throwing line, Sora called, "Your cast or mine, Wink?"

Fifty paces ahead of her, the chunkey stone, round and about the width of her hand, rolled like the wind.

"My cast!" Matron Wink shouted from her right. When her foot hit the casting line, she launched her spear. Thirty-six winters had passed since Wink's birth. More gray than black shimmered in her long braid, and wrinkles incised laugh lines around her ample mouth. Her given name, the name bestowed upon her at her initiation in the woman's house, was Marsh Wren, but she'd had a bad habit of winking at people. The nickname had stuck like boiled pine pitch.

Wink's spear arced upward, and hundreds of onlookers made awed sounds. One of the opposing headmen reached the casting line and hurled his spear. For a deadly serious game, the rules of chunkey were relatively simple. Whoever hit the stone earned two points. Whoever's spear landed closest to the stone earned one point. They played three games, each to a score of six.

Sora slowed to watch the two spears sailing toward the rolling chunkey stone. Her white dress, made from combed palmetto threads, fluttered in the wind.

Wink stopped beside Sora, breathing hard. Though Sora was four winters younger, they'd been friends since childhood. While Sora had ascended to the chieftainship, Wink had become matron of their Shadow Rock Clan. They both wore elaborately incised copper breastplates that signified their status. Sometimes she thought she knew Wink better than she knew herself. The reverse was certainly true.

"That's Chief Short Tail's spear right behind yours," Sora said.

Wink glanced at Short Tail and Pocket Mouse. Both chiefs wore red knee-length shirts decorated with shells from the far western ocean. "I know. I saw the moron cast."

Sora suppressed a smile. Wink's candor was legendary—though few people appreciated it. In fact, most of the other matrons and chiefs heartily disliked her because of it.

Wink groaned when the heavy stone slowed and fell onto its

side just before the spears landed. Almost at the same time, her spear lodged in the ground a good pace from the stone. Chief Short Tail's spear landed ahead, but it looked to be about the same distance away.

"Oh, gods, what do you think?" Wink asked.

"I can't tell."

As the judges trotted out to see who had scored, Sora's heartbeat quickened and her head grew light. People shoved to the very edge of the field, trying to get a better look.

Sora whispered, "If you scored, we win, and it's over. If not . . ."

"If not"—Wink inhaled a deep breath and let it out in a rush— "we have one more cast to stop a war that will surely destroy our people."

One of the judges, old Club-in-His-Hand, pulled a coil of twine from his belt. The other judge, the young warrior Far Eye, held the end of the cord against the stone while Club-in-His-Hand extended it out to Short Tail's spear point. They made an odd pair. Club-in-His-Hand was short, with a full head of gray hair, while Far Eye was tall and lean. Tattoos covered every part of his body. His long black hair hung to the middle of his back. Wink called him her nephew, though that wasn't technically true. Wink's brother had married a woman from the Water Hickory Clan, and since the Black Falcon Nation traced descent through the female, that meant Far Eye was really Water Hickory Clan, not Shadow Rock Clan. But Wink loved the youth as if he were her own nephew.

Hisses of disapproval went up from Sora's side as the judges lifted the twine for the audience to see the measurement. Short Tail's people remained silent, gazing wide-eyed at Wink's spear. They seemed to be holding their breaths. On the sidelines, warriors marched back and forth, eyes blazing.

As the judges moved to measure Wink's cast, Sora's gaze drifted around Blackbird Town.

Four of the great flat-topped mounds rose directly in front of her. The largest, upon which her magnificent pitched-roof home stood, was six times the height of a man and measured one hundred paces along each side of its square base. To her left, the crystal green water of Persimmon Lake glistened. In the winter, when everyone returned from their summer farming plots, the population of Blackbird Town swelled to almost one thousand. Two hundred small houses, the homes of commoners, ringed the shore. Animal bones covered the roofs like glistening white sticks. The bones of animals caught in snares or traps were never thrown away, but respectfully hung up or placed on the roof of the hunter's house. If this ceremony was not followed, the trap would become useless because the Spirits of the animals would be offended and their relatives would refuse to allow themselves to be caught.

"Please, Skyholder," Wink murmured to the Creator, "for the sake of everyone, let us win."

"What's taking so long?" Sora asked.

Wink shook her head. "The casts are too close; they're measuring each again."

Chunkey games were sacred contests where the players represented the primordial heroes of creation: the forces of Light and Dark, Peace and War, Female and Male. Villages routinely wagered everything they owned on the outcome of a game, but this was more. They played to decide a tie vote in the High Council. If Shadow Rock Clan won, there would be peace. If Water Hickory Clan won, they would be at war tomorrow. The Loon People, east of the Palmetto River, would fall like autumn leaves before the warriors of the Black Falcon Nation.

Wink made a small sound of dismay just before riotous cheers went up from Short Tail's side of the field. The judges held the two lengths of cord side by side, showing that Short Tail's cast had been closer, by a finger's length, to the chunkey stone.

"We're tied. The next point will determine the game."

Wink shook sweat-soaked strands of graying black hair away from her face. "If we're lucky Short Tail's manhood will wither and fall off before he can cast again."

Sora gave her a peeved look. "Don't you think it would be more practical to wish that his hand fell off so he couldn't throw accurately, or maybe his feet, so he couldn't run so fast?"

"Don't be ridiculous. He has the souls of a thirteen-winters-old boy. His manhood is his entire world. Crush it and you crush him." Wink calmly straightened her enormous engraved copper breastplate; it gleamed against her white dress. She gestured to Short Tail. "Look at him. Can you believe that man has seen thirty-eight winters?"

Chief Short Tail jumped up and down like an exultant child, slapping his teammate, Chief Pocket Mouse, on the shoulder and whooping, much to the delight of his kinspeople, who roared their approval.

Club-in-His-Hand trotted down the field with the chunkey stone and gave it to Sora.

"It's your roll, Chieftess," he whispered, and desperately glanced around. "Make it a good one."

Sora nodded. "I'd better."

She and Wink marched back to the starting line. While she waited for Short Tail and Pocket Mouse to finish their conversations, Sora's gaze moved down the field to where her husband, Rockfish, stood. He had been very handsome in his early days, tall and slender, with a triangular face and large dark eyes, but he'd started to show his sixty winters. His hair had gone completely gray, and his muscles had evaporated. Though he still carried out most of his husbandly duties—hunting, fishing, and advising her on clan matters—each was becoming more difficult for him. Their marriage had been one of convenience, an alliance of political advantage, but she genuinely cared for him. It worried her that his strength had begun to fail.

They'd married three winters ago, after her first husband, Flint, set her belongings outside the door and headed home to his mother's village. The divorce had disgraced Sora. Not only that, she'd loved Flint. She'd made a fool of herself, running after him, begging him to return. When he'd shoved her away, she'd been consumed by despair. The simplest daily tasks, getting dressed or making a pot of tea, had seemed overwhelming.

In response, her mother, High Chieftess Yellow Cypress, had selected Rockfish as her new husband. He came from a renowned family of Traders who lived far to the north. It had been a good choice—for both of them. Since her mother had no sons, and the chieftainship was a hereditary position destined for the eldest daughter, Sora had become chieftess after her mother's death two winters ago. What she gave Rockfish in prestige, he gave her in Trade goods. The day of their joining, a flotilla of canoes had appeared, filled to overflowing with rare cherts and mica, silver nuggets, pounded sheets of copper—and the Trade goods had never stopped coming. Every moon, another flotilla arrived. Rockfish was much older than she and knew things about people that she did not. Sora was often deeply grateful for his wisdom. He negotiated the Trade, making certain his people received things they needed: extraordinary seashells, dried holly leaves to make sacred Black Drink, fine fabrics, and exquisite pottery. He also made sure Sora's people received precious goods in abundance, which Sora generously distributed among the other Black Falcon villages. They loved her for it.

Rockfish was talking with a burly man who held a painted box clutched to his chest like a precious child.

She knew him, didn't she? From this distance, she wasn't certain.

Short Tail trotted up and grinned like a wolf with a rabbit in sight. His clan, the Water Hickory Clan, had a bloodthirsty reputation. Only last winter, they'd voted to make war upon the Conch Shell People to gain control of their oyster beds. The winter before, they'd wanted to kill the Red Owl People to capture their buffalo-hunting territory. Sora and Wink had blocked them by convincing the other clans it was far more profitable to work out Trade agreements than to lose their own warriors in a war over lands they could occupy but never fully possess.

"Are you ready, Chieftess?" Short Tail asked. His two front teeth had rotted out long ago, and the few remaining were well on their way.

"I'm ready."

He chuckled. "Good. Before you make your throw, I want you to know that tomorrow, when I lead our warriors east, yours will be out in front."

Sora gave him a suspicious look. "You will honor them by allowing them to lead the War Walk?"

"Of course." He grinned. "Why should my people die when your young men and women can block the first barrage of arrows?"

Wink's eyes narrowed. "I wish you'd try impersonating a dung beetle, Short Tail; it would take a lot less effort than pretending you're a chief."

His grin sagged. "Roll the stone, Sora, so we can settle this before I'm forced to strangle your matron."

In the shadows of the mounds, huge pots of stew bubbled on the cook fires. After dried venison was pounded up, it was dipped in salty moss that had been dissolved in water, then boiled in hickory nut milk. To make the milk, they mixed the nut meats with water and pounded until they became a delicious white liquid. The stew would be served with cornbread fried in bear grease and dipped in plum oil, which they obtained by boiling acorns, then skimming off the sweet oil and mixing it with dried plums. The rich scents mingled together and wafted across the playing field.

Sora took a deep breath and whispered, "Are you ready, Wink?"

"Yes. Let's see whom the gods favor."

Sora bowled the chunkey stone down the field. The four players broke after it, racing to the throw line. Cries rose from the crowd: some people cheering, others hissing.

As Sora ran, she caught the glances of the men standing at the edge of the field. She ran lightly for a woman who had seen thirty-two winters. Their gazes followed the curves of her tall body as though they could see through her thin white dress.

She gave Rockfish a worried smile as she raced past. He nodded his encouragement, silently telling her he didn't doubt for an instant that she would win. The burly man who stood beside him watched as though his very life depended upon the next cast. . . . *Grown Bear. That's War Chief Grown Bear from the Loon Nation.*

Short Tail and Pocket Mouse reached the throw line first. Pocket Mouse cast.

The crowd roared and pointed as the spear arced heavenward with the white chert point glittering in the morning sunlight.

When they were five paces from the line, Wink called, "You or me?"

Sora mouthed a prayer and shouted, "Me!"

She quickly judged the speed and direction of the rolling stone, then, as her foot hit the line, cast her spear. Its flight was birdlike, sailing up into the cloud-strewn blue sky like a falcon.

Pocket Mouse's spear plunged down first. It landed ahead of the still-rolling stone.

"Oh, gods," Wink groaned. "The stone is headed for his spear. At this speed, the stone will fall right beside it."

Sora's heart hammered against her ribs. She slowed, waiting for the final moment . . .

And felt eyes upon her—not the ordinary watchfulness of the crowd, but something more intense. She glanced down the field, past the multitude of onlookers, and directly at Skinner. His expression was calm, intimately knowing, as though her darkest secrets belonged to him.

Terror shot through her veins.

What's he doing here? I haven't seen him in three winters, and suddenly . . .

Wild cheers went up from the crowd, and she jerked her gaze back in time to see her spear bounce off the chunkey stone and cartwheel away across the grass.

"You did it, Sora! *You did it!* We win! There will be peace!" Wink hugged her hard enough to drive the air from her lungs. People rushed onto the field, shouting and embracing each other, the judges, the opposing villagers—anyone who didn't shove them away.

Rockfish trotted up and, in her ear, said, "You just saved lives. I'm proud of you."

"It was a lucky cast."

"Luck is the tool of the gods, my wife."

Shoulder-length gray hair fell around his wrinkled face as he bent to plant a gentle kiss on her mouth. At moments like this, when relief overpowered everything else, she felt genuinely contented.

"The Loon People secretly sent a representative to watch the game today," Rockfish whispered. "He wishes to speak with you."

"I thought that looked like War Chief Grown Bear. He's brave—I'll say that for him. Tell him I'll speak with him this evening."

"I will."

Rockfish backed away to allow Short Tail and his clan matron, Wood Fern, to approach. Wood Fern, almost blind, held tight to her chief's arm. She had seen fifty-seven winters. A white fuzz of hair covered her old head. She wore a buckskin cape adorned with iridescent circlets of conch shell and had a buzzard feather prominently displayed in her hair. She was known to be a great Healer. Buzzard feathers were worn only by those who could Heal arrow wounds. Fox skins were worn by those who could Heal snake bites; and if a person wore an owl feather, it meant he or she could trail an enemy in the dark.

"You won today, Chieftess Sora." Wood Fern cocked her head in a birdlike fashion, not quite certain where Sora stood. "But our problem remains. The Loon People are holding eleven men, women, and children from Oak Leaf Village hostage, and Chief Blue Bow says he will kill them if we try to reach our root grounds again without paying him the ridiculous amount of rare Trade goods he demands."

Sora stared into the woman's white-filmed eyes for a long moment before saying, "I hear you, Wood Fern. Truly, I do. Chief Blue

Bow assured me only six days ago when I was in Eagle Flute Village that they genuinely want peace. He claims the hostages are being well treated. I promise I will work out an agreement that is fair to both sides. I just need more time."

"Time will not change the greedy nature of the Loon People. You'll see. In the end, your negotiations will fail. Killing the Loon People will be the only way we can rescue our hostages and maintain what is ours."

Sora mopped her sweating brow with her sleeve. "Your nephew, Walking Bird, died to save me from a Loon arrow, Wood Fern. I have not forgotten his sacrifice. If our negotiations fail, my warriors will proudly lead yours into battle."

Short Tail gave her a grim smile. "I would speak with you about that. I think it is wise to discuss a war plan now, in case your efforts fail and we must act quickly to defend ourselves."

"I will be happy to discuss it—providing you help me lay out a peace plan first."

He inclined his head. "Of course."

As more and more people crowded around her, asking questions, Sora felt as though she were being crushed. She glanced down the field and said, "Please excuse me. I must see to the feast preparations."

She trotted away with people slapping her back and calling congratulations.

"Excellent cast, Matron!" Wink's son, Long Fin, yelled.

"I'm fortunate, that's all," she responded.

"You mean *we* are fortunate! To have you as our chieftess!"

She smiled. To the north, in front of her, stood the seventh mound they'd built for War Chief Feather Dancer. Their newfound wealth had allowed them to undertake several mound-building projects, both here and elsewhere in Black Falcon country, that would have been impossible before her marriage to Rockfish. The effect had been stunning. As they raised mounds so that Grandmother Earth could touch fingertips with her daughter, Mother

Sun, their lives improved dramatically. It was as though the gods saw and approved. The bright fabrics, elaborate copper and silver jewelry, and glittering shell beads were testaments to a time of riches beyond anyone's belief.

Unfortunately, the other thing that came with wealth was power. She was always uncomfortable when people lifted their chins and got that superior glint in their eyes. It seemed that half her life was spent in the vain attempt to dampen the fires of conceit.

Her favorite slave, Iron Hawk, stirred the main stew pot with a long wooden paddle. The rich scents of venison and moss filled the air. "Is everything ready?" Sora asked.

Young, with a heart-shaped face, Iron Hawk nodded. "Yes, Chieftess, just as you requested. We may have to ladle out smaller portions, but I think we can feed everyone who came for the game."

"If you have any doubts, come to me immediately," Sora instructed. "I will order the storerooms opened. We cannot afford to offend any of our honored guests."

"I will, Chieftess."

People had gathered in knots around the plaza, talking, laughing, and complaining. A few foul glances were cast her way. Most of them came from warriors who'd been looking forward to killing Loon People. Sora shook her head. The cool flower-scented air invited breathing. The redbud trees were in full bloom. She took deep breaths and let them out slowly. For a brief time, there would be peace. But who could say how long it would last? Wood Fern was right about the Loon People; as the wealth of the Black Falcon Nation increased, the Loon Council demanded more and more for crossing what they considered to be "their lands," despite the fact that those gathering grounds had belonged to the Black Falcon People for generations. Negotiations would be neither easy, nor swift.

When she turned to head back to Rockfish, she saw War Chief Skinner walking purposefully to Wink, and blood surged so powerfully in her veins, it left her feeling shaky.

Skinner bowed and pulled Wink aside to speak with her alone. As he talked, Wink's expression grew increasingly more severe.

Sora had known Skinner for more than half her life. His gestures, the way he stood, told her he brought dire news.

The edges of her vision suddenly went gray and sparkling, and an irrational fear possessed her.

"No," she whispered, "not now . . ."

As she had a thousand times, she spread her legs to brace herself and forced deep breaths into her lungs. All of her life an evil Spirit had tormented her. As her vision went black, it came like a hot glittering torrent, and before she knew it she was lying flat on the ground with her limbs jerking and her teeth gnashing.

She'd been seven winters old when the first attack came. She didn't remember it. She never remembered them. She just awoke in a sea of people with a mouthful of blood, feeling exhausted.

Throughout her childhood, her mother had forced her to see one Healer after another. She'd eaten so many Spirit Plants even the smell of them now sickened her. Nothing had worked. As she aged, the Spirit seemed to come less often, but she still felt him watching her. He was always there, right behind her eyes, ready to leap for her throat when she least suspected it. Stress seemed to bring on his attacks.

During her tenth winter, she'd named him: *the Midnight Fox*.

Sora hurried toward the Chieftess' Mound.

As she started up the steps, she couldn't help it. She looked back.

Skinner studied her with a predator's unwavering attention. He'd been her first husband's best friend—and a good friend to her. She hadn't seen him in three winters. He wouldn't be here if it weren't absolutely necessary.

Obviously trying to make certain she didn't miss it, he stepped several paces away from Wink, out into the open, and placed two fingers beneath his nostrils in an eerie gesture of respect. Then he tipped his head slightly to the left. His smile turned seductive, as though they shared something she'd forgotten.

Sora hesitated, startled. Deep inside her, long-dead fear fluttered its wings.

She rushed up the steps. Every time her foot landed, she had the overwhelming urge to run. She made it to the top of the mound before her knees started to tremble.

Torches burned on either side of her doorway, the flames waffling in the cool breeze that swept the lake. Made of logs set into a rectangular wall trench, the house measured fifty paces wide by seventy long. The roof soared four times the height of a man. On the very peak, an enormous wooden carving of Black Falcon perched. His seashell eyes glistened in the morning light.

"Sora?" Rockfish called as he trotted up the steps behind her. "Are you all right?"

She sucked in a breath. "Yes, fine."

The polished mica birds encircling the collar of his blue shirt flashed as he walked toward her. "I saw you run up the steps. You didn't look well."

She made an airy gesture. "It's the upcoming negotiations with the Loon People."

"We'll work it out," he assured her. "We always do. It does no good to worry."

She forced a smile. "You are, of course, right."

Rockfish tenderly pushed away the sweat-soaked ends of black hair that stuck to her forehead. He looked like he wanted to say something, but didn't know how.

Sora said, "What's wrong?"

"I don't know. Something. Matron Wink asked me to tell you that she'll be up as soon as she can get away. She's talking with the Loon People's representative, but she needs to speak with you immediately."

As though Sora's souls knew something her heart couldn't stand to believe, she stiffened. "What did War Chief Skinner want?"

"I couldn't hear. He spoke with Wink in private."

"A man I haven't seen in three winters walks into our town and goes straight to the high matron? Something terrible has happened, hasn't it?"

Rockfish put his hands on her shoulders and looked into her eyes. "He is the war chief of Oak Leaf Village, Sora. Perhaps he came at Chief Fireberry's request, to offer his warriors. It is their people who are being held hostage by Blue Bow. They stand to lose more than we do from a war with the Loon People."

She gently pushed away from him. "Fireberry would never offer us his warriors. Skinner would vote against it."

"Why do you say that? Do you know him so well?"

Rockfish folded his arms defensively, and Sora knew she'd just swung out over a precipice on a very thin rope.

"No," she lied, "not really. He was a friend to my first husband. But I hear things, Rockfish. He is reputed to hate us. Not only that, Oak Leaf Village is Water Hickory Clan. If he did come to offer warriors, he should have gone to his own clan matron, Wood Fern, first. Instead, he went directly to Wink."

Rockfish gave her a look like he suspected she'd been Skinner's lover. He wouldn't ask, of course. If she'd slept with Skinner while married to Flint, it would have been a crime worthy of banishment. Commoners could dally with each other's spouses and people just glared and hissed behind their hands. If adultery occurred among the elite clans, it was dealt with swiftly and harshly. Because leadership was hereditary, matrons had to *know* a child's parentage.

Rockfish turned away and gazed out over Blackbird Town. As Mother Sun rose into the bright blue sky, her light streamed through the trees like shafts of honey. A dappled patchwork of shadow and light played over the mounds.

"Well, it's probably nothing. War chiefs visit other towns and villages routinely, just to keep up with what's happening."

Relieved that he'd let it drop, she said, "Yes, I'm sure he . . ."

Her words died when Wink trotted to the top of the steps and marched forward with a dark expression. She took Sora's arm in a strong grip and pulled her toward the door to the house. "Please come with me."

When Rockfish started to follow, Wink called, "I must speak with her alone, Rockfish."

"Of course."

Sora glanced over her shoulder before she ducked beneath the door curtain. Her husband stood quietly. The slant of sunlight cast shadows over every wrinkle in his elderly face. It made him look a thousand winters old.

2

THE CHIEFTESS' HOUSE WAS DIVIDED INTO SIX CHAMBERS—
the four small chambers in the rear were for personal use, and two
large chambers in the front served as community rooms. The council chamber stood on the left, and a temple dedicated to the worship
of Black Falcon stood on the right.

As Sora turned left and ducked into the council chamber, she
swung around. "Tell me, Wink. Quickly. Why is Skinner here?"

The lines around Wink's mouth deepened as her lips pressed
into a tight white line. Twenty torches stood in holders around the
walls, casting a molten amber gleam over her round face. The gray
and black wisps of hair that fringed her cheeks glistened.

"I'm sorry it took me so long to get here. I knew you'd seen him
speaking with me. The Loon People sent a war chief to watch our
game today. I had to talk with him first. He is very eager to—"

"I want to know about Skinner."

Wink inhaled a breath, as though to fortify herself. Through a
taut exhalation, she said, "He came to tell us that Flint is dead."

"D-dead?"

She slowly eased down to the log bench that ran the length of the wall. Deep inside her a voice cried, *No, no, he can't be!*

She could barely hear her own voice ask, "How? What happened?"

Wink sat down beside her and took her hand. Her dress looked startlingly white against the dark wood of the bench. "I know you never stopped loving him. I'm sorry. I don't know much about it. Skinner said he found Flint in the forest three days ago. He wants to tell you the details himself."

She felt like she'd been punched in the belly. She couldn't seem to get any air. "Was he wounded?"

"No, I don't think so. Skinner found him just moments before he died. Apparently, Flint asked Skinner to deliver a message to you. It was his last request."

Sora watched the flickering patterns of torchlight dance over the cold hearth in the middle of the chamber. Fragments of burned logs lay in a gray bed of ash. The rich, pungent smell from the burning cedar bark torches filled her nostrils. Flint smiled at her across a gulf of time, and her heart ached for him.

He had always been a lightning bolt waiting to strike. Everyone who'd ever stood beside him had felt it. In a crowd of hundreds of warriors, he'd stood a head taller, but what attracted the eye was his face. Stunningly handsome, his expressions were always fierce and bright. In the fourteen winters they'd been married, he'd killed three men for looking at her the "wrong way." Each had been a fair fight, but that didn't change the fact that three men she'd barely known had died for nothing.

"Tell Skinner I need some time. He'll understand. I will see him tonight."

Wink rose to her feet. "What about the Loon war chief?"

A bone-numbing grief was spreading through her. She had to force herself to think. "I'll meet him before I meet with Skinner. Is that acceptable?"

"Yes, of course. Do you want me to be there?"

"No." She shook her head emphatically. "Whatever he wants, it will give us more time if I tell him I have to discuss his words with you."

Wink placed a hand on Sora's hair and petted it lightly. "You should bathe and rest before you see anyone. I'll send in two slaves to help you. I suspect tonight is going to be more difficult than you imagine."

Sora looked up, and their gazes met. Wink squinted slightly, as though wishing she hadn't said that.

"Why? Did Skinner say something else? Something you haven't told me?"

Wink let her hand fall to her side. At the end, just before Flint divorced her, Sora had spent nearly every day in Wink's lodge, desperate to talk to her, to beg her old friend for advice.

"There was just . . . one other thing." Wink's gaze lifted, and for a time, she seemed to be examining the brain-cakes that hung from the massive roof beams. They resembled festoons of dark green bread. Their people preserved brains, for use in tanning hides, by smearing the brains on hanging moss, molding them into round cakes, poking a hole in the center, and hanging them up to dry on hooks or sticks. Buffalo brains were considered the most valuable, but bear and deer were also used. When the time came, they would pull down the cakes, soak them in water until the liquid was thick and soapy, then add their hides to the pot.

Wink looked back at Sora, and her fists clenched. "Skinner said Flint died with his own hands wrapped around his throat. He had to pry Flint's fingers loose to hear his last words."

3

LIKE A LOST SOUL, SORA WANDERED THE SMALL CHAMBER at the very rear of the Chieftess' House. This had been her childhood bedchamber. She touched precious belongings, things she'd long ago put away so that she could concentrate on adult concerns. A fire burned in the hearth, fluttering yellow light over the pinepole walls.

The chamber measured five paces square. Baskets and pots nestled in every corner. Buffalo hides draped the sleeping bench along the wall to her right. The fine brown hairs glittered as though sprinkled with gold dust, but she knew her slaves had really scattered the hides with the powdered flesh of a fisher bird. The musky odor of the bird's flesh drove away moths and insects.

She reached up to the shelf of cornhusk dolls that stood to her right, near the doorway, and touched them gently. They were old and brittle—their painted faces had faded; the red mouths were now a pale pink, the black eyes gray—but she didn't care. Her father had made them for her. She'd barely seen seven winters when he died.

She let her hand fall and looked around. After she'd bathed and eaten a meal of roasted turkey and persimmon bread smeared with palm fruit jam, she'd come here to open the big basket on the rear wall. She'd been wandering the chamber for a full finger of time, but hadn't faced the basket yet.

Her clean white dress rustled as she forced herself to cross the room. She'd unbraided her long hair and left it to fall loosely about her shoulders. In the firelight, the thick waves shone blue-black.

The basket stood eight hands tall and about four wide. It was a beautiful thing, red zigzagging lines alternated with black from lip to base.

She knew each item by heart, even where it rested in the carefully organized basket; the brilliant headdresses, breastplates, anklets, bracelets . . . The basket was more a shrine than a collection of belongings.

Light-headed, she pulled the lid off.

On the left, a shell pendant that had belonged to her dead sister rested beside one of her mother's copper bracelets. On the right sat a wooden box filled with pendants. Magnificent copper falcons, an elaborate Birdman, images of antlered snakes, and deer with human faces stared up at her. Flint had been a master copper worker. People had come from a moon's walk in every direction to Trade for his artistry. He'd breathed his soul into each one, giving them life. Over the past three winters, Sora had frequently heard them calling to her—but she'd never been able to face them.

She murmured, "I'm sorry I've been away so long."

As she lifted the Birdman pendant, its soft voice whispered to her. It still had a leather thong attached. She tied it around her neck and said, "I'm here now. Everything is well. Don't worry."

The size of her hand, it hung to the middle of her chest. The copper had tarnished, but the image was crystal clear; a Dancing Birdman strutted forward, one foot lifted, a war club in his right hand and the severed head of his enemy hanging in his left. He was half man and half falcon. His human face had a bird's beak, and behind his human arms, gloriously detailed wings spread.

Flint's warmth and strength seemed to ooze from the pendant. It filtered through her chest, and she could almost feel his powerful arms around her.

"What happened, Flint?" she whispered in a tortured voice. The old heartache spread across her chest, as painful today as it had been three winters ago.

When he'd divorced her, she'd placed every precious thing he'd ever given her in this basket and never opened it again. Wink had asked her many times why she didn't give them away, or ritually bury them.

She should have.

She just couldn't.

Having them close was like having a part of him close.

The copper was cold beneath her fingers as she traced the lines of Birdman's wings. She often dreamt of coupling gently with Flint. Other times, when the responsibilities of being chieftess seemed overwhelming, those dreams became fits of dark passion.

In the past few days the dreams had intensified dramatically, waking her three or four times a night. It was as though her souls were desperate to be with him. Perhaps the gods had been trying to warn her. . . .

She clutched the pendant as tears welled hotly in her eyes.

Her people believed that each person had three souls: The soul that traveled to the afterlife lived in a person's reflection. Another soul lived in the shadow, and still another could be seen in the pupils of the eyes. It was the shadow-soul that walked in dreams.

One of the Black Falcon People's greatest fears was that they might catch a dying person's last breath, because it was at that moment that the reflection-soul and shadow-soul slipped out together. If a living person was too close to the breath, the shadow-soul, desperately looking for a new home, could shoot like an arrow into the living person.

The shadow-soul was terrifying because at death all the evil leached from the other souls and settled in the shadow-soul. That left the reflection-soul pure, fit to live among the blessed ancestors, while the cleansed eye-soul stayed with the body forever.

A sudden chill went through her. Wink said he'd died three days ago. The evil shadow-soul wandered the earth for seven days after the body died, then it usually disintegrated into the air. Unless it sneaked into a new body.

What had she been loving in her dreams?

She stared wide-eyed at the wall.

. . . The *"fingers beneath the nostrils" greeting.*

Before they'd married, they'd had to undergo six moons of preparation: sanctification rituals, ceremonies of purification and absolution. In the midst of one of the rituals, surrounded by dozens of priests and family members, the greeting had been his way of saying, *Meet me at my canoe. I'll show you how much I love you.*

"No," she murmured to reassure herself. "No, it's not possible." A swallow went down her dry throat. "Is it?"

Footsteps sounded in the long hallway outside.

Rockfish called, "Sora? The Loon war chief is here to see you."

"Please tell him I'll meet him in the council chamber."

"He's already there," he said, but he didn't walk away. She could hear him shifting outside; his woven palmetto moccasins scraped the hard-packed dirt floor.

Sora slid the lid back onto the basket and turned. As she walked toward the door curtain, Rockfish asked, "Do you want me to go with you?"

She ducked out into the torchlit hall and stared up into his soft brown eyes. He looked like a faithful sad-eyed old warrior. Clean gray hair fell around his triangular face.

"Of course I do. What would I do without you?"

He smiled and slipped his arm through hers. As they walked down the hall, he explained, "War Chief Grown Bear comes as an emissary of Chief Blue Bow."

She frowned. "I just spoke with him. Why would he send me a messenger so soon after our meeting?"

"Apparently he has important news."

She heard the subtle irony in his voice. "What do you mean?"

"Grown Bear brings a gift."

"What gift?"

"He wouldn't show it to me. Which means he's either afraid I'll deem it too paltry to grant him an audience with you, or he wants to see your face when he reveals it."

Sora looked at him from the corner of her eye. "My belly already aches."

She ducked beneath the door curtain into the council chamber and walked toward the central hearth, where the war chief sat. He leaped to his feet and rushed to meet her.

Sora held out her hands, palms up, and he put his hands atop them, then knelt before her.

"Chieftess Sora, I thank you for agreeing to meet with me."

The central fire hearth blazed. Those flames, along with the torches that lined the walls, gave the air a honeyed glow.

"I am here to serve, War Chief. How may I help?"

Grown Bear was a burly man, of medium height. One long slash of white scar tissue cut across his cheek and nose, making it appear that his face had two halves. He wore a rabbit-fur shoulder cape over a knee-length yellow shirt. No jewelry adorned his wrists or ears, but elaborate geometric tattoos decorated his face.

He mouthed the ritual greeting, "I pray our ancestors fill the room around us, to help guide us."

"As do I."

He stood up. "I must tell you I was deeply grateful you won the game today. I knew I'd have to run for my life if you lost."

Sora smiled faintly. "Even if we'd lost, I would have given you safe passage back to your people, Grown Bear. We are not monsters." Sora gestured to the six log benches around the fire hearth. "Please, let's sit down and talk."

He bowed and followed as she led the way to the benches. Rock-fish sat to her left, as was appropriate for the chieftess' husband.

Grown Bear sat to her right and pulled a small, elaborately painted box from his belt pouch. He clutched it to his chest.

"My husband tells me you bring important news."

"Yes, Chieftess." He nervously wet his lips. "Chief Blue Bow apologizes for the recent confusion surrounding the death of your warrior Walking Bird and asks that you hear and consider his proposal. He offers this gift as a token of his loyalty."

"Loyalty?" she said suspiciously. "He's holding eleven of our people hostage. He told me he was going to roast them over a slow fire if I didn't—"

"He regrets his words, Chieftess. Truly, he wishes nothing but friendship with the Black Falcon People. He says if you agree to his proposal, he will return your hostages and you may cross his lands freely, without payment, at any time."

He held out the box, and Sora took it.

"And in return, he wants . . . what?" she asked.

Grown Bear gestured to the box. "Please?"

She opened it.

Rockfish sucked in a surprised breath.

The enormous brooch was stunning. Rimmed in pure glittering gold, it was the size of her two hands put together and made of a green translucent stone that very few people among the Black Falcon Nation had ever seen before.

"I feel like I'm looking into the richest depths of the Lake Spirit's heart. What is it?" Rockfish asked in awe as he touched the stone.

Grown Bear smiled. "It's called jade. My clan paddled south along the coastline for sixteen days until we encountered the Scarlet Macaw People. They are idolaters, with strange ways, but we Traded with them." He pointed at the brooch. "They consider this common. They're willing to fill our canoes with this stone."

Sora glanced at Rockfish. His natural Trader's instinct had been roused. His brown eyes sparkled, but it was with a mixture of suspicion and desire.

Rockfish cocked his head. "Who is *'our'*?"

Grown Bear leaned forward. "Whoever has the strength to help the Scarlet Macaw People defeat the owners of the quarry."

Rockfish sank back on the bench and exhaled hard. She could see thoughts roiling behind his eyes.

Sora said, "I'm not sure I understand. Are you asking us to commit warriors to a war party you will lead south to attack the enemies of the Scarlet Macaw People?"

"Yes. Chief Blue Bow promises you half of everything we obtain."

Rockfish gestured derisively to the brooch. "Is this paltry jade all they have to offer? Or will they Trade more valuable things?"

Eagerly, Grown Bear answered, "You won't believe the things they have to Trade. Their fabrics are extraordinary. And the things they do with gold! I could barely believe my eyes! If you will commit just two hundred warriors—"

"It sounds like a fool's errand to me." Sora halted the discussion with a wave of her hand.

For more than six thousand winters, the Black Falcon People had ruled this land. Though she had never seen a Scarlet Macaw Trader, her grandmother had told her many stories about them, none of them complimentary. More than three centuries ago, they'd begun showing up with beautiful pieces of jewelry—gifts for the clan matrons. *"Every time one of the Scarlet Macaw People leaves our village we find things missing. They steal our sacred art and stories! They rob our graves! They are idolaters who want nothing more than to strip us bare before they send their warriors in to conquer us! Have no dealings with them. Ever. They are not trustworthy."*

"Don't be hasty, my wife," Rockfish said. "We should at least consider this proposal."

"I will discuss this with Matron Wink, of course," she answered, "but I think it's too risky. Blue Bow is asking us first to ally with him; then he wishes us to send our warriors south to ally with another people, to fight against a foe whose numbers and strength we do not know, to gain access to a quarry that may not even exist."

Her delicate black brows plunged down over her pointed nose.

She handed the box back to Grown Bear. "If it was solely my decision I would refuse to send our young men and women into such a situation. However, I would tell Chief Blue Bow that if he obtained the stone, we would be happy to pay him well for it."

"But, Chieftess, we cannot obtain it alone! We are a small clan. We need help." Grown Bear held the box to his heart, as though afraid to set it down for fear it would suddenly disappear.

Sora studied his half-panicked expression. "What do the other Loon chiefs think of this? Have they agreed to send warriors to fight this unknown people?"

Grown Bear swallowed hard. "They will not help, Chieftess. Like you, they are timid."

Rockfish lunged to his feet with fire in his eyes, ready to lash out at the insult. Sora gripped his arm and silently ordered him to sit back down, which he did, but reluctantly.

In a deadly quiet voice, Rockfish ordered, "Do not ever insult our chieftess again—not if you wish to make it home alive."

Grown Bear lifted both hands, as though in surrender. "I meant no disrespect. It's just that this is such a rare opportunity! If we do not act now, the Scarlet Macaw People will find other allies, and we will be cut out of the Trade. We have to—"

"If the Scarlet Macaw People had other allies," Sora asked, "do you think they would have approached you, an utter stranger?"

That seemed to stop him. For several moments, he blinked and stared at her like a duck hit in the head with a rock. "We spent seven days with them, Chieftess. We became great friends. That's why they decided to include us—"

"Yes, I'm sure," she said coldly. "I give you my oath that if the Scarlet Macaw warriors survive the battle with the people who control the quarry, we'll discuss this again."

"But their chances of success are much greater with us than without us, wouldn't you agree?"

Sora gracefully rose to her feet. Grown Bear's eyes followed her; he resembled a man awaiting execution. "As I said, I will speak with Matron Wink about this, but you should not get your hopes up."

Grown Bear blurted "Thank you!" and fell to his knees to kiss her sandals, a gesture of deepest respect. "Blessed be the name of the Black Falcon People. You will not regret this. I—"

"I just said we would discuss it, Grown Bear. That's all. Will you wait for our matron's answer? Or shall we send a runner to Chief Blue Bow when we've decided?"

"I will wait, Chieftess. How long do you think the discussions will take?"

"I will speak with Matron Wink tomorrow morning. You should have your answer by tomorrow night."

He looked up at her with shining eyes and handed her the box again. "I will wait, Chieftess, but please, you must take this back. Chief Blue Bow said it was yours regardless of your decision."

She gestured to Rockfish. "Deliver it to Matron Wink, and tell her I would like to speak with her about it in the morning."

Rockfish took it and clutched it against his chest like he could barely stand the thought of letting it out of his sight. "Of course, my wife."

"Also, make certain that War Chief Grown Bear has a comfortable chamber to sleep in," Sora added.

"I'll put him in one of the chambers we reserve for visiting chiefs." Rockfish gestured to Grown Bear. "If you will follow me."

Grown Bear rose, nodded to Sora, and followed Rockfish out of the council chamber.

When they were gone, Sora rubbed her arms. Despite the blazing fire, she felt icy inside and out. Cold pimples dotted her skin. She paced before the fire. The watery way alliances ebbed and flowed never ceased to astound her.

Voices rose in the hallway. Rockfish lifted the curtain, his elderly face pinched with concern.

"My wife, War Chief Skinner is here to see you. May I send him in? Or do you wish some time?"

Her stomach muscles clenched. She wanted this over with. "Send him in."

Rockfish dropped the curtain, and Sora watched the leather sway in the firelight.

An eternity seemed to pass before Skinner ducked under the curtain. Tall and broad-shouldered, he had a strong, sun-bronzed face. A waist-length black braid draped his right shoulder. The style accented his high, arching cheekbones and straight nose, and made his deeply set black eyes look cavernous. Dressed in his knee-length buckskin shirt, he looked like a war god.

They stood in silence, staring at each other, and images of Flint flashed across her souls: she and Flint running through head-high palmettos, laughing; lying together in the cool spring grass, the air filled with the sweet voices of songbirds. Loving each other . . .

As she looked at Skinner, she realized for the first time that there truly would be no tomorrows. The sodden lump in her throat was the death of a precious dream.

Did I hurt you so much, Flint? Was it my fault?

"Sora," he said in a deep voice. "I'm so sorry."

She closed her eyes. Just hearing his voice made her hurt.

"Come and sit down with me, Skinner. I want to know everything."

He crossed the floor, took her arm like the old friend he was, and slowly guided her to the bench.

After they'd seated themselves before the fire, he released her and bent forward to prop his forearms on his knees. In an intimate voice, he asked, "Are you well?"

"I was. Until I saw you this morning. I knew something was wrong or you wouldn't have come."

"Forgive me. I wanted to, a long time ago. Things were just difficult. You know as well as I that he would have seen it as a betrayal."

"Yes. You were always more his friend than mine."

He bowed his head, but made no effort to deny it. When they'd been boys, Skinner and Flint had been inseparable. Though Skinner was a winter older, Flint had been the stronger, more dominant personality. Skinner had always reminded her of a wide-eyed puppy trailing behind a larger-than-life dog, trying very hard to keep up.

He said, "I needed to see you, Sora. You and I . . . we were the only people in the world he trusted. The only people who understood him."

She wrapped her arms over her chest, hugging herself, and her white dress fell around her sandals in firelit folds. His eyes took in her every movement, as though comparing it to his memories.

She had tears in her voice when she said, "After Wink told me, I realized that for three winters I've been secretly hoping he'd come back to me, that someday he would realize he needed me as much as I needed him. Now . . ." Emotion welled in her throat, cutting off her next words.

Skinner took her hand. His fingers felt large and calloused. "And what would you have done? Divorced Rockfish and taken him back?"

"Probably," she granted without hesitation. "Even though it would have ruined me and devastated my clan."

He cocked his head in disbelief. "Your clan would have declared you Outcast, given all your belongings to Rockfish's people, and replaced you as chieftess with . . ." He tilted his head thoughtfully. "Who would they choose to replace you?"

"Long Fin. Since I've yet to bear a child, Wink's eldest son is next in line. He's a little young, sixteen winters, but someday he'll make a good chief."

"So you would have given up everything to have Flint back in your life? Even knowing his jealousies, his wild passions?"

She sighed. "He was the one great love of my life. Which certainly proves I'm a fool."

"No," he said tenderly. "It proves you loved him. As I did."

For a long time, the soot-colored shadows of the empty council chamber wavered about them in gray veils, silken and quiet but for the distant voices of people in the plaza. The mossy fragrance of the lake and the acrid odor of smoke clung to him. He sat so still that one of his eyes caught the firelight and held it like a polished copper mirror. The only thing that moved was the steady rise and fall of his chest.

"I know a person never really gets over a love like the two of you had, but I was really praying you would find someone who drove his memory away, or even better, obliterated it."

"Tell me what happened," she pleaded. "Was he wounded in a raid? Did he die of a fever?"

His bushy black brows drew together, and he frowned down at her hand. "He wasn't wounded; he hadn't been ill in moons. I wish I knew what killed him. I don't."

She shook her head. "I don't understand."

He looked up, and his eyes were deep and dark, like bottomless wells. "A Trader brought news that our fishing grounds were being raided by the barbarian Lily People. We didn't really believe it, but we went out to scout the perimeter of our territory. Just the two of us. I woke up in the middle of the night and discovered his blankets empty."

He paused to massage his brow, as though his head throbbed. "I found him dying in the forest two hundred paces from camp. I carried him to Minnow Village as quickly as I could. It was the closest help."

From the despair in his voice, it obviously hadn't been quickly enough.

"Skinner, Wink told me you found him . . ." She couldn't say the words.

"Yes." He nodded. "I had to pry his fingers from his throat to hear what he was trying to tell me. It was about you, Sora. He wanted you desperately. I think you're the only woman he ever truly wanted."

An eerie sensation filtered through her. His voice sounded different, intimate in a way she did not want to think about. It was probably the stress of the situation, but she drew her hand away from him and laced her fingers in her lap.

He smiled his understanding, and for one stunning heartbeat, it looked so much like Flint's smile that she flushed. Even in the fire-light, he saw the mottled red spread across her cheeks. His eyes flared with interest.

Defensively, she said, "I don't know what's taking Rockfish so long. Delivering a box to Wink and showing Grown Bear to his chamber should have taken a few hundred breaths. When he returns, I'll have him show you to a chamber where you can rest."

He boldly reached out and lifted her Birdman pendant from between her breasts. "I'm surprised you kept this. I thought you would have ritually buried it."

Sora looked down. Against his large hand, the pendant appeared small and fragile. "Part of him lives in this pendant. I couldn't let go of it."

He released the pendant and clasped her hand again. When she tried to pull it back, his grip tightened until it was painful.

"Please, Skinner, let go."

For several moments, he rubbed his thumbs over her skin as though drowning in the feel of her. "You know, don't you?"

"What are you talking about?"

"Flint's last words. You know what they were, don't you?"

She stared at him with her mouth open and her heart racing. Fear uncoiled like a snake in her chest. "How c-could I?"

Just as he leaned toward her, to kiss her, Rockfish's steps padded down the hall. Sora shoved away and called, "Rockfish!"

He hurried into the chamber. Obviously, her tone had alerted him. He stared at Skinner with hostile intent. "What is it?"

Breathing hard, Sora said, "Please show Fl–Skinner to one of our guest chambers."

The slip shocked her. *Dear gods, I almost called him Flint.* His death must have shaken her reflection-soul loose.

"Certainly." Rockfish not-so-subtly held the door curtain aside.

Skinner smiled at her, rose to his feet, and walked across the floor. Before he ducked beneath the curtain, he turned, mouthed the words *"I still love you,"* and strode past Rockfish.

Her last glimpse of him was a swirl of buckskin shirt and a flash of red legging.

Rockfish asked, "Is everything all right?"

"Yes." She waved a hand dismissively. More softly, she said, "We'll discuss it later."

He nodded and hurried to escort Skinner to the guest chambers.

As the sound of their steps receded, she realized she hadn't taken a breath in a long time. Her lungs were starving. She sucked in air, and the world took on a strange shimmer, as though sparks floated all around her.

She walked out of the council chamber and across the hall to the temple. At the opposite end of the large chamber, the Eternal Fire burned. Behind it, three steps led up to a raised altar where an enormous wooden carving of Black Falcon hung on the wall. Though he stood upright, twice the height of a man, Black Falcon looked dead. He had his eyes closed, his head tilted to the right, his wings folded over his belly. In the Beginning Time, many birds had tried to fly to Mother Sun to get fire for human beings. Only Black Falcon had succeeded. He'd done it by flying into her heart. His feathers had burst into flame, and he'd tumbled through the sky like one of the Meteor People, rolling over and over until he hit the earth, where his flaming body started a great forest fire. When it ended, humans gathered up burning chunks of wood and used them to start new fires to heat their homes and cook their food. Sora's ancestors had found Black Falcon's charred body and brought it home to become part of the Eternal Fire, the fire that was never allowed to go out.

Black Falcon had given his life for humans.

She walked up the steps and knelt on the altar at his feet. As she spread her arms to him, she prayed harder than she'd ever prayed in her life.

"Blessed Black Falcon, please, *please* tell me this is all a lie."

4

"SORA, YOU'VE BEEN A UNDER A GREAT STRAIN—THAT'S ALL it is. War talk, eleven hostages taken, and the news of Flint's death."

Wink handed her a cup of hot tea and sat down on the opposite side of the fire. Sunlight streamed through the roof's smoke hole and landed like a dropped scarf on the hem of Wink's yellow dress. Woven from the inner bark of mulberry trees, the extremely fine threads had a silken, knobby texture that was very pleasing to the eye. Wink wore her graying black hair up today, in a bun on top of her head. It made her round face look moonish.

Sora clutched the tea cup in both hands. Wink's personal chamber spread ten paces long by twelve wide. The plastered walls had been painted white and decorated with the images of the gods who watched over the Black Falcon People. To Sora's right, Mother Sun's golden hair streamed out from her face in flaming spirals. To her left, Comet People streaked earthward with their long blue-white wings tucked behind them. Over Wink's head, on the wall directly in front of Sora, a stylized image of Black Falcon flying into Mother Sun's heart blazed in brilliant shades of red, purple, and yellow.

"He said he still loved me, Wink. Why would he say that?"

"You and Skinner were never lovers?"

She shook her head vehemently. "Never. We both knew Flint would kill us if we so much as looked at each other fondly."

"So it's not that you didn't *want* to be; you just knew you'd couldn't risk it."

Sora shrugged. The idea made her as uncomfortable today as it had ten winters ago. "I wasn't interested in him, Wink."

Wink grunted as though she didn't believe her and threw another branch into the fire. As flames crackled up, she said, "Skinner has quite a reputation among the neighboring villages. Apparently, women fight to get beneath his blankets."

"Why would that matter to me?"

War chiefs often acquired such reputations. Being great lovers added to their images as great men.

"Well, most women would at least consider it interesting," Wink responded.

Sora massaged the back of her neck. Her muscles felt like chunks of granite. "What about the greeting?"

"He put his fingers beneath his nostrils. In many parts of our territory that salute is accompanied by a buffalo's deep-throated rumble and is considered an honored salute."

"It wasn't just the fingers to the nostrils. It was the seductive smile, the expression on his face. Everything."

"Oh, don't be a dull-wit. What do you think Flint talked about after he left you? Who do you think he talked to?"

Sora sank back on her mat. How odd that it had never occurred to her that after the divorce, Flint might have revealed every detail of their life together . . . especially to his best friend, Skinner. Perhaps he'd kept nothing sacred.

Wink sighed at the hollow expression on Sora's face and toyed with her tea cup, moving it in little circles on the floor mat. "Don't look so shocked. Divorced people hurt each other. You know that."

"Do you think Flint told him every private moment?" she asked.

"Probably. It wouldn't be unusual."

She stared down into the pale green liquid in her cup and murmured, "I've kept those moments locked in a sacred chamber in my heart. It's just hard to believe he might not have."

"Men are curious creatures, Sora. They don't have the responsibilities that we do. Men can afford to be gossips; women can't."

Women were responsible for deciding when and what to plant, when to harvest, when to go to war. Women negotiated marriages to distant clans, established political alliances and critical Trade agreements. Men were responsible for hunting, fishing, and fighting—and making certain their sisters' children received the proper upbringing. Even when a woman's son ascended to the position of chief, he followed the orders of the clan matron. She always had the final word. The world's welfare rested on women's shoulders.

As the angle of the rising sun changed, the splash of sunlight that had been on Wink's yellow hem crawled imperceptibly across the mat-covered floor toward the door curtain.

Sora watched it. Very soon, Rockfish and Long Fin would arrive for their scheduled meeting to discuss the jade brooch that sat in the painted box near the fire. They didn't have much time.

"I swear to you that my reflection-soul is not out wandering the forest, Wink." That's what caused insanity—the reflection-soul drifted out of the body and got lost in the forest. Only a powerful priest could bring it home again and make it stay. "Something's wrong with Skinner. It's as though . . . he's not Skinner."

Wink exhaled so hard the tea in her cup rippled. "How long has it been since you've seen him?"

"After Flint left me, I never saw him again."

"Three winters?"

"Yes."

"People change. Three winters is a long time. Maybe he's just a different person now."

"But"—she struggled to say this right—"he reminded me so much of Flint. As though . . ."

Wink's mouth quirked. "Stop it. Friends pick up each other's mannerisms. I mean, Blessed gods, every time I wave my hand to dismiss someone, it reminds me of you. Because I learned it from you."

Wink was right; they frequently imitated each other. It came from a lifelong friendship. Sora tossed her head when she was angry in exactly the same way Wink did.

Wink glanced at her and hesitated before saying, "Flint was crazy. You know it. Every time he challenged someone to a fight because the poor man smiled at you, I saw the looks you and Skinner exchanged. You were always attracted to each other. Don't deny it."

"That's not true," she objected.

"Sora, everyone saw it, including me. Now that Flint is gone, maybe Skinner has finally decided to go after the woman he's wanted for eighteen winters." She leaned toward Sora with her graying brows lifted. "Did that occur to you? If he really did say 'I still love you,' maybe he meant it. *He* loves you."

Sora stared at her. Of all the possibilities, that made the most sense. She took a long drink of her tea, hoping it would settle her roiling stomach. Made from the inner bark of the honey locust tree, the bitter brew eased nerves and purified the blood.

She whispered, "I hadn't thought of that."

"Perhaps you'd better start."

Sora's gaze drifted around the chamber. Pots and baskets lined every wall except for the wall behind Sora, where Wink's sleeping bench stood covered with finely woven blankets. It was a narrow bench, designed for one person. After the death of her childhood love five winters ago, Wink had remarried, as was appropriate for a clan matron, but it had been purely a political alliance. Sora wasn't even certain that Wink and Sumac slept together. They occupied separate chambers in the Matron's House and barely spoke together in public.

Wink said, "I surprised you with that one, didn't I?"

"Yes," she admitted. "Either I'm blind or—"

"You're blind. You always were when it came to Skinner. Any

other woman would have jumped into his arms, but you ignored him because you were drawn to his insane friend. Incidentally, that says something about you that's a little scary."

Sora laughed.

They both sipped their tea, smiling at each other when their gazes crossed.

After a time, Wink said, "What are you thinking about?"

"Oh, human frailties."

"Skinner's frailties?"

"Yes."

Wink frowned into her tea cup. "He *was* a curious child. After his little brother died from that fever, Skinner barely spoke for two winters. Do you remember that?"

"Yes. I'd seen six winters, but I remember. After that, he always went out of his way to help any child in need." She paused a long moment before adding, "He loves children so much I've always wondered why he never married and had his own."

Wink gave her a bland look. "You're *much* more blind than I thought."

"Oh, Wink, I don't think he's spent eighteen winters pining for me. I think . . ."

Wink lowered her tea cup to her lap. "Finish that sentence. You think what?"

"Well, I've always wondered if perhaps he isn't *berdache*."

Berdaches had male bodies but female souls. They were divine bridges between Light and Dark, Male and Female, War and Peace. In most villages they were prized as sacred beings. Often, the greatest of warriors took a berdache as his wife.

Wink tilted her head, as though thinking about that.

Sora could not say how many times they'd sat like this—too many to count. After the death of her father, Sora's mother had gone mad for a time. She vividly remembered her mother running up and down the hallway screaming and slamming her fists into the walls. Sora had been lying on her sleeping bench with hides pressed over her ears when Wink had come in, curled up against Sora's back, and stroked her hair softly. She'd seen seven winters; Wink had seen eleven. She didn't remember them exchanging more than a few words, but Wink had been there every time her mother had burst in and started ranting at Sora. While Sora shivered, Wink had screamed back, trying to protect her. The love for Wink that had been born in Sora's heart in those few terrible days would never go away, no matter what Wink did, or failed to do.

Wink said, "Tell me something? Skinner courted you right after you were made a woman, didn't he?"

"Oh, yes. My mother gave many feasts to introduce me to elite young men. Skinner was always invited, but he was too timid for me. Too sensitive."

"Really?" she said as though in disbelief. "That's a part of him no one mentions these days."

"Well, he's a war chief now. I'm sure he doesn't want that widely known."

Out of respect for Skinner, she wouldn't tell Wink, but she knew exactly why she and Skinner had never gotten together. He'd wept too often for her tastes, especially for a man destined to be a war chief. She remembered stumbling upon him in the forest one day when she'd seen ten winters; he was crouched before a wounded fawn, stroking its side with tears in his eyes. The fawn was near death, and Skinner turned to her and said, *"I did this! It was a poor shot!"*

Sora had blinked in confusion and answered, "We need the meat, Skinner. Kill it and let's take it back to your village. Your mother will be proud of you."

He'd jerked his chert knife from his belt, wiped his eyes on his sleeve, and slit the fawn's throat; but as its blood drained out onto the forest floor, Skinner had hung his head and silently wept.

At the time, she'd wondered how he would ever be able to kill an enemy warrior when he couldn't even kill a fawn.

Voices sounded down the hall, and Wink said, "Your problem is easier to solve than you think."

"How's that?"

"When you see Skinner next time, you can either ask him straightly if he's a berdache, or just invite him into your bedchamber and see what happens." She picked up the painted box and headed for the door.

"Blessed Ancestors, do you have to be so blunt?"

"Yes," Wink answered.

Sora sighed and followed her down the hall to the meeting room at the front of the Matron's House. The house, which sat upon the second-largest mound in Blackbird Town, measured eighty paces long and thirty wide. Though this mound wasn't nearly as tall as Sora's, it still stood three times the height of a man. No torches lit the hallway, but a pale stream of light penetrated around the curtain that draped the front door.

As she walked, Wink said, "Incidentally, we must do something about young Touches Clouds. He stole his cousin's knife yesterday."

"How many does that make?"

"Three knives in one moon. Apparently he's hiding them somewhere, because his family has repeatedly searched his belongings. They've found nothing."

"Do you think it's time to arrange a Healing Circle?"

"Yes. We can't let this go on. Nothing his uncles say seems to make any difference to him."

Touches Clouds was an unruly boy of eight winters. He'd begun stealing about three moons ago, little things at first: a polished bead, a bit of copper, a wooden spoon. His family couldn't prove he'd taken them, but they suspected the worst by the violent way he reacted when they questioned him about the missing items. His uncles had been counseling him for the past two moons, explaining their values, trying to convince the boy that his actions hurt the people who loved him most. Apparently their words had done no good. It was time to take more dramatic action.

Sora said, "Make the arrangements. Let me know when the Circle will be held."

"Very well. I'll speak to his uncle this afternoon."

But for treason, the Black Falcon People did not punish wrong-doers as other nations did; they almost never killed a criminal. Instead, they gathered him in their arms and told him how much they loved him, all the while explaining how his actions hurt others.

As they neared the council chamber, Long Fin and Rockfish ducked beneath the front door curtain.

Rockfish gave her a concerned smile. He'd pulled his gray hair away from his wrinkled face and tied it in back with a cord. His plain brown shirt was cinched at the waist with a bright red sash.

Long Fin held the chamber door curtain aside for his mother, then Sora.

As she ducked in, Rockfish whispered, "Are you well? You were up early this morning?"

"I won't be well until all these negotiations are over and done."

He squeezed her shoulder gently. "Tell me what I may do to help you."

Four benches surrounded the fire hearth. Wink and Long Fin sat on the north bench, to Sora's left. She and Rockfish sat on the west bench, their backs to the door. A tripod with a tea pot stood at the edge of the fire, near Wink. Cups rested on the hearthstones, keeping warm.

Long Fin said, "May I dip a cup of tea for anyone?"

"Yes, I'd like one." Rockfish smiled his thanks.

As Long Fin went to the tripod and dipped the ceramic cup full, Rockfish asked, "Did you two have a chance to discuss the strange new stone?"

Wink and Sora blinked at each other. They'd been occupied discussing far more important things, like forbidden love and disembodied souls.

"Some," Sora lied. "What do you think about it?"

Long Fin seated himself beside Wink and leaned forward to brace his elbows on his thighs. "I think we should do everything we can to obtain it."

Taken aback, Sora said, "Why is that?"

Wink exchanged a strange, secret look with Rockfish, then said, "Rockfish told us last night how lucrative the stone could be. How can we say no?"

After a morning of trust and soft words, Sora felt suddenly betrayed. She glanced around the fire. Had Wink already made the decision to go after the stone?

She glared at her husband. He lowered his eyes, obviously shamed by his duplicity. Is that what had taken him such a long time last night? While she'd been speaking with Skinner, he'd had a discussion with Wink and Long Fin? What surprised her most was that she had not foreseen it. Of course he wanted the stone. His people would give their very lives to . . .

She went still inside, as though the eyes of her souls had just come upon a hidden snake. Was he thinking that? That if the Black Falcon People did not want to take the risks his own people might?

Dear gods, he didn't tell Wink that, did he?

Wink said, "Sora, listen, I was up all night thinking about this. Rockfish suggested that his people might be willing to send two or three hundred warriors. With our two hundred, and Blue Bow's two hundred, who could stand against us?"

Long Fin eagerly nodded. "We would all benefit enormously."

Sora gave Wink a look of disbelief. "Who could stand against us? I'll tell you who: An army with a thousand warriors. An army that knows the terrain better than we do. An army that, if endangered, has relatives in a dozen nearby villages who will appear at the fall of an arrow to support them." Her voice had gradually been rising until now it was almost a shout. "If we do this at all, we should dispatch a very small war party to minimize our risk! What's the matter with the three of you? We could be sending our warriors into a trap. Even more important, what makes you think Blue Bow will keep his word about sharing the stone?"

"Well . . . ," Long Fin said with a casual smile. He was a handsome youth with large brown eyes and perfect white teeth. "If we have five hundred warriors there, and he has two hundred, we can take what we want, can't we?"

Sora looked at Wink's stiff face, then at Rockfish. His wrinkles had rearranged into apologetic lines. Yes, Long Fin was obviously sixteen.

"Do you truly think Blue Bow hasn't thought of that?"

Long Fin's smile froze. "What do you mean?"

"I mean, he's not a fool. He contemplated every twist and turn long before he dispatched his war chief. We are no friends to him. He must have planned for the possibility that we will betray him and take the stone for ourselves. Wink," she pleaded, "we just went to great effort to keep peace with the Loon People. Do you now want to do something that will cause war? That's what will happen if we do as your son suggests."

"My Chieftess," Long Fin defended, "I did not mean to suggest that we take the stone, only that if Blue Bow goes back on his agreement, we *could* take it."

Rockfish slid around on the bench to face her. In his softest, most persuasive voice—the voice he used when negotiating Trade—he said, "How do you think we should protect ourselves? I may be able to pull more warriors from distant villages, but it will take time that I'm not sure we have. Should I try?"

"What do I think?" She blinked in surprise. "I don't want to do this at all. It's political suicide! Please, listen for a few moments." She extended her hands to them. "Imagine what the other villages will think if we do not invite them to send warriors south. They will rightly feel slighted. On the other hand, if we do ask them, and they commit warriors who are then slaughtered in some faraway land, they will blame us. This stone may cause an irreparable rift between the Black Falcon clans. As well as war with the Loon People! And maybe war with a distant people we do not even know!"

Long Fin picked up the painted box and opened it. The huge jade brooch shimmered in the firelight. Longingly, he said, "With this stone, we could become the preeminent chieftainship in the world. It seems hasty to me to dismiss this matter so quickly. Perhaps we should gather our elders and ask for their guidance?"

The lines at the corners of Wink's eyes tightened, obviously torn between supporting her son and supporting Sora. "Rockfish? What is your opinion?"

He glanced at Sora, then grimaced at the floor. "I support whatever my wife decides."

Wink said, "Sora? Shall I make the decision, or should we gather our elders to discuss this further?"

These were three of the most important people in the Black Falcon world. If they thought the stone was worth risking the lives of five hundred warriors, they could certainly convince the elders. Her words would be considered, of course, but in the end the elders would choose to join the war party.

Anger swelled her chest. Sora couldn't help but think that if she'd talked to Wink and Long Fin before Rockfish had, this discussion would not be taking place. His disloyalty stung. It might cost the lives of hundreds or, if warfare erupted over the stone, thousands of men, women, and children.

"Sora," Wink said, "all we're saying is that we should seriously consider Blue Bow's proposal."

Curtly, she replied, "Since we disagree, we should gather the elders and ask their views."

Wink relaxed and started to say something, but from down the hall a man called, *"Matron?"*

Wink gestured to Long Fin. As he rose, he said, "I'll return shortly, forgive me."

He left the chamber, spoke softly with the runner, and called, "Mother?"

Wink crossed the chamber with her yellow dress fluttering around her legs. When she ducked out into the hallway, she said, "What's wrong?"

The voices outside went too low to hear.

Rockfish turned uneasily to Sora. "It just happened, Sora. I delivered the stone, and when Wink opened the box, she started asking me questions. What did I think about the stone? Was it worth as much as Blue Bow suggested? Could we gather the warriors to mount an attack on the quarry? I had to say something."

"You were supposed to arrange a meeting to discuss it. Nothing more."

As though angry, he bowed his head. "I try to serve you as best I can, but I always fail, don't I?"

Irritated by this common litany, she snapped, "Not always, Rockfish. I just wish you had—"

"*Sora?*" Wink called and shoved the curtain aside to look in at her. "May I see you?"

The taut tone made Sora leap to her feet and hurry across the chamber. When she ducked out into the hallway, Wink ordered, "Long Fin, please continue your discussion with Rockfish."

"Yes, Mother."

Wink waited until her son had disappeared beneath the curtain and she heard him talking with Rockfish before she gave Sora a wide-eyed look. "The runner came for you."

"What's wrong?" Dread prickled her chest.

"The runner said a man paid him very well to bring you a message."

"Yes? What is it?"

"The man said he has to talk to you. He's waiting for you in the place where he always stowed his canoe."

Meet me at my canoe. I'll show you how much I love you.

Sora's stomach flip-flopped. She couldn't find the air to speak.

Wink grabbed her arm, as though to hold her up. "That's where you used to meet Flint, isn't it?"

"Yes, I—I . . ."

"Let me go, Sora. I'll find out what he wants and tell you."

A potent brew of fear and curiosity shot through Sora's veins. She shook her head. "No. I have to do this. If I'm not back for a while, can you make some excuse for me?"

Wink released her arm, but glared at her. "If you're not back in one hand of time, I'll come looking for you with a war party."

5

SHE CROSSED THE BRIDGE THAT SPANNED RACCOON CREEK and walked out onto the lakeshore trail. The small houses of commoners dotted the way. At the very end of the lake stood an enormous burned-out tree. She resolutely marched toward it.

"I have to find out what he wants, why he's doing this," she whispered.

To her left, fish tails glinted as minnows fed in the shallows. People waded through the water with green cane spears tipped with the spikes taken from the tails of horseshoe crabs. Several people watched her pass, but she was obviously in a hurry and no one dared speak to her.

Sora tramped past the burned tree and turned right onto the deer path that led into the depths of the forest, where only pinpoints of sunlight speckled the mossy deadfall. The beautiful songs of warblers filled the giant oak trees.

She'd come to this place a hundred times after Flint left her to lie in the cool shadows where his canoe had always rested and to dream of him. What bitter days those had been, filled with despair and wrenching anger that had made her sick to her stomach.

A rattlesnake shook its tail at her as she thrashed through the palmettos that choked the path. Sora backed up, said, "Forgive me for disturbing you, Sister," and took a new path.

Though snakes were thought to portend misfortune, no one among the Black Falcon Nation would knowingly harm them. Just after the Creation, Mother Sun had become angry with human beings and decided to destroy them. It was Rattlesnake who had saved humans by killing Mother Sun's daughter and turning her anger to grief. She . . .

Wind swept the forest, and Sora saw Skinner just ahead, partially concealed behind a long swaying beard of hanging moss. He held a huge oak leaf in his hand, which he lazily twirled.

He called, "He asked me about you. Did he tell you?"

She stopped. "Who?"

"Your husband, when he was showing me to the guest chambers. He's very curious about us."

Inexplicable anger possessed her, as though Rockfish had said something that would hurt her. Ordinarily, it would never have occurred to her, but after the meeting with Wink and Long Fin over the jade brooch, she no longer knew what he might say or do.

"What did he ask?"

"He wanted to know if I'd *done* something to you in the council chamber."

When she'd called out last night, her tone must have frightened Rockfish.

"What did you say?"

Skinner leaned a shoulder against the enormous trunk of an oak and looked at her. His deeply set black eyes glistened. He'd left his waist-length hair loose. It draped the front of his long buckskin shirt like a gleaming jet curtain. "I didn't tell him any of your secrets, if that's what you're worried about."

"You don't know any of my secrets."

The silence stretched.

He started pulling the leaf apart, slowly, a vein at a time. The green wisps fluttered to the ground at his feet. "Rockfish seems to think we were lovers."

She ducked under a thick curtain of moss and tramped closer to him. "You told him no, of course."

"I told him that not once in the entire time I'd known you had I betrayed your trust. I said that whatever had happened between you and me was ours alone."

Which means that any lingering doubt Rockfish might have had about us being lovers vanished.

Upset, she said, "You and I never touched each other, Skinner. Why did you say that?"

He gave her a strange look, penetrating, then tore off another piece of leaf, which spun to the ground like a wing seed. "Why don't you just have your warriors escort me out of your village?"

"You are a visiting war chief. Why would I do that?"

"Because you're afraid of me. You always were." He gazed at her unblinking, like a big cat about to leap for her throat.

She stiffened. This was not at all the timid youth she remembered. "Why are you here, Skinner?"

He threw the leaf down and stepped toward her, his movements graceful for a man his size. "I came because I needed to tell you Flint's last words."

"Then tell me and go."

His gaze traced the smooth line of her jaw, lingering on her pointed chin, then lifting to her full lips. "He still loves you."

"What are you talking about? He died four days ago. You told me so yourself."

"Yes, but you knew it wasn't true."

Stunned, she stammered, "Are—are you telling me he's alive?"

"Let's stop this foolish bantering. You recognized me the instant I stepped into your council chamber."

Frightened by the strange glow in his eyes, she started to back away.

He grabbed her arm and jerked her against him. In a low, pained voice, he murmured, "You said I didn't know any of your secrets, but I do. All of them."

As panic burned through her, she struggled to get away. "I don't know what you're talking about."

He leaned down until their lips almost touched, and murmured, "I know you killed your father."

She felt as though she'd been struck from behind. "Wh—what?"

Tenderly, he said, "Who else but me knows, Sora?"

Me.

The ground seemed to fall out from under her feet. She was floating, weightless, only his hand tying her to the forest.

Skinner smoothed his fingers over her long hair. It was a lover's touch, a preamble to lying down together.

"It wasn't your fault," he said softly. "Instead of hiding her Spirit Plants from you, your mother should have taught you about them from the time you could walk. You were just making supper for your father while your mother was in a council meeting. You thought it was another herb."

He must have seen the utter terror on her face. He added, "I've never told anyone. Not even when I hated you the most. You must believe me. I love you too much to hurt you that way."

He let go of her arm, and she stumbled backward like a wet cornhusk doll, her legs barely strong enough to hold her.

"Why did you come here?" she asked, too frightened to break eye contact with him.

He cocked his head in a way she'd seen a thousand times. *Friends pick up each other's mannerisms. That's all it is.* "I need you, Sora. More than I ever did when I was alive."

"I'm tired of this! I'm going home!"

As she started to turn, he said, "Please stay. I beg you. I need to hold you, Sora, like I used to." He held out his arms.

As though her most desperate hope had just slipped from the empty place between her souls, she started shaking. "You're frightening me, Skinner. I'm leaving."

She turned to walk away.

He called, "Do you remember the Moon of Swallows, on the red hill? I held you so tightly. My souls tore apart when you gave birth to our tiny son in the forest, but I never let go of you. Do you remember? I held you for four days, feeding you broth and tea, weeping with you. I need to hold you like that again. Please, please, come back."

She spun around to stare at him.

His eyes had a bright watery sheen. "Who else knows that your pains began just after sunrise, during a rainstorm? Did you tell anyone that I sang lullabies to you through the whole terrible thing?"

One of her knees gave way. She stumbled.

I told Wink about losing the baby. Right after Flint set my belongings outside our door.

Had she also told Wink about Flint singing her lullabies? Or the rainstorm?

For moons, she'd been so distraught she'd done and said things she didn't even remember. Wink had had to remind her of promises she'd made to village chiefs or clan matrons, things she could not afford to forget. But she had forgotten.

In an agonized voice, Skinner said, "I've never stopped loving you, Sora."

It took almost more strength than she had to keep from running back to the safety of Blackbird Town, but she just stood there, unable to break the dark spell his voice had cast upon her. "You told me you had to pry Flint's fingers from around his throat to hear his final words?"

"Yes. He was very strong, he—"

"How close were you when his last breath escaped?"

He walked closer, leaned down, and whispered, "Very close."

Horror exploded in her chest.

"Leave me alone!" She wrenched free of his hand and ran like a madwoman, thrashing through the palmettos to get to the lakeshore trail.

People whispered as she ran by, and their gazes turned to follow her.

In the plaza, men laughed as they knapped out new stone tools. Children raced up and down the lengths of the chunkey field, kicking a hide ball. Four pots of yucca blades boiled in the lye of wood ashes at the base of Wink's mound. Three women stood around with long paddles, stirring the blades. When the pulp washed away, they would comb the stringy fibers and twist them into very fine white ropes.

"A pleasant morning to you, Chieftess," one of the women called.

Sora hurried by, climbing the stairs to the top of the mound two at a time. When she reached the last step, she spied Wink and Long Fin sitting on the benches in front of the matron's tall pitched-roof house. The wind had torn graying black locks loose from Wink's bun; they blew around her face in wisps.

Sora didn't have to say a word.

When Wink saw her pale face, she leaped to her feet and ran. "What is it? What's wrong? You look like—"

"We have to go somewhere and talk. Now."

Wink looked over her shoulder at the tall, slender young man who still sat on the bench with a curious look on his face. "I'll return in a few moments, my son," she called, and gripped Sora's arm.

As they walked away, she hissed, "What happened? Did he hurt you?"

"No," she managed to say through a taut exhalation. "Please, let's walk to the far side of the house. I don't want anyone to overhear us."

Wink swiftly led the way around to the rear of the Matron's House, where a series of benches looked out at the three other clan mounds across Raccoon Creek to the south. "Here, sit down. You look like you're ready to fall on your face." Wink gestured to the bench at the very edge of the mound.

Sora gingerly lowered herself to the massive log. Forty hands below, Raccoon Creek ran clear and clean. Though they tried to keep the banks cleared of brush, the palmettos grew too fast for anyone to keep up with. They cast wavering shadows over the pale green water.

Concerned, Wink asked, "Was he waiting for you where he said he'd be?"

"Yes, he was there." She forced herself to take a deep breath. "How long has it been since you've seen the matron of Minnow Village?"

Wink stared at her for a few instants. "Five or six winters. Why?"

"Could you send a runner to her? Ask her what actually happened the day Skinner carried Flint into her village? I have to know."

Wink sat rigid on the bench beside her, her yellow dress waffling in the breeze. "Skinner told you something terrible, didn't he?"

"I don't want to discuss it until we've heard from Matron Wading Heron. If I reveal any of the details he told me, I'll be suspicious of whatever the runner says." She ran a hand over her numb face. "I'm praying this is just a trick."

Wink tucked a lock of gray hair behind her ear. "What kind of a trick?"

"I don't know."

"Sora, please, you have to tell me something."

She shook her head.

Wink's gaze darted over the mounds across the creek, as though she was thinking. While Wink was the matron of the Shadow Rock Clan, there were three other clans among the Black Falcon People: Matron Wood Fern ruled the Water Hickory Clan; Matron Black Birch headed the Bald Cypress Clan; and Wigeon was in charge of the Shoveler Clan. Each matron had her own mound. All three stood in a line south of the creek, and paralleled the northern line created by Wink's mound, Sora's mound, and old Priest Teal's mound. People moved around the bases, going about their daily duties. The bright reds and blues of their clothing created a beautiful mosaic against the dark soil.

"Do you think Skinner might be tricking you about Flint's death?"

Sora jerked around in surprise. "Why did you say that?"

"Well, if not Flint's death, what?" Wink pressed.

When Sora didn't answer, Wink said in a stern voice, "Is he still proclaiming how much he loves you?"

Sora squeezed her eyes closed.

"Hallowed gods, Sora. Why are you so upset by this? You should be honored that he—"

"I'm *terrified*."

Wink scrutinized Sora's tortured expression. "Why did you say it like that? With such desperation?"

"I . . ." She fumbled with her cold hands. "I asked him how close he was when Flint's last breath escaped."

Wink didn't ask about the answer. She could see it in Sora's eyes. The color drained from her face. "Sora, are you telling me you believe Flint's shadow-soul is hiding inside Skinner?"

Their gazes held for a long time.

Sora's skin prickled as though Skinner's hands were moving over her body. His very presence, the way he moved, the sound of his voice, had reminded her so much of Flint that she'd actually started to believe it. "Gods, maybe my reflection-soul *is* out wandering lost in the forest."

"That's one possibility," Wink admitted in a wry voice, "but I hope not. If so, I'll have to hire a priest to go search for it, which will cost me a fortune. Then, if the priest can't find it, one of your relatives will be responsible for whacking your soulless body in the back of the head. I don't want it to be me."

Wink's sense of humor had never been less amusing. "That wasn't funny, Wink."

"Especially not if Flint's shadow-soul *did* sneak inside Skinner, but I suspect your first instinct is correct: Skinner is tricking you. In that case, he's the one who deserves to be whacked in the head."

Sora mulled over her words before she said, "There's another possibility, one we haven't considered."

"What's that?"

"This could be Flint's reflection-soul. I've heard priests say that sometimes the reflection-soul lingers on earth, completing tasks, saying things to loved ones that need to be said before it travels to the afterlife."

"If it's his reflection-soul, it has to leave within ten days of his death, or it will become a homeless ghost wandering the earth forever. This is the fourth day after his death, which means it has six more days to remain here."

"Then, in six days, we'll know. Isn't that right?"

"Don't be ridiculous," Wink blurted. "Do you want to take that chance? What if it is his shadow-soul? Or what if Skinner is tricking you in order to hurt you, or Shadow Rock Clan?"

A gust of wind blasted through the forest and swept old leaves around them. They both turned their faces away until it raced past, whirled down the face of the mound, and out into the plaza, where dogs barked and ran away with their tails between their legs.

"Stay away from him, Sora, until I can get this sorted out."

"Blessed gods, do you think I'm an idiot? Of course I'll stay away from him." Despite her words, longing rose, and she knew she *needed* to see him again. She had to be sure.

"I see that look on your face," Wink said in disbelief. "Don't even think it. If the worst is true, he's *not* Flint. Shadow-souls are filled with all the evil that ever lived inside the person. He's dangerous."

But he hadn't felt evil. He'd felt *Powerful*—as though a hurricane lived inside him, which he held at bay through sheer force of will.

"You know what we'll have to do if we find out it is Flint's shadow-soul?" Wink asked.

The thought chilled her. Shadow-souls rarely rested in one body. Once, when she'd been a child, her mother had ordered three people killed to stop the shadow-soul of an old priest who wouldn't leave his family alone. He'd kept slipping from one unsuspecting person to another, hiding until discovered, then moving again. Because shadow-souls resembled breath, they could slip from one mouth to another barely noticed. Whispering usually passed the soul.

Wink rose to her feet. "I'm going to instruct our guards that Skinner is not to enter this town again." She remained standing there, looking down at Sora as though she expected her to object.

"Thank you. That's a good idea," Sora said.

"I'm glad you agree."

Wink marched up the trail—a woman on a mission.

Sora continued to stare blindly out across the forest at sprays of flowering redbud. Blossom-scented wind, blowing off Persimmon Lake, tousled her long black hair around her shoulders. As Mother Sun rose higher into the morning sky, the shadows of the mounds stretched toward her like long, pointing fingers, silently accusing her.

Of what? What had she done?

For three winters, I've been longing for him . . .

Fifty heartbeats later she found herself striding down the mound steps, past the women who stirred the yucca blades. They cast fearful glances her way and whispered to each other.

She hurried along the north side of her mound. To her left, across the broad plaza filled with commoners and racing children, War Chief Feather Dancer stood atop his mound, practicing with his war club. He swung the massive copper-studded club over his head, then slashed downward, as though cutting an opponent across the belly. When he saw her, he bowed.

She dipped her head in acknowledgment. A very tall, muscular man, he'd seen twenty-six winters. She'd chosen him as her war chief when she'd ascended to the chieftainship—a reward for extraordinary bravery while serving her mother. Not only that, the former war chief, White Pelican, was old and always too eager for war.

Feather Dancer had sided with her in the council, speaking against war with the Loon People. She wondered how he would feel if he knew that his matron was now considering another war, with a people he did not know at all, over a green stone he'd never seen before.

As she rounded the northeastern corner of her mound, her white dress flapped around her legs. Despite the thousands of times she had climbed these fifty-four steps, she still counted each as she trotted to the top. She did that: counted things unconsciously, like the angles in a painting or the leaves on a palmetto. Counting seemed to order her chaotic heart.

From the crest, the view was stunning. She could look out across the top of Priest Teal's mound to the lake, where ducks and cormorants paddled the green water, coming to within a few body-lengths of the people fishing onshore. The birds never got too close. They just seemed to want to watch for a time; then they veered away, leaving a wake of silver rings bobbing behind them. All around the lake, for as far as she could see, farm plots, patches where the trees and brush had been cleared, resembled irregular green squares. The corn, beans, and sunflowers that sustained the Black Falcon People had just begun to turn their faces to Mother Sun.

Far down the lakeshore someone shouted in glee and pulled a wriggling fish from the water. His family gathered around as he used a hook to draw the intestines out through the anus without cutting the fish open, then skewered the fish, tail to jaw, with a cotton-wood stick. His wife covered it with mud and put it in the embers of their breakfast fire. When the mud cracked off, it would be ready to eat. The cottonwood gave the meat a pleasantly tangy flavor.

"He is *not* Flint," she whispered to herself. "He can't be. Skinner is tricking me, but why?"

In the dark place deep inside her, where her own shadow-soul walked, fear rose. If all the evil had been sucked into Flint's shadow-soul at his death . . .

It would come looking for me.

She entered her house and stood for a moment in the cool

hallway, listening. Rockfish must be away. The silence pressed against her ears like huge hands.

Though her mother had always insisted that her slaves live in this house, Sora had sent them away the first day she'd become the chieftess. They lived in slaves' quarters out on the lakeshore, came when she asked for them, and left when she ordered them to. This house was the only place on earth where she had any privacy. She wanted to keep it that way.

Sora walked into the temple. The low flames of the Eternal Fire cast a soft, flickering light over the enormous figure of Black Falcon that hung on the wall.

It took a few moments for her to realize that a special offering lay on the altar at Black Falcon's feet: a necklace of copper hands connected by a leather thong. From the palm of each hand, wide-open eyes, embossed by a master copper worker, stared out at her. *A circle of disembodied eyes.*

Every time they'd argued, Flint had left her a gift in this very spot. It was his way of apologizing without having to say the words.

As her heartbeat increased to slam against her ribs, she had the terrifying sensation that he was here, very close by.

Sora glanced around the temple. Nothing moved except the shadows cast on the walls by the flames.

She climbed the altar steps and went to touch the necklace. It was warm. Had it just been pulled from around someone's throat and placed here?

The door curtain behind her whispered.

"I didn't mean to frighten you," he called softly.

Sora swung around. He must have been waiting in the council chamber across the hall. "Skinner, I told you to leave me alone."

The shark's teeth on his buckskin shirt flashed as he walked toward her. "Yes, today you did, but last night you said you would give up everything for me, including your husband. I'm here, Sora. I want you as much as you want me."

"Leave. Now!"

His gaze focused on the fists she'd clenched at her sides, then moved to the necklace on the altar behind her. "I made that for you the day I died. I had to bring it to you myself."

"You are not Flint! Stop pretending to be!"

"Please, please, listen to me," he pleaded. "From the instant my souls seeped from my body—"

"Skinner, I beg you not to say these things! If *you* feel this way, then just tell me and we'll—"

"I knew I had to see you before I traveled to the Land of the Dead. There are so many things I must tell you."

She stepped backward, almost into the Eternal Fire. Maybe it was his reflection-soul? *I'm insane. I should run to a priest and ask his advice.* "Then you're not Flint's shadow-soul?"

So much hope filled her voice she could barely stand to hear it herself.

A sad look came over his handsome face. "How does a person tell, Sora? Please, I need you to help me figure this out."

He made a helpless gesture with his hand and turned slightly away from her. As he stood in profile, his solitary eye squinted as though in confusion.

She said, "Can you tell me what happened at the end? What's the last thing you remember?"

"Skinner started sobbing and gasping for breath and I . . . I knew."

"You knew what?"

"I knew I was dead."

Hearing him say it made her ache as though she'd just received the news for the first time. "And then?"

He clutched the fabric over his heart. "A deep sense of gratitude went through me, and I realized it wasn't me feeling it."

"You mean, Skinner was feeling grateful? That—that you were dead?"

"No, I think he knew my soul had slipped inside him. He could feel me there, and didn't mind. In fact, he seemed deeply relieved."

Breathlessly, she asked, "Did he tell you that?"

"Yes. Later. Now, we talk often."

She edged around the circumference of the fire pit. His one eye followed her. He knew she was getting ready to bolt.

"You're toying with me, Skinner. You know how much I loved him. Are you trying to hurt me?"

He got down on his knees and spread his arms wide in a warrior's gesture of surrender, exactly the way Flint used to do when he was begging her to listen to him. "Give me three more days, Sora. Just three days of your life. Please, there's something I must ask you, and so many things I must tell you."

The crackling of the Eternal Fire seemed suddenly unbearably loud.

"If I agree, will your reflection-soul be at peace and able to go on to the Land of the Dead?"

Tears beaded his lashes. "Yes. I think so."

A battle raged inside her: good sense warring against an emotional need so deep and dark it wrung her souls.

"Wink told the guards you are never to set foot in this town again."

"Then I won't. We can meet in the forest, like we used to."

Slowly, as though trying not to frighten her, he rose to his feet and stepped forward. "Please, Sora, let me hold you. I need to feel you in my arms."

She shook her head. "No. I—I can't do that."

He extended his hands, and her muscles seemed to freeze solid.

She just watched as he slowly came forward. When he embraced her, a stunning wave of calm flooded her veins. She felt as though for three winters her body had been wound up like knotted strips of rawhide, waiting for his arms so it could relax. She leaned against him, and he kissed her.

Against her lips, he whispered, "Forgive me for ever leaving you. But you know why I did it."

"No. I never knew why."

The only sound in the world was the roar of blood rushing in her ears. When his kisses grew more passionate, she shoved away and stared at him.

"I—I have to think about this. About the three days. When I decide, I'll send word. Where will you be?"

He exhaled haltingly and clenched his hands into fists at his sides. It surprised her that he was shaking. "Don't send a messenger, Sora. After all we've been through together, if you're going to tell me to go away, I expect you to do it yourself."

Skinner held her gaze for several long moments before he turned and walked out of the temple.

As soon as he ducked through the front entrance, shouts rose. Sora sprinted from the temple and threw back the curtain.

"Weapons aren't necessary!" Skinner shouted.

Wink hurried toward him with five guards. Her graying hair and yellow dress whipped in the wind that blasted the mound top.

Two guards grabbed Skinner's arms, while the other two kept their spears aimed at his belly. The remaining guard, Far Eye, trotted toward Sora.

Skinner said something to Wink—something Sora couldn't hear—and Wink gave him a small, satisfied smile that made Sora's spine stiffen. What had he said?

As the guards dragged him away, he struggled to look back, to glance over his shoulder at her.

Just before the guards hustled him down the stairs, out of her sight, he shouted, "Sora, come to me!"

Wink's eyes shot to Sora and narrowed, as though daring her to answer.

When she didn't, Wink followed the guards down the stairs.

Far Eye bowed. "The matron instructed me to guard your house, Chieftess. I'll be outside this door if you need me."

In a low voice, she asked, "What did War Chief Skinner say to Wink before they hauled him away?"

Far Eye straightened. The geometric tattoos that covered his face and arms looked faint against his brown skin. "He said, 'I just need a few more days.'"

"Did the matron answer?"

"Yes, but I didn't hear her words, I'm sorry."

What had Skinner meant? A few more days to do what? To finish saying the things he needed to? Wink would not have given him a satisfied smile if she'd thought that's what he'd meant. She would have snarled some unpleasant comment. Had they been talking about something else?

She walked back into her house, down the dim hallway, and straight to the chamber where she'd spent her childhood.

She lifted the curtain and stood in the entry, her fists clenched, staring at the basket.

She'd been hearing them since dawn, but in the past hand of time their voices had grown much louder. The pendants, the headdresses, the anklets he'd made for her . . .

They wept.

6

LATER THAT AFTERNOON, ROCKFISH PACED BEFORE THE FIRE in their personal chamber, his brown shirt waffling around his legs. His gray hair reflected the orange shade of the firelight. "Wink wouldn't tell me why she ordered War Chief Skinner out of town, but one of the guards said he'd been harassing you. Is that true?"

She had never seen him like this, seething, his eyes flashing.

"Not harassing—that's too strong a word," Sora said as she pulled her dress over her head and tossed it onto their sleeping bench. She had a council meeting with the elders in one hand of time. She needed to change and prepare before they arrived.

"What does he want?"

Sora propped her foot on the bench to unlace her leggings. "I don't really know, Rockfish," she lied. "When he first arrived, he said that before Flint died, he asked Skinner to bring me a message."

"What was the message?"

Naked, she walked to the basket where her clean clothing lay folded and removed the lid. Rockfish's eyes traced the lines of her slender body, lingering on her full breasts, then dropping to her long legs.

As she sorted through the dresses, she said, "He still hasn't told me the message."

"Why not?"

"How do I know?" she replied, irritated. "He seems to think this is some sort of guessing game."

Rockfish smoothed his hand over his wrinkled forehead, as though exasperated. "How old is he?"

She gestured lightly. "I don't know. My age. Thirty-two winters or a little more. Why?"

"Because he acts like an insolent boy. I saw the way he looked at you, Sora."

From a locked chamber inside her, Flint's voice seeped out: *"He looked at you the wrong way, Sora!"*

She jerked out a red dress with yellow diamonds woven around the throat and hem. The warp of the cloth was combed cane threads; the weft was finely spun buffalo hair.

As she slipped it over her head, she curtly said, "What way was that, my husband?"

With a distinct chill in his voice, he said, "He looked at you like the two of you were lovers."

"I'm with you every day, all day, Rockfish. How could we possibly—"

"I wasn't with you when you went to negotiate the release of the hostages with Chief Blue Bow. You told me you didn't want me there."

"That's right. I needed you here while I was away." She pulled her long black hair out of her dress and fluffed it around her shoulders. "So, you think I really went north to Oak Leaf Village to sleep with my new lover? Is that what you're saying?"

"No, I . . ." He stopped, shook his head, and turned away. "Gods, I don't know what I'm saying."

For the past ten or eleven moons, he'd been progressively less able to perform in their bedchamber. She suspected that's what this was really about. She always told him it didn't matter, that they'd try again later. But when later came, he was sound asleep. In truth, it didn't bother her. Not really. There were times when she longed for a more vigorous man, but not often. The only time her desires had almost driven her to someone else's arms was that morning— and she regretted the incident with Skinner.

He said, "I know I don't have the energy of younger men, Sora, and because I'm not always there when you need me, I—"

"You *are* always there when I need you. What is this sudden insecurity?"

"Don't patronize me. You are a woman of great passions. That's one of the things I love most about you, and"—he paused to glance at her—"and I saw the way you looked at *him*, Sora."

The dread in his voice touched her. Honestly, she said, "Skinner was my former husband's best friend. For a long time, he was my friend. I *do* love him. But not in the way you think. Skinner and I have never been lovers, Rockfish. Please put that worry out of your heart. We have more important things to think about. The elders will be here soon."

She walked to the place where she'd left her copper falcon pendant and fumbled to tie it beneath her hair.

"Here, let me help you." He came across the floor, gently pushed her hair aside, kissed the back of her neck, and finished tying the leather ends. "I've never been a jealous man. You know that. I just—"

"Don't explain. It's over. By now, he's on his way back to Oak Leaf Village, and I'll probably never see him again. *You'll* never see him again."

Rockfish sighed in relief and gave her a remorseful smile. His wrinkles suddenly looked deeper, their patterns more intricate. He stroked her hair. "I love you very much, Sora."

"And I love you." She brushed his arm with her hand. "Now, let's get to the council chamber in case someone arrives early. I don't want any of the elders to have to wait for me."

He nodded and followed her to the door and down the torchlit hallway.

As he pulled back the council chamber curtain, he softly said, "Forgive me. I don't know what came over me."

She looked up into his sad brown eyes and smiled. "If I ever had any doubts about your affection, I don't now. Perhaps this has been good for us."

She ducked into the council chamber.

In the short time he'd been in Blackbird Town, Skinner had disrupted every part of her life, and the lives of the people who mattered most to her. He was like a spark thrown into a pile of dry tinder.

Despite what she'd said about it being good for them, she feared the spark was just about to catch.

7

SORA SAT ON A MAT BEFORE THE FIRE IN THEIR BEDCHAM-
ber, staring at the low flames that danced in the fire hearth.

The council meeting had been heated. At the end, she'd begged
the elders to consider sending only a small war party, as a show of
their support, and only in exchange for the release of their hostages.
War Chief Feather Dancer had taken her side, flatly stating that he
would strongly recommend against sending large numbers of warriors into an unknown land to fight an unknown people. But that
hadn't settled the matter. The matrons' votes had been split. Wink
and Black Birch, matron of the Bald Cypress Clan, had voted in favor of joining forces with Chief Blue Bow to try to obtain the stone;
Wood Fern and Wigeon against. Wood Fern and Wigeon despised
the Loon People. They refused to establish an alliance with the people they had, only two days past, voted to wage war against. It had
been their council votes that had forced Wink and Sora into the de-
cisive chunkey game.

Why didn't I foresee that this might happen?

The council members had finally agreed to delay their vote until
they had more information. They had called in War Chief Grown

Bear and sent him back to Blue Bow with a message that they wanted to speak with Blue Bow in person before they made such a momentous decision.

It did not end the matter, but it bought Sora a little time to work on the individual matrons, especially Wink. If she could convince her old friend this was a bad idea, it would secure the vote.

Sora was dead tired, but her body refused to sleep. After three hands of time tossing and turning, keeping Rockfish awake, she'd risen and built up the fire to stay warm while she considered the other matter that demanded her attention.

What was she going to do about Skinner?

Was he, even now, waiting for her in one of *their* places in the forest?

She closed her eyes.

Why was he doing this?

Skinner might be insane. In that case, if she was truly his friend, she would hire a priest to find his lost reflection-soul and bring it back to his body.

The one possibility neither she nor Wink had mentioned was the frightening thought that Skinner might be a Raven Mocker.

Of all the witches, Raven Mockers were the most dreaded. They flew through the air in fiery shapes, their arms outstretched like wings, with sparks trailing behind them. They could take any shape they wanted: that of an owl, a cougar, or a wolf, whatever allowed them to get close to the person they desired to harm. When their victim was finally dying, they searched out his reflection-soul, usually as seen in a cup of water, and swallowed it, hoping to add days or winters to their own life. For a time after the reflection-soul had been swallowed, it waged war on the Raven Mocker's body, trying to take it over.

But if she had actually spoken to Flint's reflection-soul, surely he would have told her that Skinner was a Raven Mocker. She felt certain he would have pleaded for her to help him.

Please, there's something I must ask you.

She ran a hand through her long black hair. Too many questions without answers.

As though her souls were struggling to get her to connect the disparate pieces of a puzzle, she kept thinking about Rockfish's discussions with Wink about the jade, and the satisfied smile Wink had given Skinner. It seemed odd that Skinner had appeared on exactly the same morning as War Chief Grown Bear.

Could they be working together?

A wave of fear coursed through her. Perhaps Oak Leaf Village had made a secret alliance with Blue Bow to weasel into a more favorable Trade relationship. Or perhaps, in exchange for the return of their hostages, Oak Leaf Village had agreed to send warriors after the jade?

Then again, what if it was more than a village-to-village agreement? What if the matron of Water Hickory Clan knew about it? Like all Water Hickory Clan villages, Skinner's chief, Fireberry, answered to Matron Wood Fern. Was that why Wood Fern had voted against allying with Blue Bow? She already had a secret agreement to get the stone?

Sora massaged her brow. If Water Hickory Clan won a glorious victory and returned home with canoeloads of jade, it would elevate them above the Shadow Rock Clan. That would mean Wink would have to step down, and Wood Fern would replace her as the high matron of the Black Falcon Nation.

She heaved a tired sigh. While that made some sense, it didn't explain why Skinner would pretend to be Flint. Skinner would have been as much a distraction if he'd blurted out that he loved her as he was trying to act like her former husband.

The simplest explanation, she hated to admit, was still the most frightening—he *was* Flint. He was Flint, and he desperately needed to talk to her.

"Give me three more days."

She silently rose to her feet and ducked beneath the bedchamber door curtain. At this time of night, only two torches lit the long hallway, both in holders near the front entrance.

She tiptoed through the darkness until she reached the curtain, then walked out into the gusting wind. Her long black hair swirled around her face, almost obscuring her vision of Far Eye until she captured it in her hand.

"Chieftess," Far Eye greeted and bowed. "Do you need something?"

"I'm going for a walk. There's no need for you to come. I'll just be wandering around town."

"But Matron Wink said—"

"Your aunt ordered you to guard my house, not me."

Far Eye seemed to be mulling that over. "Are you certain you don't wish me to accompany you?"

"I prefer for you to stand guard here. If my husband wakes, explain where I am."

"Yes, Chieftess."

Sora pulled her feather cape tightly around her shoulders and walked to the stairs. As she climbed down, she gazed out across the seven mounds of Blackbird Town. Moonlight glittered from the rooftops and silvered the dark, swaying trees.

On a windy night eighteen winters ago, she'd sneaked out of this house to meet Flint. She remembered it as though it were yesterday. She'd become a woman three moons before, and her heart was flushed with the newfound freedom. Her mother had been carefully arranging feasts for her to meet elite young men from advantageous clans. Unfortunately, when a feast was given, it was impossible to screen out all of the less-desirable suitors. Skinner, the son of Oak Leaf Village's matron, had been invited. Flint had not, but he'd tagged along to keep his best friend company on the journey.

When Sora had first been led into the crowd of young men by her mother, dressed in a brilliant red feathered cape and copper headdress, all of the warriors had stared in awe. Not only was she destined to be high chieftess of the Black Falcon Nation, as the daughter of Yellow Cypress she was considered divine, descended directly from Black Falcon himself.

She had smiled out at the men and seen Flint standing slightly behind Skinner. His mouth had opened, and he'd stared at her as though she were too beautiful to be real. While the other warriors attempted to impress her, he'd stood at the edge of the gathering, smiling shyly every time he caught her eye. He was such a handsome youth, a head taller than anyone else, muscular, with large black eyes. Toward the end of the feast, Skinner had introduced Flint. She'd extended her hands, palms up, to greet him, and when he'd placed his hands atop hers, it was as though she'd been struck by lightning. A jolt went through her. He'd felt it, too. She could tell from the strange sparkle in his eyes.

At nightfall, just before she was to retire, he'd slipped through the crowd, taken her arm, and pulled her close to whisper, *"My canoe is stowed in the forest just past the burned-out tree. Meet me. Please."* Then he'd bowed and placed two fingers beneath his nostrils.

In that instant, a common gesture of respect had become something more. . . .

She'd found him sitting on the gunwale of his dugout canoe, waiting for her. They'd talked of their lives, and dreams. He'd longed to be a Spirit Healer. She wanted to be a good chieftess. He'd made her laugh. When they'd climbed into the canoe together, he'd kissed her with more passion than she'd ever thought possible. At last, he'd pulled her dress up over her hips, but instead of immediately coupling with her, like every other young man she'd loved in the past three moons, he'd just stared at her, his eyes like enormous dark moons. Reverently, he'd whispered, "May I touch you, Sora?"

"Yes. I want you to."

Instead of touching her with his hands, as she'd expected, he'd touched her with his mouth, his lips moving expertly, leisurely, striking fire wherever they lingered. Without even realizing it, she began to lift rhythmically against his mouth. When she thought she couldn't stand it any longer, the sudden warmth of his tongue startled her.

"Don't be afraid, Sora."

"I'm not afraid."

He'd moved her legs farther apart, then kissed his way down to her opening and slipped his tongue inside. He'd alternated between wet hot strokes and murmuring about how beautiful she was, how soft her skin.

They hadn't coupled that night. She hadn't even seen him again for three days, but every day had been filled with a sublime euphoria of anticipation.

When Sora's sandal reached the last stair, she strode down the path, past Priest Teal's mound, and crossed the bridge that spanned Raccoon Creek. The water burbled as it flowed over rocks into Persimmon Lake.

Just as she had that night eighteen winters ago, she stepped onto the lakeshore trail breathing hard. Ahead of her stood a slithering line of dark houses. The homes of commoners measured three or four paces wide and perhaps six long, tiny in comparison to the grand, elite buildings that graced the mound tops. She quietly walked past them. A few dogs, sleeping outside, growled at her until they realized who she was; then they flopped back down and watched her with moonlit eyes. Occasionally a tail thumped the ground.

By the time she reached the burned-out tree, she was cold to the bone. The wind had whipped her long hair into a wild wealth of tangles. She lowered herself to a fallen log on the shore and gazed out across the wind-churned water. Silver-crested waves curled across the surface like ribbons.

If he was there, at their secret place in the forest, he would see her and come.

She clutched her feathered cape closed and shivered. The first six moons after she'd met Flint had been like riding a hurricane. Her mother had ordered her to stay away from him, explaining that Flint wasn't a high-status man, that maybe in the future, when he'd proven himself in war, Sora could see him. Seven days later, she'd traveled with her mother to Oak Leaf Village to work out a Trade agreement. Skinner had come, supposedly to court her. Instead, he'd told her Flint was waiting for her in the forest. She'd sneaked out at midnight and run all the way.

That night, he'd lain back in the fragrant spring grass beneath the overarching branches of a redbay tree and propped his head on his hands. Smiling at her, he'd said, "Stretch out beside me, Sora. I've dreamed of nothing but you for days."

"You've filled my dreams, too."

His gaze admiringly went over her face, then dropped to her dress front. As he began to loosen the ties, she bravely moved her hand down his shirt until she felt the swell of his manhood.

Against her lips, he groaned, "Take me in your mouth, Sora."

She lifted his war shirt awkwardly, not really certain what to do, but as his manhood thrust up, her own desires stirred. She used her lips and tongue to gently stroke him until he grabbed her head and began pushing her down on him.

"Like this," he moaned. "I won't break."

She'd used more and more force, until he was thrusting into her throat so continuously she couldn't breathe. He seemed to realize it. He withdrew and crawled on top of her. For ten heartbeats he just lay there, panting against her hair; then he whispered, "I'm going to join with you now, Sora. Is that all right?"

She smiled. "Yes, I've been waiting for that."

His hand was shaking when he opened her and slid inside. Through gritted teeth, he said, "I'll try to be gentle, but I'm—"

"No, don't. I want to feel what you like."

He reached up to tenderly touch her face. "All right, but tell me if I hurt you."

He tried to start slowly, but his movements quickly built to fierce thrusts that jolted her body. The sensations were overpowering. He lifted his head to stare into her eyes, watching as the waves of pleasure shook her. When she cried out and fell back in the grass, his seed spilled inside her.

As she'd stroked his hair, Sora had whispered, *"Teach me everything, Flint. I want to know how to please you . . ."*

Grief cramped her stomach. Sora doubled over, light-headed, and watched the water that splashed onto the shore three paces away. The pungent scent of damp wood permeated the air. The wind had died down a little, but the oak branches behind her continued to saw back and forth, producing a sound like huge cricket legs being rubbed together.

As she lifted her head, she heard steps coming up the lakeshore path. Familiar steps.

In a worried voice, Rockfish asked, "What are you doing out here? Far Eye said you went for a walk in town. I looked everywhere for you."

"I needed to be alone."

"Are you all right?"

"I'm just worried about the things that were said in the council meeting."

He sat down on the log beside her, and his gray hair blew around his wrinkled face. "Nothing has been decided, Sora. There's no sense in worrying until Blue Bow actually accepts the council's invitation to come here and discuss the matter. Which I suspect he won't."

"Why not?"

He shrugged. "It's too risky. If I were Blue Bow I'd be nervous that you wanted to lure me into your territory to kill me."

She stiffened. "Why would he think that?"

"As you pointed out in council, he's not a fool. He must realize that once we know the way to the quarry, he will be an impediment. We won't need him or his warriors."

"But we don't know the way to the quarry, Rockfish."

"I've been thinking about that. I was going to discuss this with you early tomorrow, but this is actually better. We're alone out here. No one can overhear us."

Her suspicions roused, she slid around on the log to face him directly. He looked oddly like a dog with a fresh bone. "I'm listening."

"I've decided that you're right. An alliance with the Loon People is unwise."

She blinked. "But I can tell from your voice you haven't given up on getting the stone. What are you thinking?"

"I'm thinking that we could still catch Grown Bear on the trail. He brought back the jade. He knows the way. With the proper persuasion, I'm sure he would tell us—"

"Absolutely not."

He lifted both hands in a consoling gesture. "I just want you to consider it. We have until midmorning before we must dispatch the war party. After that, he will be too close to home for our warriors to safely apprehend him."

Moonlight shadowed his wrinkles, but his eyes had an inhuman glow. As though seeing him for the first time, Sora noted the web of lines that crisscrossed his fleshy nose, and the way his withered lips curved downward.

"Do you want the stone so badly that you would torture an innocent man to discover what he knows?"

He leaned forward. "Sora, I swear to you that once we know the way, I can gather enough warriors to undertake the journey. Then the stone will be ours alone. We won't have to split the Trade with anyone."

"Except with your people, you mean. They will get half of everything."

"Well, yes, of course, but that's just a two-way split, not a three-way split."

She sat there staring at this man she had thought she knew. "I can't believe you're suggesting this."

He opened his hands to her. "If this truly bothers you, let's discard the idea. I give you my oath I won't mention it to anyone."

Wind flapped his cape around his legs. From his fanatical expression, she could tell he wasn't going to let this go so easily. He'd become obsessed with the stone.

"Good," she said. "Then let's drop the idea."

"Fine, but"—he rushed to say—"please consider one last option."

An owl sailed over the lake, its dark wings flashing in the moonlight. She let it distract her for a few moments before she asked, "What option?"

"We may also be able to find the way by ourselves. If we just follow the coastline for sixteen days, as Grown Bear said he did, we may stumble upon the Scarlet Macaw People."

"And we may stumble upon their enemies. What if they have discovered that the Scarlet Macaw People made an alliance with northern barbarians to come and steal their jade? They could be lying in wait for us."

"Well"—he waved a hand dismissively—"that's possible, but I doubt—"

"If you want to throw away lives, my husband," she said without thinking, "you have my permission to go home to your own people to try and pull together this raiding party, but leave the Black Falcon clans out of it. I value the lives of our warriors too much to sacrifice them for a few boatloads of stone."

Rockfish folded his arms tightly across his chest. "Will you give me a few days to consider this?"

She nodded once.

He smiled, trying to make light of their discussion. "Now that we've settled that, why don't you walk back with me, Sora? You're tired and worried. You need to sleep."

"I'll be along shortly," she said in an icy voice. "You may go."

Surprised at being dismissed, he stared at her before rising to his feet. "I'll wait for you." He leaned toward her to kiss her cheek.

Sora pulled away. "Don't. I may be here a long time."

Rockfish appeared to want to say something else, but he just sighed and reluctantly walked up the shore.

She waited until he was out of sight; then she slumped forward on the log and squinted at the wind-blasted lake.

It took another hand of time, sitting in the cold, before she realized she was waiting for someone who wasn't coming. A man who couldn't come.

He'd been dead for days.

8

"I WAS UP HALF THE NIGHT RELIVING THAT AWFUL COUNCIL meeting," Wink said, crossing the floor to greet Sora as she ducked into the Matron's House the next morning. "I should have known old Wood Fern would wind up shouting and waving her fists in everyone's face."

"Especially mine," Sora said unhappily.

"Yes, I know. I'm sorry about that."

The room smelled of burning cypress and damp wood. Sora had run through a downpour to get here. Her black-and-white feathered cape shimmered with raindrops. As she removed it and shook it out, she asked, "Is that why you sent for me? You want to discuss the council meeting?"

"Partly. Our runner also returned. Let's go into the council chamber and talk about it."

Sora followed her down the hallway to the chamber. "The one we sent to Blue Bow? How could he be back so quick—"

"The runner I sent to Matron Wading Heron in Minnow Village." Wink ducked beneath the door curtain and gestured to the four benches around the central fire pit. "Come and sit down."

Wink walked over and sat on the closest bench with her back to Sora. The posture unnerved Sora. Wink had coiled her graying black hair on top of her head and fastened it with a carved deer-bone pin. Oval pieces of pounded copper glittered across the back of her blue dress.

Sora removed her woven mulberry bark hat and hung it on a peg by the door, next to her cape. "What is it, Wink? You're scaring me."

Wink waited until Sora sat down beside her; then she turned and gave her a somber look. "Didn't it surprise you when Skinner told you that he and Flint had gone out to scout the perimeter of their territory for raiders?"

Sora frowned. "Yes. Ordinarily a war chief would dispatch low-level warriors to complete that task. He wouldn't go himself."

Wink nodded. "Wading Heron said that Skinner was panicked, drenched in blood, when he carried Flint into her village. He kept spouting nonsense about being ambushed by someone they were supposed to be meeting."

"Why is that nonsense? Maybe the Lily People—"

"Didn't he tell you he woke in the middle of the night and found Flint's blankets empty?"

"Yes. Why?"

"Wading Heron said he stumbled into her village in the late afternoon."

Sora shrugged. "We don't know how far from Minnow Village they'd camped. Maybe it took him several hands of time to get there."

Wink's gray-shot black brows slanted down. "They weren't out searching for raiders, Sora. They had gone to meet someone."

"Perhaps they found the raiders and set up a meeting with the leader of the war party. Who knows?"

The lines around Wink's mouth deepened when she pressed her lips into a thin, disbelieving line. "You and I think too much alike for you not to have thought about the same possibilities I have."

"What possibilities do you mean?"

"I mean, what if Chief Fireberry dispatched Skinner and Flint to meet one of the Loon People? Blue Bow may not have come to us first about the jade."

Sora warmed her cold hands before the fire, remembering the thoughts that had roiled her souls last night on the lake. "I did think of that, but I dismissed it."

"Why? What if Water Hickory Clan has a secret alliance with Blue Bow? Do you know what that could mean to us? To Shadow Rock Clan?"

"If he already had an alliance, he wouldn't have sent Grown Bear to try to convince us to join him."

Wink leaned forward to prop her forearms on her knee. The copper bangles on her blue dress glittered. "Unless it's some kind of diversion. Maybe while we're arguing about his proposition, he and Water Hickory Clan are plotting to overthrow us."

"Wink, stop. I think we're seeing evil Spirits where there are none."

"Maybe, but I doubt it."

Water dripped in the far corner, creating a dark spot on the hard-packed floor. Last night's ferocious wind had probably torn loose a portion of the thatch roof. They would have to repair it before the next storm.

"Sora, what did you and Skinner discuss yesterday before I had him dragged off?"

"I think he knew my soul had slipped inside him. . . . We talk often."

If she told Wink the truth, Wink would order Skinner hunted down and clubbed to death.

"He asked me to give him three days."

"Three days to do what?"

"Talk to me. He said there are things he must tell me."

"Do you still think Flint's shadow-soul might be hiding inside him?" When Sora hesitated, Wink ordered, "I want the truth."

"I don't know. I don't think he's evil."

"Oh, well," Wink said with exaggerated politeness, "that's *very* convincing."

Sora searched Wink's face. "Why did you give him that satisfied smile after he told you he just needed a few more days?"

Wink scowled at her. "Because I *did* feel satisfied. I was looking for him and I found him. What surprised me was that I found him in your house. I thought you said you were going to stay away from him."

Sora waved a hand. "I was in the temple when he walked out of the council chamber and came up behind me. I didn't know he was there. If I had, I wouldn't have gone home."

Wink's expression softened. "I'm sorry. I should have ordered the guards to search there first. It never occurred to me he would be that bold."

"It doesn't matter now. Did Wading Heron say anything else?"

"Yes. Apparently the thing that worried her most was that Skinner was drenched in blood, but neither of them seemed to be wounded. She said her own personal Healer looked each man over carefully and found no injury that would explain the blood."

"Skinner may have killed someone trying to protect Flint."

"Did he say that?"

"No." She shook her head. "Did her Healer have any idea what caused Flint's death?"

"Not really, though he suspected poison."

"Poison?" Sora whispered. Her heart fluttered. "What kind of poison?"

"Wading Heron didn't say."

Behind her eyes, images passed as though painted in sequence . . .

From the time he'd been a boy, Flint had longed to be a Healer, not a warrior, as his grandmother insisted. He'd always experimented with Spirit Plants, and become quite fond of nightshade berries and buckeye nuts—both deadly poisonous to the uninitiated. She'd found him lying in the forest on numerous occasions locked in visions, his arms and legs trembling while he stared at the sky with huge black pupils. Usually, he would linger in that state for about six hands of time; then his soul would return to his body, and he'd spend the rest of the night throwing up. He'd even gone to study with the renowned Healer Long Lance, whom many called a witch; but Flint had come home after a single moon, saying the old man had already taught him what he needed to know. He'd tried very hard to find a Spirit Helper, but none would come to him.

Sora squeezed her eyes closed.

Wink said, "What's the matter?"

"I was remembering the time Flint ate too many nightshade berries. Do you remember that?"

"How could I forget? The convulsions lasted most of one day; then his soul was lost for another two days before Teal found it wandering alone in the forest and brought it home to his body. Do you think that's what happened?"

Sora opened her eyes. "Just before he divorced me, he started eating more and more Spirit Plants. On several occasions, I thought he was dead. He told me he could feel his Spirit Helper's wings beating just beyond his reach. If he could just fly a little higher, he knew he could climb onto the giant bird's back."

"The idiot."

"I begged him to seek guidance from Teal. He told me he didn't need another old fool whispering ignorant comments in his ear."

"That sounds like Flint. He always hated to have people interfere when he was set on destroying himself."

For all his strength and audacity, Flint had never figured out exactly what he wanted. He'd used Spirit Plants as much to fly away from himself as toward a Spirit Helper.

Sora flushed. Suddenly, she knew beyond a doubt where he was waiting for her. The one place, the one event, she would never forget. Her body wouldn't let her.

Sora rose to her feet.

Wink said, "Are you going to give him another two days?"

"I haven't decided."

"You're such a liar."

"I am not," she protested.

Wink rolled her eyes. "If I were sure it was just Skinner who was interested in you, I'd tell you to go do what you've both always wanted to do. Just be discreet. I'll protect you as best as I can."

Wink was giving her that *look*, as though she could see straight to Sora's adulterous heart.

But if anyone ever found out, the truth was that Wink would have no choice but to banish her. Sora responded, "I won't need your protection, Wink, but thanks for offering it."

Wink gave her a hard stare. "Don't say that until you know for sure."

"I *do* know for sure."

Wink shrugged and looked away; then she said, "Before you go, there's another matter I want to discuss with you. I've set the Healing Circle for tonight, just after sundown."

"Does Touches Clouds suspect he's being followed?"

"His uncles don't think so. They've been very careful. Everything is prepared."

Sora nodded and headed for the door.

Before she left, she said, "Come and get me when you're ready."

9

OLD TEAL STOOD AT THE EDGE OF THE PLAZA FROWNING AT Sora as she walked westward toward the bluff. In his conical rain hat and cape, he looked oddly unreal. Toothless, bald, his back hunched from age, he might have been a walking skeleton rather than a living man. His face was all sharp angles, which gave his white-filmed eyes a hauntingly dead look.

He lifted a gnarled hand and beckoned for her to come to him. She pretended not to understand, waved, and climbed the trail to the bluff top. The last thing she wanted was to speak with him. Teal had a way of seeing into people's souls. She was afraid he would see her guilty thoughts as plain as her face.

Light rain fell through the maple and oak trees. But for the steady hiss of drops, the world had gone quiet and still. Birds perched on the branches with their feathers fluffed out, and the insects had all crept beneath fallen leaves or into cracks in the bark to keep their wings dry.

When Sora came to the faint path that angled out into the moss-cloaked forest, she stopped. Tracks dimpled the sand. A man had walked here before the rain, yesterday probably.

Skinner?

Anxiously, she shoved aside the massive curtains of moss and wound along the path toward the meadow. The raindrops that beaded her cape reflected the rich green shades of the forest, giving the white feathers an emerald tint.

She ducked beneath the last whisker of moss and emerged at the edge of the palmetto-choked meadow. The fronds dipped and swayed in the rain. She hadn't been here in four winters, but she remembered everything: the red clay hill at the opposite end of the meadow, the gray rocks, the giant sycamores that ringed the base of the hill.

She didn't see anyone.

By the time she reached the sycamores, her feet were soaked and cold. The trail led straight up the face of the hill to the top, where a small ramada sheltered a fire pit. In the depths of winter, hunters often came here to keep an eye on the animals that wandered into the meadow.

She took a deep breath and climbed to the hilltop. The air was heavy with the scent of spring blossoms.

The ramada, four upright logs roofed with grass thatch, measured five by seven paces. The fire pit inside was cold. All of the ash had been blown clean, leaving a few chunks of blackened wood. A short distance away, a pile of freshly gathered wood had been carefully stacked. She looked around at the forest. Dead limbs had been cracked off the *west* side of a persimmon tree. Sora's gaze darted around, finding the same thing on several sycamores and oaks.

She involuntarily took a step backward.

The Black Falcon People always gathered dead limbs, roots, or bark from the *east* side of the tree. That was the good-luck quarter and stood for strength, while the west side represented weakness and death. Malevolent Spirits lived to the west, and it was the quarter from which witchcraft emanated. Only evil people gathered wood from the west sides of trees.

A witch might have walked this trail and gathered wood, but he hadn't built a fire, or . . .

"I'm not a witch. Is that what you're thinking?" he softly asked, and walked up the trail from the opposite side of the hill.

Startled, she stammered, "No, I—I wasn't."

His gaze went over her with infinite care. "It took you a long time to get here. Did you go to the place where I stowed my canoe first?"

"Yes."

"Any others?"

"No."

He leaned his shoulder against the ramada pole three paces away. His loose black hair looked freshly washed, shiny. Raindrops glistened on his handsome face and beaded the shark's teeth that covered the front of his buckskin shirt. His leggings, like the red sash around his waist, were damp.

"Where's your rain cape?" she asked.

"Skinner left our capes in the forest the night I died. I haven't had a chance to Trade for a new one."

Everything, even the way he clamped his jaw, reminded her of Flint.

"What happened here, Skinner? On this hilltop? Do you know?"

He hesitated for a long time before he replied, "I stole something very precious to you."

Heat flushed her body. There was nothing in his voice. No anger. No regret. Only a frail tremor, as though he didn't like remembering. "What happened?"

"I fed you a Spirit Plant."

"What plant?"

He clenched his fists at his sides. "Water hemlock. I put it in your stew. That's why you lost our son."

Even now, the loss ate at her souls. In her dreams, her shadow-soul walked with that little boy, watched him grow, heard his laughter, felt his arms around her neck.

When her child died, she'd wondered if perhaps Flint hadn't been feeding her small amounts of hemlock for a long time.

"What happened to the Trader I'd been talking with?"

Skinner made a futile gesture with his hand. "I followed him when he left Blackbird Town. Though it took me a full moon before I had the opportunity to slip poison into his tea pot."

A chill ran down her spine. She had never known for certain that Flint had killed the man.

Five winters before her mother stumbled over the edge of the bluff and fell to her death, Sora began taking over more and more of her mother's duties, negotiating fishing and hunting agreements, feasting visiting dignitaries, meeting with Traders. She couldn't even remember the man's name. He'd come from the southern islands to Trade pearls for fabrics. She'd been laughing at a funny story he'd told when Flint walked into the council chamber. Flint's gaze had cut back and forth between them, noted their smiles, and his eyes had narrowed in fury.

He'd disappeared for two moons.

When he returned, he'd been withdrawn, living in some inner cocoon. Sora had dared to ask what he'd done. He wouldn't answer. They'd eaten together in utter silence, a simple meal of catfish stew and maypop cake; then she'd walked into the forest to be alone. The gut-wrenching cramps had doubled her over almost on the very spot he was standing. The instant she'd cried out, he was beside her, stroking her hair, covering her face with kisses. *Forgive me, forgive me, I love you so much. You must believe me! This is for the best!*

All night long, she'd begged him to go find Teal or another Healer. He'd just rocked her in his arms, weeping like a child, and telling her he loved her.

"Forgive me, Sora. I know I almost killed you, but I wasn't—"

"Yes, I know. You weren't trying to kill me."

He lowered his head, and tears beaded his lashes. "No. I wanted to make certain you could never give birth to another man's child."

"Instead, you made certain I could never bear children at all."

He stared at the ground.

She asked, "Where did you learn that water hemlock could make a woman barren?"

He shrugged. "Long Lance taught me. I know I acted like a fool, Sora. That's why I finally had to go away. My love for you was an inferno consuming my insides. I couldn't stand to be away from you. I was afraid to allow anyone to talk to you when I wasn't there. Try to imagine what's it's like to be that afraid. Every instant of every day, I thought about your scent, about the feel of your fingers on my skin . . . and about another man thinking those same things."

"That's obsession."

"You think I don't know that? That's why I finally divorced you. I was terrified that someday in a jealous rage I might kill you."

The words took her by surprise. She had feared the same thing, but she'd loved him so much, she'd never allowed herself to believe it. "You did insane things when you were hurting. I understood that, Flint. I just—"

"No, you didn't understand anything." He slowly walked toward her. In an agonized voice, he asked, "Don't you see? I left because my love for you was killing *both* of us. And . . . I didn't feel like I was helping you anymore."

His tormented expression lodged in her heart like an arrow. She hurt for him, as she always had when he'd begged for forgiveness. Wink had told her many times that she was just as crazy as Flint, that no other woman would take a man back after the things he'd done to her. But she'd loved him.

He came toward her slowly. "Sora, will you take a walk with me? I promise we won't go far. I know you're afraid to be alone with me, and the gods know I understand that. I just—I don't want to talk to you here."

What harm could taking a walk do? It wasn't like there was a stew pot close that he could drop a Spirit Plant into. The fact that she even considered it, though, made her shy away from his hand.

"All right, but I must return to town soon. I don't have much time."

He nodded.

They walked down the opposite side of the hill and along the trail through the oak grove. The branches intertwined over their heads—dark filigree against the gray sky. Thick beards of hanging moss blocked most of the rain, leaving only a sprinkling of drops in the patches of dry grass beneath the trees.

She and Flint had taken this very trail a thousand times, laughing, playing hide-and-seek in the hanging moss, and her heart had not forgotten. The farther they went from the red clay hill, the more longing tore her souls.

She watched his broad shoulders sway. His body might have been Skinner's, but he moved with the fluid, catlike grace of Flint.

Confused, oddly happy, she didn't know what to think. For three winters, she had begged the gods to bring him back to her, and now, apparently, he'd returned.

When he held aside a curtain of moss for her, she stopped in front of him and looked up with her whole heart in her eyes.

"Are you Flint? Really?" The desperation in her voice stunned her. Had she wanted this all along? Just as Wink had suggested?

He touched her cheek, smoothed his hand down her jaw to her pointed chin, whispered, "Yes."

He bent down and kissed her mouth, then planted a dozen tiny kisses over her forehead and cheeks. As he gently embraced her, he said, "Holding you eases my fears, Sora. Gods, how I've needed this."

He untied the laces on her cape, and let it fall on the ground, but he kept kissing her, moving from her shoulder, down to her collarbone. With a tenderness she remembered in perfect clarity, he opened the laces on the front of her dress and freed her breasts.

"Please don't; I—"

"No one will know, Sora. I give you my oath."

"But Rockfish . . ."

As his gaze drifted over her body, he whispered, "Last night, you said I was the one great love of your life."

The shock of those words coming from Skinner's mouth affected her like a hard slap in the face. She blinked and stepped away from him. "Blessed Ancestors, what am I doing? You have me believing you're Flint! I should never have agreed to go for a walk with you."

"I am Flint. Let me prove it to you!"

She let out a small cry when he grabbed her, but it took barely five heartbeats for him to swing her into his arms and lay her flat on the ground. He jerked his war shirt aside, pried her legs apart, and shoved his rigid manhood inside her. The wave of pleasure that surged outward from her loins left her breathless. He took his time, each thrust going a little deeper, until he felt like a smooth wooden beam moving inside her.

The world seemed to come into sharper focus. The raindrops on her flesh pricked her with such superb reality they might have been icy needles. Before she was even aware she'd done it, she had locked her arms around his back and was matching him thrust for thrust.

"Yes," he whispered against her throat. "I knew you needed me as much as I needed you."

Their coupling became urgent, frantic.

She looked up. His dark eyes were glazed, on the verge of ecstasy. His thrusts began to come faster, pounding her against the ground.

When a dark shimmer began at the edges of her own vision, she whispered, "Flint, we mustn't make a sound. We can't take the chance that someone might hear us."

"I know." He clamped his mouth over hers to stifle her breathless moans while the contractions in her womb spread like tiny clenching fists. It lasted much longer than she remembered.

Just as the stunning intensity began to lessen, he whispered, "Forgive me. I can't hold back any longer," and the curtain of his hair trembled around her while he groaned against her throat. Sora worked to wring the last instants of pleasure from his body.

Finally, they lay side by side, staring up into the falling rain. The drops tumbled as they fell, flashing and winking like gray veils dropped by the Star People.

He lightly stroked her hair. "Are you all right?"

"Yes. Dear gods, I don't understand this, but I feel as though I just loved my husband. That's all."

It did not matter that he was no longer her husband—that, in fact, her husband was probably looking for her at this very moment, wondering where she'd gone.

"And I loved my wife." He rolled over, took her breasts in his hands, and began kissing them. "Tell me the truth. When we were joined, were you dreaming about me or Skinner?"

The words sent a shiver through her. "What are you talking about?"

"I know you wanted him at one time. I saw the way the two of you used to look at each other when you didn't think I'd notice."

The incongruity stuck her as bizarre. This could *be* Skinner, testing her, trying to find out if she really wanted him.

She said, "I was dreaming about you."

"Are you lying to me?"

He smoothed the raindrops from her neck, and his fingers stretched two-thirds of the way around her throat. His fingers tightened, pretending to strangle her. They had often done that while loving each other. It was an erotic game. When she neared climax, he would cut off her air, and then, when it was his turn, she would cut off his; it intensified their pleasure enormously.

"Why would I lie to you?"

"Because you're worried about him. I can tell by the way you say his name."

"Yes, of course I am. If I could just speak with him for a few moments, I—"

"No." As he tucked his hair behind his ear, the damp ends pulled across her chest; they felt silken and cool. He had a faraway look in his eyes.

"Why not?"

Ominously, he said, "He loves you, too, Sora. He's dreamed of coupling with you for eighteen winters. If he can get rid of me, he'll have you to himself."

That strained tone that signaled poorly concealed jealousy made her sit up.

"You told me Skinner didn't mind carrying your soul."

"He didn't at first; then he started screaming and wouldn't stop."

Sora stared at him. "When did this happen?"

"When I saw you on the chunkey field."

Almost too terrified to ask, she said, "Was he screaming in fear?"

"Rage. I think."

He flexed his fingers, then reached inside her open dress front to caress her breast. "Let's go where people can't possibly hear us, Sora. What about the cove near the shell midden?"

"No, I have to get back."

For several heartbeats, he ignored her to suck her breast. To her disbelief, she felt herself responding again. His mouth was warm, his lips soft. When he lowered his hand and tucked two fingers inside her, she said, "Please, Flint, I have duties."

"You're not going to run away with me, are you? You'd rather stay with that feeble old man."

His fingers probed deeper.

"Don't ask me. Not yet."

He kissed her while his fingers moved in long and languid strokes, as though he was petting an animal's soft fur.

"I'm sorry. I know it's too soon."

He lifted his head, and a strange light entered his eyes. After more than a decade of watching him, she had learned to recognize that light. She had to leave. Now. Or he wouldn't let her go.

To calm him, she said, "You asked if I still loved you."

"Yes," he softly answered, and tucked a third finger inside her. His rhythm changed; he used short stabs to strike fire along her nerves.

When her body began to quiver, she arched against his hand. "I long for you nearly every moment of my life. I do still love you."

He gripped her shoulder with one hand to hold her in place, and drove his other hand into her like he was repeatedly ramming a stiletto into the body of an enemy warrior.

How could I have forgotten this?

Every part of her body flamed. She half sat up, gripped his hand, and forced it deeper. She felt nothing else. Saw nothing else. The ragged cry that burst from her lips rang through the forest.

"Shh!" he urged, and quickly covered her mouth with his own.

She fell back to the ground, panting, staring wide-eyed into his handsome, knowing face. His fingers continued to move inside her until she stopped shuddering.

Then he removed them, cleaned them in the damp grass, and smiled.

"Are your souls completely here now, Sora?"

Panting, she said, "Yes, and I—I must leave." She rose unsteadily to her feet. "I have to get back to town."

He picked up her cape. As he draped it around her shoulders, he whispered in her ear, "I'll be waiting for you tonight. Midnight. At the eastern end of the bluff."

"I don't think I can meet you. Not tonight."

"Nonetheless, I'll be there."

She backed up the trail.

When he made no attempt to follow her, she turned and walked away, but every time her sandal landed, she listened to see if he was behind her, stalking her—as he had the last few moons they were married.

She walked briskly past Wink's mound and across the plaza toward the stairs that led up the face of her own mound. Rain had drenched Blackbird Town. Even the slaves had retreated inside. Puddles filled every low spot, shimmering like hundreds of wide-open eyes.

She rounded the corner of her mound and stopped.

Old Teal sat on the bottom step. He'd been sitting there for some time. The rain sheeting from his hat and cape had created a glistening ring around his body. He stared at her with naked understanding.

"Teal," she greeted as she walked forward. "What are you doing here? Did you need to speak with me?"

He tipped his skeletal face up, but for a long time, he didn't speak. His white-filmed eyes looked opaque. Finally, he said, "I thought perhaps you needed to speak with me."

"Why would I need to speak with you?"

He rose to his feet and adjusted his rain hat to shield the back of his neck. As he propped his walking stick, he said, "You've already started calling him Flint, haven't you?"

She could barely manage to breathe. "Who?"

Teal peered directly into her pupils, as though searching for something. "So far, you're alone in there, but you won't be for long, Chieftess. I can already see the nest he's making for himself."

"What nest?"

"It will happen in an instant. You'll barely have time to realize you've said yes. You'll be talking with him, feeling happy for the first time in moons, and somewhere inside you, you will wish you could feel this way forever. You may not have intended to grant him permission, but in less time than it takes you to blink, he will seep inside you."

She just stood there staring at him, unable to speak.

Teal pointed a bony finger at her heart. "There are ways to keep him out. If you decide that you want to fight him, come to me. You don't know it yet, but I am the last friend you have in the world."

He walked away into the mist like a ghostly wraith.

10

SORA RUSHED DOWN THE HALL TO HER BEDCHAMBER, UNTY-
ing the copper Birdman pendant as she went. When she ducked beneath the door curtain into the firelit stillness, the pendant rested in
her palm. Beautiful, the forked eyes flashed as she carried it across
the room to her personal basket.

A yellow dress with blue diamonds woven around the collar
rested on top of the basket. She pulled it out and tucked the pendant into the folds of a pale purple dress.

"What's *wrong* with me?"

She tugged her soiled dress over her head and threw it at the
floor.

Blessed gods, I just betrayed my husband.

If her clan ever found out, they would remove her as high chieftess and order her never to set foot in a Black Falcon village again.
She would lose everything—yet she didn't care. Her body lingered
in euphoria, and she knew if he ducked beneath the curtain right
now, she would lie down with him in the very bed she shared with
Rockfish.

As she slipped the clean yellow dress over her head, she looked around the bedchamber. Two copper-covered wooden celts, cere-monial clubs, hung side by side over their hide-covered sleeping bench. Symbols of office, they had belonged to her mother.

Chieftess Yellow Cypress had detested Flint, but she'd finally given in to Sora's pleading and conferred with Flint's mother—a common weaver—to arrange their marriage. Perhaps believing that Sora would get over him, or get bored with him, her mother had ensured that the marriage preparations lasted six moons.

"Six moons of quivering," she whispered to herself.

It was customary to wrap the young couple in a blanket every morning before the instructions began, symbolically joining them, but Flint had taken advantage of the cover to sneak his hand beneath her dress. While they listened to the sacred words of the elders, he had stroked her. He always seemed to know when she was on the verge, because he'd slip a finger inside her to feel her muscles twitching, then deeply probe her until she finished. How they got away with it, she never knew.

As a smile curled her lips, she suddenly felt sick, as sick as she had right after Flint divorced her and she'd been consumed by these same memories.

Sora knelt before their sleeping bench and pulled out the wooden box where she kept her ritual jewelry. A large circular rattlesnake gorget stared up at her with one huge eye. Carved from a conch shell, the stylized serpent coiled back and forth, forming spirals around its central eye. "Brilliant lookers," they were called, because their bright unblinking eyes had the power to kill. Priests coiled enormous spiritual snakes around the houses of sick people to keep Raven Mockers and evil Spirits away, leaving only a narrow space between the head and tail for relatives to enter and exit. They used rattlesnake fangs to mark the spots where they would place their buffalo-horn sucking tubes to suck out magical amulets shot into the bodies of the sick people by witches.

Teal had given her this gorget a moon after Flint left.

"Wear this."

"Why?"

"It will protect you from his witchery."

"You think he's a witch?"

"A very Powerful one."

He'd slipped the necklace over her head and ordered her never to take it off.

But when her mother died, she'd put away the rattlesnake gorget and began wearing elaborate copper breastplates that befitted her new status as high chieftess of the Black Falcon Nation.

Smoothing her fingers over the cool conch shell, she wondered if she should have obeyed Teal and never taken it off.

She tied the necklace around her throat and turned to—

Rockfish stood in the doorway behind her, holding the curtain aside. Raindrops glinted in his gray hair. Shocked to see him, she sucked in a breath.

"I'm sorry," he said. "Did I frighten you?"

"Yes. A little."

He stepped into the chamber and let the curtain fall closed behind him. "I was hoping to speak with you for a few moments."

A curious expression lined his elderly face, and for one stunning moment she feared someone might have seen her and Skinner in the forest and told him.

"Of course."

She went to sit on a mat before the fire. Instead of sitting beside her, as he always did, he crouched on the opposite side. The wrinkles around his mouth deepened.

"Sora, I've made my decision." He glanced up at her from beneath stubby lashes.

"What decision?" she asked, confused.

"You told me I had your permission to go home to my people to try to pull together a raiding party to go after the jade."

"You're going?"

"Yes. I've spoken with Wink about it, and she told me that if you did not object, she didn't either."

After their conversation earlier, Wink probably thought it was Sora's way of getting her husband out of town while she dallied with Skinner. No wonder she hadn't put up a fuss. She was trying to "protect" Sora, just as she'd promised to.

"I'm going to leave today, if you don't need me for more pressing concerns."

A hollow ache spread through her chest. She'd been so stupid to tell him he could go. Those few careless words might cost the Black Falcon Nation dearly.

Trying to sound calm, she asked, "When will you return?"

"Three days, maybe less. I'm taking four men with me. We'll alternate, paddling day and night."

Neither of them spoke for a time.

Finally, she said, "Give Chief Tenkiller my fond regards and return as quickly as you can. I'll miss you, my husband."

Surprised by the affection in her voice, he hurried around the fire to embrace her. As he kissed her hair, he said, "I'm doing this for *our* good, Sora. I swear it. You'll see."

Tenkiller is a wise leader. Surely he will say no to this insanity.

She patted his wrinkled hand. "I know you wouldn't do anything to harm me, or my people. I just wish we agreed on this matter, but since we don't"—she gestured her frustration—"do what you must and come home."

Relief slackened his face. "I'll pack my things and go now. That way I'll be home sooner."

As he rushed around their bedchamber, stuffing things into his pack, he periodically turned to smile at her, and a weightless sensation filled her—as though she were not quite in the chamber. Her souls had drifted out to the forest, and she could *feel* Flint thrusting inside her.

11

TOUCHES CLOUDS HELD HIS COUSIN'S NEW RED CHERT KNIFE to his heart and smiled as he trotted down the twilight trail toward his secret hiding place beneath the rotting log. His cousin, Sharp Nose, had left the knife in plain sight and walked out his door, leaving Touches Clouds alone with it. Of course he'd taken it. Sharp Nose was a stupid boy. He didn't deserve to have a knife like this. Touches Clouds was a much better hunter and fisherman. He *needed* the knife. Besides, even though he'd wanted it badly, he'd left Sharp Nose's magnificent ritual knife, the knife his cousin used in sacred ceremonials.

Parting the hanging moss, he stopped to look around. It had been raining off and on all day. The dwindling gray light sparkled on the wet leaves of the palmettos and created a lacy veil in the moss. Twenty paces ahead, the rotting log fell across the trail like a huge dark arm.

Joyous, he raced to it, removed the rock that covered his stolen prizes, and carefully tucked the new knife into his collection. It looked beautiful resting alongside the other knives and surrounded by his precious beads and bits of pounded copper. More than anything, he loved sitting here touching them, looking at them. If only he could . . .

Whimpers came from the forest to his left.

Touches Clouds jerked around to look, but as he did so, crying started on his right.

He leaped to his feet and spun around in a circle. It was getting very dark now. He couldn't see anyone, but other people began crying. Children, men, and women out in the trees.

"Who's there?" he called in panic, and backed up to block the sight of his collection beneath the log. If anyone saw this . . .

Shadows moved.

All around him, the hanging moss swayed, as though being parted by dozens of hands.

One by one, they stepped out. His young cousins came first, their eyes filled with tears as they walked toward him. Each carried a knife in his hand. Behind them his mother and father emerged carrying baskets, then his uncles and aunts. Finally, his grandparents and Matron Wink and Chieftess Sora stepped out.

Terrified, he tried to run, but they closed the circle around him. All of them were crying now, loudly. It sounded like a funeral. His mother wept so hard she might have been suffocating.

His four cousins came forward with their knives and tucked them into his clothing. Two went in his belt, two in his sandal lacings. Touches Clouds looked down. They were his cousins' best knives! They had given him their most valued possessions—their ritual knives! Sobbing, they backed away and walked out into the forest while his mother and father, uncles and aunts came forward. They formed a very tight ring around him. Each placed a basket at Touches Clouds' feet. When he looked inside them, his mouth gaped. His mother's basket contained the precious hair comb her great-grandmother had given her just before she'd died. Mother loved that comb! She'd once said that losing it would tear her souls from her body!

Touches Clouds' Uncle Cooter knelt in front of him and spread his arms wide, in a warrior's gesture of surrender, and the other adults joined him, spreading their arms, their fingers touching.

It's a Healing Circle. Blessed Ancestors! They think I'm soul-sick!

The thought shocked him. He knew he shouldn't take things—his uncles had told him often enough—but it had never occurred to him that he might be sick! He started to tremble. Sometimes, he did feel like an evil Spirit lived inside him—maybe that's why he had to take things that didn't belong to him? Did his family care so much about his illness that they would give him their most precious belongings to keep him from stealing them?

"Mother?" he said in a quaking voice. "Am I sick?"

"Yes, my son." She wept and reached out to touch his hand. "You are. We love you very much. Sit down. Let us Heal you."

His relatives joined their arms around him in one enormous embrace. As their tears fell upon his face and shoulders, he suddenly understood how much he'd hurt them, how much they wanted him to get well. It was as though the water falling from their eyes cleansed his souls and forced out the evil Spirit that made him do bad things. He could feel it. It flew away into the darkness like a poisoned arrow. His heart hurt as though a huge hole had opened in it. He shouted, "I'm sorry! Mother, I'm sorry! Father, I'm sorry!"

Matron Wink and Chieftess Sora stood up.

Matron Wink lifted a bag of corn pollen and sprinkled it over Touches Clouds' head while she sang the Healing Song:

A long way to go,
A long way to climb,
A long way to Skyholder's arms,
But no evil can enter that embrace.
Skyholder, never let this boy go.
Keep him close to your heart,
As we will. Always.

We will keep Touches Clouds close to our hearts,
   And no evil will enter him.
Climb now, Touches Clouds; climb into our arms.

He lunged to embrace each person around him, sobbing, "I'm sorry, Uncles! Aunts!"

Chieftess Sora hesitated, and all eyes turned to her as she pulled a "brilliant looker" pendant from around her own throat and draped it over Touches Clouds' head. It rested against his chest like an enormous coiling serpent.

"Never take this off, Touches Clouds," she softly instructed, and petted his hair. "It will protect you if the evil Spirit tries to come back."

He grabbed her hard around the neck and wept. "Thank you, Chieftess. I'll be good now. I swear it!"

Far off in the trees, he saw a shadow move. The man just stood there.

Watching.

SORA REMAINED BEHIND IN THE DEEPENING VEIL OF DUSK, allowing Wink to lead the Healing Procession back to Blackbird Town, where Touches Clouds' family would have a small private feast to celebrate his Healing. If she followed them, someone in town would see her and feel compelled to stop to discuss the boy's future or some other clan issue that needed her attention. She longed to avoid that.

After the day's events, she had begun to wonder if perhaps she, too, wasn't soul-sick. There had been a moment during the Healing Circle when she'd felt her own souls lighten, as though the Midnight Fox had lifted his ugly head and begun to leach out, draining away like water through a cracked pot. But before he could fly away, he had hardened into a black lump that settled in her belly like bad food.

She sank down atop the rotted log where Touches Clouds had hidden his stolen treasures, lifted her cold hands, and rubbed her temples.

"Blessed gods," she whispered aloud. "I think I'm in trouble. Maybe I really do need Teal's advice."

In the distance, the forest murmured with talk. It was soothing, the voices warm and concerned, not the usual banter of people going about their evening duties. She could make out Wink's voice, then Touches Clouds' voice. For the next few days, Wink would be responsible for monitoring Touches Clouds to make sure the evil did not sneak back inside him.

Sora lowered her hands and studied them in the gray light. The first Star People had awakened, and their gleam silvered her fingers. They looked like her hands, but they felt like someone else's. Memories of the different textures of Skinner's body seemed to be locked in her tingling fingertips.

And I cherish each one.

She clenched her fists to keep those precious memories from slipping away.

A cool breeze meandered through the forest, shoving the hanging moss back and forth.

His voice came to her very softly: "I thought you might stay behind to think about what happened today."

Sora's spine prickled. She turned.

For what seemed an eternity she gazed across the ten paces that separated them, into his starlit eyes. She must have been little more than a pale shadow against the darkening background of trees, but he seemed to see her perfectly. He never blinked.

She rose from the log, and as though they'd both planned it, they hurried through the palmettos to step into each other's arms. All that existed was his mouth on hers, sweet with the tastes of roasted catfish and plum jam.

"I think I'm going mad. I crave you constantly, Skinner. I can't—"

"We're both mad, Sora. We always have been." He smiled against her lips. "Ask anyone."

He's right. Neither of us has been sane since the day we met.

Her fingers dug into his broad back, and she clutched him more tightly. The hot river that flooded through her left every hair on her body flaming. Their mouths collided violently.

I called him Skinner. Didn't he notice? Why didn't he correct me?

By the time they parted, panting, to get a few breaths into their starving lungs, they were both shaking, and his eyes were filled with tears.

"What's wrong?" she asked. "Are you all right?"

He wrapped his arms around her and held her as though he would never let go. "Sora." He seemed to be fighting to keep his voice from breaking. "You asked to talk with me, so he's giving me a few moments. That's all."

She pushed back and stared up in confusion. "Who? Who's giving you a few moments?"

"He—he's very Powerful. I can't come out unless he allows it. So, please, *please listen to me!*" He stroked her hair with a trembling hand. "He was right when he told you that I loved you. It was agony for me when the two of you were married. You hurt each other so much, and I always thought that if it were me you were married to—as it should have been—I would have petted you and protected you. I would never have hurt you."

She gazed up into his tormented face. His demeanor had completely changed. The strong, forceful person she'd loved that morning was gone, replaced by this tender, much too sensitive man. Fear spread its wings in her chest.

"Listen to me!" he said, and shook her. *"He truly is trying to help you. Do as he says. Do* exactly *as Flint says. He knows what you did, and he's working very hard to—"* His head snapped back as though he'd been slapped. He stumbled.

She lunged to grab his arm before he fell. "Skinner? What do you mean Flint knows what I did?"

Through gritted teeth, he ordered, "He told me everything, Sora. Just this once, let him help you. You need his help desperately."

"Why? What's—"

"Stop playing the fool! We know the truth, Sora!" He took her shoulders in a painful grip. "Soon everyone will know. Do you understand? All of your dark secrets are about to be revealed. Go home. Go home and prepare yourself."

He shoved her hard in the direction of Blackbird Town and ran away through the forest like a man fleeing a war party. Branches and twigs cracked in his wake.

13

WHEN SORA LEFT HER HOUSE LATER THAT NIGHT, THUNDER rumbled in the distance. She'd talked Wink into dismissing Far Eye, and with Rockfish gone, there was no one to see her as she walked down the wet steps. Every house around Persimmon Lake was dark and quiet. Only the frogs serenaded the darkness. She pulled up the hood of her goose-feather cape and trotted toward Teal's mound. Orange firelight gleamed above his smoke hole. He must still be awake.

Elaborate paintings decorated the clay-plastered walls of the Priest's House: life-size images of Dancing Birdmen, mountain lions with the feet of eagles, and coiled snakes with human smiles. His house was separated into two chambers. In the front, a small private room opened into the charnel house—the place where he prepared the dead for the journey to the afterlife. Row upon row of clean dry bones rested on the wall shelves. Tucked into ceramic pots, or wrapped in cloth bundles, they represented the last remains of the elite rulers of Blackbird Town. Sora frequently came here to seek advice from her mother's eye-soul, the soul that remained with the body forever.

As she neared the door curtain, she called, "Teal? Are you awake?"

A hoarse old voice answered, "Yes, I've been waiting for you."

She ducked beneath the curtain and found him sitting on a mat before his fire, sipping a cup of tea. The interior walls also bore the life-size images of the gods. He seemed to paint a new one every winter, and now a crowd of divine eyes gazed down upon her.

Teal rose to his feet. His bald head and age-bowed back reminded her of a plucked bird. "Please join me, Chieftess," he said, and gestured to the mat across the fire.

Sora knelt on the mat and shifted uncomfortably. "I need your help."

"I know that better than you do." His eyes glowed whitely in the firelight as he filled and handed her a cup of tea. "Drink this," he ordered. "It will help to cleanse you."

She took it and watched him gingerly lower himself to the mat again. He wore a coarsely woven white robe that hung over the skeletal frame of his body. The knobs of his shoulders resembled knots beneath the fabric.

"He's already coaxed you into his arms, hasn't he?" Teal asked.

She swallowed hard and whispered, "How did you know?"

"I could see it on your face when you returned from the forest. Did your husband know?"

"No. I don't think so."

"Then you are more fortunate than you deserve. But take care with Matron Wink. She knows you better than Rockfish does. What are you going to say when she questions you?"

Sora clutched her cup in both hands. "I'm going to lie."

He nodded, and his bald head shook on the slender stem of his neck. "Yes, that's how it generally goes. You'll lie to her, and to your husband, and to anyone else who might suspect. Then you'll meet him in the forest again. Sooner or later, someone will see you."

Her face felt hot, prickly. "No, Teal, I swear to you—"

"I've seen seventeen shadow-souls in my life, Chieftess. I tried to observe each very carefully, because I knew I would be called upon to cast him out of the body he inhabited. Usually, I could do it. Do you remember the three people your mother ordered killed when she was trying to stop Blue Manatee's soul from jumping around the bodies of his family?"

"I remember them very well."

"Blue Manatee was a strong one. Stronger than me." Teal sucked his lips in over his toothless gums and stared at the fire as though distastefully remembering the battles. "I couldn't help them because they wanted Blue Manatee inside them."

"I don't understand. Why would someone—"

"Don't lie to me. You *do* understand. I wasn't just fighting Blue Manatee. He only entered people who loved him so much they would have done anything to keep him alive. I had to fight to get him to leave, and to get them to let him go. I wasn't strong enough to fight all of them."

She stared at him. "They wanted to keep him alive?"

"Of course. Just as you want to keep Flint alive. Everyone has his own reason for committing spiritual suicide. Blue Manatee's wife couldn't imagine life without him; his daughter loved him very much; I think his brother wanted his power and wisdom. To have him close, to talk with him for the rest of their lives, they were willing to give up their own bodies."

She sat up straighter. "Teal, how does a person know that a shadow-soul has entered her body?"

He tilted his head, and his white-filmed eyes flashed. "Eventually, you realize that two people are looking out your eyes."

"Eventually?"

"It depends on how clever they are. Shadow-souls are frail at first. If they think you will fight them, they rest for a time inside you, days or even moons, while they gather their strength. That's when the fight begins."

"The fight?"

"The fight to keep your body as your own. Blue Manatee's wife didn't realize what had happened for three days. She thought her reflection-soul had begun to wander the forest. Finally, he spoke to her, telling her not to be afraid. He told her he was using her, but that he loved her very much and would never hurt her. What would you do if you heard Flint's voice say that?"

Three winters ago, she would have cherished the idea that he was alive inside her. They would have been closer than ever possible while they inhabited two separate bodies. But now . . .

"I'd be terrified, Teal."

"Would you?"

His harsh tone made her go rigid. "Yes."

"Then we have nothing to worry about." He gave her a small smile. "When will you see him again?"

Startled, she said, "After what you just told me, I'll never see him again."

Teal rose to his feet and crossed the chamber to a wooden box that rested beneath his sleeping bench. As he tugged it out, he said, "You must."

"But I don't want to."

The damp leather hinges squealed when he opened it. Wrapped in purple cloth, a small pot sealed with a wooden stopper lay on top. "I want you to give him a pinch of this."

Teal carried the pot over and handed it to her. She smelled the stopper; it had an acrid scent. "What is it?"

"The juice of fermented hominy mixed with bloodroot."

Sora stiffened. "But that's poison. Won't that kill Skinner?"

"One pinch isn't enough to kill, but it will make him very ill. When the vomiting is over, he will long to sleep. If Flint is in command, it will give War Chief Skinner a chance to take control of his own body again. That will help us."

"How?"

"Presumably Skinner wants Flint gone as much as we do. Once Skinner is back in control, I will start giving him a series of strong potions; it will still be a difficult battle, but at least we will have a chance of casting him out."

He flicked a hand at her. "Now leave. You're supposed to meet him tonight, aren't you? Didn't he tell you where?"

The eastern end of the bluff . . .

"How did you know that?"

"All shadow-souls have a single goal, Chieftess: They want to find someone who will cherish having them inside. He thinks you are that person. That's why he came to you. He can't afford to waste time. Nor can you." He pointed a crooked finger at the door.

She tucked the pot into her belt pouch and uneasily got to her feet.

Teal peered up with nearly blind eyes. "Hurry. I'm sure he's waiting."

14

SHE CUT ACROSS THE PLAZA AND HEADED TOWARD THE eastern end of the bluff that formed the northern boundary of Blackbird Town. Spark flies flashed as they flitted through the towering oaks. The mist had turned into a fog that eddied with the breeze, twining like ghostly arms around the massive trunks.

Emotion tightened her throat. Could she do it? Could she slip poison into Skinner's drink?

It won't hurt Skinner. It will help him by driving out the evil shadow-soul that's stolen his body.

"But Flint . . . Flint, forgive me."

When she passed beyond the gleam of Blackbird Town, she slowed down and carefully picked her way over the uneven ground. Some of her earliest memories were tied to walking this trail. When she was a child her mother used to take her to the small pond that glistened at the end of the bluff to gather duck eggs. She could still recall the laughter of the women and children who combed the reeds for nests, still see the mother ducks soaring overhead, squawking in dismay. Later, after they returned to Blackbird Town, the rich scent of eggs frying in deer fat had filled the air.

As she followed the bend in the trail, her souls filled with other recollections . . . nights of wild excesses with Flint. Toward the end of their marriage, when the strain was almost unbearable, he used to demand that they row out onto the pond in their canoe and love each other through the night. It was an odd routine where they would sleep for a hand of time, then one of them would wake, leisurely begin touching the person who still slept, and perhaps another hand of time later, couple again. *Nights of moonlit eyes, smiles, and soft words.*

Those dreamlike moments, however, always shattered at dawn when she woke and wanted to return to town. He never wanted to go back. He would beg her to stay in the canoe with him. His protests grew so desperate they frightened her. At the very end, she was so afraid he might not let her go home that she started refusing to leave town with him. He grew truly sullen after that. His eyes became dark abysses that seemed to suck the life from her souls.

"Sora?"

She stopped and stared at the hanging moss ahead of her. She could make out the shifting forms of trees, but nothing human. Sister Moon must have crested the horizon, because the mist had taken on a frosty shimmer.

"Skinner? . . . Flint?"

"I'm over here."

She angled away from the trail toward the sound of his voice. Palmettos rustled against her goose-feather cape as she walked.

"Where are you? I don't see you."

"At the edge of the pond. You remember."

She shouldered through thick curtains of moss until she saw him kneeling before a small fire dressed only in a breechclout and leggings. Long black hair fell down his back, but the wet sheen of mist outlined every muscle across his naked torso.

"I was afraid you wouldn't come," he said.

"I had to. There are things I must know."

He reached into the darkness behind him, pulled out two folded blankets, and spread one over the sand. "Come and sit beside me."

She sat down cross-legged. At first she avoided his gaze. Through a break in the clouds, she could see Sister Moon hanging over the treetops like a round ball encircled by a gauzy orange halo. The pond, which measured thirty paces across, rippled silver. Everything was starkly beautiful.

Sora turned and found him watching her with luminous, unblinking eyes.

"Do you ever think about the nights we spent together on this pond?"

She nodded. "Often. Those times were very precious to me, Flint."

Clearly happy that she hadn't called him Skinner, he knelt beside her on the blanket and smiled. "Those nights kept me sane. I had you all to myself. I didn't have to be afraid that another man was gazing at you admiringly. You were mine. Totally."

"Other men were of no interest to me, Flint. I'm just sorry I couldn't make you believe that."

He bowed his head. "My beliefs were crazy. I know that now. I see everything as if for the first time."

A chill wind breathed across the pond and fluttered his long hair over his broad shoulders. "You must be freezing," she said. "Why don't you wrap the other blanket—"

"No." He shook his head. "I feel alive. That's what I need tonight. *Life*."

The way he'd said it sent a shiver up her spine, as though being cold somehow fended off death. "What's wrong? Is something happening?"

He slowly turned, and she saw the hard line of his clenched jaw. "I have to leave soon. I've spent too much time here."

"You mean . . . tonight? You're leaving for the Land of the Dead tonight?"

He tightened his fingers over his knee. "Yes."

The pot in her belt pouch felt suddenly cold, as cold as a dead fist. If he truly planned to leave, she wouldn't have to use it, and that thought comforted her.

"That means," he said darkly, "that we must speak honestly. Ask me whatever you wish; then I'll ask you my questions."

Lightning flashed over the treetops, followed a few moments later by a peal of thunder. The storm must be moving closer.

She said, "Tell me why Skinner was covered with blood when he entered Minnow Village."

His black brows plunged down. "Who have you been talking to?"

"I asked Wink to send a runner to Wading Heron."

A swallow went down his throat. For a time, he didn't answer. "I should have known you'd do that. I don't even like remembering that day. Skinner was running, carrying me in his arms. I kept spitting up blood. I felt like my insides had been shredded by a thousand copper flakes. Every time I vomited, he clutched my body more tightly against him and told me to hold on, to stay with him, that we were almost there."

Sora shivered. When a man became sick at the stomach and vomited it was believed that a dead person had been eating out of the same dish with him.

"Did you make it to the village?"

"No, I died along the way." He rubbed a hand over his face, and grief tightened his eyes. "Gods, Skinner loved me. He'd loved me since we were children. His sobs were heartrending. I've relived those last moments many times and I—I think Skinner wanted me to live so badly that he actually 'invited' me inside him."

You give him permission. . . . It happens in an instant.

Beneath her cape, Sora's hand rose to grasp the rattlesnake pendant old Teal had given her. Her fingers found nothing, and she remembered she'd given it up to protect Touches Clouds.

"I'm sure he did invite you inside him," she said.

"Why do you say that?"

"Something Teal told me. He tried to warn me about you. He

said you'd make me happy and when I wished I could feel that way forever I would be unwittingly giving you permission to come inside me."

His eyes flared when lightning flashed through the forest, followed by the deep-throated roar of a thunderbird. In a taut voice, he said, "Yes, that's what it felt like. Skinner didn't want me to travel to the Land of the Dead. He couldn't let me go." He shook his head. "But I should have gone anyway. I know that now. This was a bad choice. I needed to talk with you, but—"

"The agony in your voice tells me you are not a shadow-soul. I don't think evil souls would ever worry about whether or not they'd made the right decision."

As though in gratitude, he reached out and placed his hand on the cape over her thigh.

"You said the two of you had gone out to scout for Lily People raiders, but Wading Heron said Skinner told her you were meeting someone in the forest." She studied his hand on her cape, saw the fingers flex. "You weren't meeting one of the Loon People, were you?"

His hand caressed her leg. "Why do you ask?"

"Who were you supposed to meet?" She held her breath, waiting for the answer.

His fingers parted the gap in her cape and moved up her leg. His touch had always affected her like a splash of hot water; it seared her flesh.

"That's what I wanted to talk to you about, Sora. I must talk to you about that. My last living words were a question for you."

He slipped his left arm around her shoulders and kissed her while his right hand moved up her thigh.

Slowly, he lowered her to the blanket and propped himself on one elbow beside her. The misty rain thickened, creating the impression that his dark face was floating above her. When the lightning flashed again, his features bleached to a silvery white. He had his jaw set, as though straining against himself.

"Are you all right?" she asked.

"I will be. You know what I need to calm me." He kissed her again. "You want me inside you, don't you?"

"Yes. Yes, I do."

He smiled as he untied his breechclout and rolled on top of her. His manhood swelled against her abdomen. It took only heartbeats for him to enter her. He groaned and arched backward.

Sora locked her legs around him and held him tightly. "I just want to feel you inside me. This may be the last time we . . ." Tears constricted her throat. She started moving.

"Blessed gods," he whispered, matching her rhythm. "You cannot know how I need this. It keeps me here. Here with you. Just as it keeps your reflection-soul home. Tell me what to do. I'll do anything you want."

She sat up with him still inside her. Over the fourteen winters they'd been together, they'd perfected this; she moved in frantic fits, bringing him close, then stopping, just petting him, before she slowly began again. He braced his chin on her shoulder, and a low moan sounded in his throat. He didn't have to do anything except give her the freedom to please him. When her own body flushed on the verge of ecstasy, he rasped, "Harder, Sora. Hurry."

She moved faster. As the fiery wave built, he gripped her hips and violently shoved her down on his manhood.

He moaned, "Oh, gods! I love you so much."

His hands moved up her arms and clenched around her throat. When she started gasping for air, it was as though white-hot fire exploded inside her. Her entire body bucked and quivered. She fell back to the blanket, and the weight of his body covered her. His wet hair fell around her like a dark curtain.

Abruptly, he lifted his head and choked out, "Who . . . who's there? Sora? Do you see him?"

"Who?"

"*Him.*"

She tried to rise to look, but he shoved her down, and his fingers tightened around her throat again. "Quickly, before he comes, tell me how you did it." He was glaring at her with huge eyes, feral eyes, more animal than human. "How did you do it!"

"Do what?" she begged, and tore at his hands. "What are you talking about?"

"How did you kill her? Did you slip something into her food? Did you hire someone to do it?"

She struck him with her fists, fighting to shove him away. *"Stop it!"*

He shook her so violently she thought her neck might snap. "How did you get that close to her camp without someone seeing you? Witchery? Did you fly in on raven wings?"

The edges of her vision went gray. Just before she lost consciousness the Midnight Fox's gleaming eyes blazed to life inside her, and she . . .

Skinner rolled off her and shouted, "No, don't! You don't understand! Talk to Wink. She'll tell you . . . *Wait!"*

Then he roared.

And kept roaring.

Like a man fighting for his life.

15

RAIN PATTERING LIGHTLY ON THE ROOF WOKE HER.

She fought her way up from a horrifying dream where she was running, running through a dark forest, utterly lost and alone.

When she opened her eyes, she blinked in shock at the familiar walls of the temple chamber in her house. A pile of hides covered her body, so many that she felt too warm—but she didn't shove them away. Not yet. She fought to remember how she'd gotten home. Had he let her go? She didn't remember anything after blacking out. High above her, the deep blue light of predawn streamed through the smoke hole. It was almost morning. Several hands of time had passed since Flint had had his fingers around her throat. The fragrances of wet thatch and bark walls filled the room.

When she heard hushed voices in the hallway outside, she started to shake. Men's voices.

Where is he?

With the stealth of a shivering rabbit, she remained still. Only her gaze roamed the temple, landing on the magnificent carving of Black Falcon that hung on the wall, then drifting down to the Eternal Fire, and finally to the swaying door curtain at the far end of the temple. The main door curtain at the front of the house must be hooked back, allowing a breeze to flow down the corridor. As the temple curtain fluttered, she caught glimpses of men in many-colored capes. At least two. Maybe three.

She sat up.

A new scent came to her. Bitter. Like poison.

She slowly turned to her left.

And looked straight into Skinner's eyes.

For a moment, she was too shocked to move.

He lay on his stomach with his arms and legs twisted at impossible angles. As wind gusted into the temple, he didn't blink. Still, were it not for the coagulated blood that had pooled in his mouth, she might have thought him alive.

As the truth sank in, she leaped to her feet and stood over his dead body trembling like a leaf in a powerful gale. Her teeth chattered. Her fists twitched.

"What *happened*?"

The voices outside stopped.

"Chieftess?" War Chief Feather Dancer drew the curtain aside and looked into the temple. Tall and muscular, he'd seen a great deal of raiding in his twenty-six winters. His heavily scarred face proved it. But he had kind brown eyes.

Feather Dancer hurried toward her, his red cape fluttering around his long legs. He wore his black hair in a bun over his left ear. "Forgive me. You were hurt so badly, we didn't think you'd wake for several hands of time. We just brought you here moments ago. Please believe me, if we'd thought you might wake so quickly, I would have never left you lying beside the criminal."

Almost without her knowing, her hand lifted to rub her swollen throat, then moved to the back of her head. A lump the size of her fist met her probing fingers.

She croaked, "What happened? I—I don't remember very much."

"You wouldn't, not after that blow to your head. Priest Teal woke me shortly after midnight. He told me he'd gone to your house to speak with you and found you gone. He ordered me to find you."

Teal must have feared the worst. Thank the gods for his prudence.

Feather Dancer examined her tormented expression, and the lines at the corners of his eyes deepened. "I woke Far Eye, and together we began to search for you. After about four hands of time, Far Eye stumbled upon the two of you near the pond. When Far Eye first flipped him over, the war chief was still alive, but by the time Far Eye shouted to me and I ran to find him, the war chief had died." He heaved a breath. "We brought you here immediately, and I sent Far Eye to notify Matron Wink. I'm sure she'll arrive shortly."

Sora shakily walked to the benches arranged around the Eternal Fire and sat down. Her rain-soaked dress stuck to her legs. On the wall, Black Falcon seemed to move in the shadows of the flames. His eyes shifted slightly to glare at her like an accusing god.

She stared at Skinner's dead body. "What killed him?"

As Feather Dancer walked forward, he threw back his cape and pulled a small pot from his belt pouch—the pot Teal had given her. He handed it to her. It was empty. "We found this beside him. Far Eye smelled the pot, then the war chief's breath; he said they smelled exactly alike. We assumed that after he hurt you, the war chief took his own life by drinking the poison."

An eerie mixture of grief and doubt swelled her chest. Skinner would have never taken his own life, but Flint . . .

During their marriage, every time he'd hurt her he'd suffered terrible guilt. She'd often wondered if that wasn't why he ate too many Spirit Plants; he was trying to atone, to find a Spirit Helper to guide his souls away from the need to hurt her.

"Please send a runner for Priest Teal. There's something I must ask him."

"Yes, Chieftess, I—" Feather Dancer swung around when loud voices erupted in the hallway.

"Where is she?" Wink demanded.

"In the temple, Matron!"

Wink burst through the door curtain with her eyes blazing. Panic lined her face. Her graying black hair hung over her shoulder in a long frizzy braid. As she rushed forward, her brown cape swept back, revealing the pale green sleep shirt beneath. She must have risen straight from her blankets.

"For the sake of the gods!" she growled at Feather Dancer and flung out a hand to Skinner. "Get his filthy body out of the temple! What were you thinking bringing him here!"

"Forgive me, Matron," he pleaded. "Where should I—"

"Take him to Teal!"

"Of course—so his body can be prepared. Far Eye! Help me carry away the war chief's body."

Far Eye ran beneath the door curtain and grabbed Skinner's legs. Feather Dancer took his shoulders, and together they muscled the dead body out of the temple.

Wink dropped onto the bench beside Sora and wrapped her arms around her in a tight embrace. "What happened? Far Eye said Skinner attacked you."

Sora leaned against her. Having Wink close was like cool salve on a hot wound. She felt safe for the first time in days. "I don't remember much, Wink. He started choking me. I blacked out. Someone clubbed me in the head. I don't even remember it."

"But you were alone. He must have done it."

". . . I suppose so."

Wink's gaze went to the pot sitting on the bench beside Sora. "What's that? Far Eye told me Skinner had apparently drunk poison. Is that it?"

Sora pulled away from her and soberly stared into her friend's eyes. "There's more to it, Wink."

"What do you mean?"

"I decided I needed help. I went to Teal around midnight. I—"

"I thank Black Falcon you had the wits to do that. He gave you the poison?"

She nodded miserably.

In fierce pride, Wink said, "You did the right thing. I assume you gave him the poison, and when he realized it he tried to kill you?"

Sora blinked. Had she done that? It sounded plausible. "I honestly don't remember. I may have."

As the shock and fear began to subside, overpowering grief set in. She felt sick to her stomach and utterly exhausted. She desperately needed to sleep.

Wink scanned her face with more than twenty winters of experience and gently said, "It's over now. Let it go. You did the right thing," she repeated. "What else could you have done?"

Tears welled hotly in Sora's eyes. *I could have run away. Why didn't I just run away?*

More voices rose in the hall.

Teal ducked under the door curtain, followed by Far Eye and Feather Dancer. The warriors took up positions on either side of the door while Teal hurried forward with his walking stick. He looked like he'd been up all night worrying. His old face was drawn and cadaverous. He wore the same coarsely woven white robe that he'd had on earlier.

"Chieftess," he said as he hobbled to stand in front of her and examine her with his white-filmed eyes. "Are you all right?"

"I'm alive."

"Which is more than we can say for War Chief Skinner," Wink coldly added. "Good work, Teal. I'm grateful for your fast thinking."

The old priest dipped his head in acknowledgment. "When she came to me last night, I knew I had to do something, so I—"

"Wink," Sora interrupted. "Could you leave us alone? I need to speak with Teal in private."

Obviously confused by the sudden change in her behavior, Wink rose to her feet. "Of course. I'll be waiting just outside the door. Call me when you're finished."

She walked away and ducked beneath the door curtain. Soft voices rose outside.

Sora inhaled a deep breath, and through the long exhalation asked, "You told me there wasn't enough poison to kill him. Why?"

"I told you one pinch wouldn't kill him. That pot is empty, Chieftess. Did you give him all of it? Not that it matters." He heaved a sigh. "I was hoping you would."

Sora leaned forward to brace her forearms on her knees. If she didn't get to bed soon, she was going to collapse. "I must have done it."

The silence stretched. She didn't know what else to say.

Teal lifted his chin. "Shadow-souls choose their victims carefully, Chieftess. He was intent upon having you. For a time you will feel guilt and regret, but what happened was for the best. You stopped him before he could enter you or someone else."

Powerful emotions seethed in her heart. She longed to weep. "He told me he was leaving. He told me he'd spent too much time here and he had to leave."

Teal reached out to put a gentle old hand on her arm. "Chieftess, please try to see this clearly. You have bruises on your throat. Someone struck you in the head. I suspect he lied to you about leaving. He must have known you were not going to invite him inside; he may have even suspected you would fight him with all your heart. He had to knock your souls loose before he could seep into you."

She opened her eyes, and her lips parted in fear. "Are you saying he might have—"

"Only that it's possible. I will keep a close watch on you for the next few moons to make sure you're alone in there."

"Thank you, Teal."

"I am, as always, your servant." He dutifully inclined his bald head and walked away. When he ducked beneath the curtain, she heard him speak to Wink, but couldn't make out the words.

Moments later, Wink came back into the temple with a frightened expression. Feather Dancer and Far Eye followed her.

"We need to get you to bed, Sora," Wink said. "Teal tells me there are evil Spirits feeding around your head wound. Your headache is going to get worse before it gets better. He's brewing a strong pot of willow-bark tea for you. It should ease your pain, but you're going to be very ill for a while."

"I'm sure he's right."

She rose and stood on trembling legs. Sparkles suddenly filled her eyes. She staggered. Was it her head wound, or was the Midnight Fox sneaking in for the kill?

"Help her!" Wink ordered.

Feather Dancer and Far Eye leaped forward to take Sora's arms, supporting her while she slowly walked down the hallway to her bedchamber. Wink brought up the rear.

By the time she sat on her own sleeping bench, she had barely the strength to lie down. Wink shouldered by the warriors and pulled the blankets up over Sora.

Softly, Wink said, "Try to sleep. I'll wake you when the pot of tea arrives."

Sora nodded and closed her eyes.

Wink and the men moved to the door, where they spoke in low voices.

"Feather Dancer," Wink whispered, "I want you to post twice as many guards, and organize several scouting parties. This news is going to travel like it's riding Eagle's wings. We must guard our borders for the next moon or so until I can work out an agreement with the matron of Oak Leaf Village to compensate her for the life of her son."

Why didn't I think of that?

When Skinner's mother learned of the death of her son, she would be outraged. No one would be able to convince Matron Sea Grass that her only son, the man destined to become the chief of Oak Leaf Village, had been possessed by a shadow-soul. She would want revenge.

Sora's eyes fluttered open. She saw Wink duck out of her bedchamber, followed closely by Feather Dancer.

Far Eye remained for a few moments longer, staring at her as he fingered his large conch shell pendant. Then he, too, was gone.

16

FOR DAYS SORA DRIFTED IN AND OUT OF TORTURED DREAMS, awaking only long enough to eat some of the broth Wink forced into her mouth or to drink more willow-bark tea. Often, she heard Wink ordering someone to be gentle as Sora was rolled onto her side and her soiled bedding removed and replaced. Every night, Wink bathed and changed Sora's sleep shirts herself; then she softly talked about the day's events until Sora drifted to sleep again.

Finally, when the evil Spirits in her brain began to die, she opened her eyes.

She was alone. Firelight flickered on the wall of weapons above her sleeping bench. The copper studs on the war clubs glinted. She inhaled a deep breath and let it out slowly. The air smelled of freshly washed blankets and venison broth. When she turned, she saw the pot bubbling in the ashes at the edge of the hearth. Someone stood outside her door. She could see feet beneath the curtain.

A guard?

Yes, of course, to protect you in case Matron Sea Grass dispatches an assassin to find her son's killer.

Wink would be leaving nothing to chance. She must have already sent the fastest runner in town to Oak Leaf Village, hoping to beat the other people who carried news of Skinner's death.

How long had she been lying here? Days. But how many? Three? Four?

Sora sat up. Her headache was no longer excruciating, but it was still there, throbbing behind her eyes. She massaged her temples with cool fingers. Fortunately the nausea had passed.

She eased forward to sit on the edge of the bench. Dressed in a long blue sleep shirt that brushed her ankles, she looked like she'd lost weight. Bars of ribs pressed against the fabric beneath her breasts, and her gaunt belly resembled a curved hole. But, oddly, the days of pain and meager food had left her vision unusually clear. The worm patterns in the roof beams seemed more beautifully intricate, the smell of the cypress fire particularly fragrant. Were it not for the headache and the fact that she still did not know what had happened the night Skinner died, she would have felt like she'd been reborn.

Why don't I remember?

Her souls had played out every possible permutation of what might have led to Skinner's death, but nothing made sense.

She hadn't given him the poison. She was sure of it. Feather Dancer could be right that when Flint discovered what he'd done, he'd drunk the poison himself, but why would he kill his best friend? Flint's reflection-soul would never have killed Skinner—he would simply have gone on to the Land of the Dead. And why would Flint's shadow-soul have killed its own vessel?

Perhaps it had another one.

Her darkest fear was that Teal was right. Flint's shadow-soul had choked her until she'd blacked out; then it had seeped inside her. She didn't feel him, but he might be waiting, allowing her fears to subside, before he spoke to her.

The guard outside the door shifted; feet moved beneath the curtain.

Sora rose on wobbly legs and made her way to the fire, where she slumped down on the mat next to the soup pot. Nested ceramic bowls and buffalo-horn spoons rested on the hearthstone beside the pot. She dipped a bowlful and picked up a spoon. Her hand shook. Half the broth spilled before the spoon reached her mouth, but she kept feeding a ravenous hunger.

By the time she'd finished, cold bumps speckled her flesh. She set the empty bowl down, walked across the chamber to her clothing basket, and pulled out her favorite dress. Made of woven buffalo wool, dyed crimson, it had cost her mother a fortune in Trade pots and colorful fabrics. Sora removed her sleep shirt and slipped the soft garment over her head. The velvety feel against her skin soothed her raw nerves. Hundreds of seed pearls ringed the collar and chevroned the sleeves. The dress accentuated her every curve, forming to her body like a second skin.

She sat down by the fire again. So much was at stake, she had to think. Rockfish had not yet returned. The things he'd taken with him—his pack, bow, and quiver—were still gone. Which meant she couldn't have been unconscious for more than two or three days. But a good deal might have happened in that interim. She had to contemplate the worst: Wink's runner had been to Oak Leaf Village and had already returned with a message. What had Sea Grass said? She was a wise old woman, generally thoughtful, but she'd loved her son very much. Perhaps Sea Grass had told Wink to prepare for war. Or worse, maybe they were at war.

"Blessed gods," she whispered. "I'm such a fool. I didn't just endanger myself. The entire town may be at risk."

If Sea Grass attacked them, it would force the other clans to choose sides. The entire nation could fray like cloth left in hot sunlight.

How could she have done this? Had her love for Flint blinded her to the political realities of her position? She was high chieftess of the Black Falcon world. Other people could make mistakes; she couldn't. From her earliest memories, her mother had imprinted that message on her souls. *"Little Doe can act like a stupid fool. She's a commoner. People will forgive her for the impetuousness of youth. If you do the same things she does, people will wrap a rope around your throat and hang you. Never forget that. You are* not *like other people. You must set the examples for what is right and what is wrong."*

Sora closed her eyes and watched the firelight play on the backs of her lids.

War stared at her from three sides now. They still hadn't resolved the problems with the Loon People over access to traditional root-gathering grounds; Blue Bow continued to hold eleven of their people hostage. Oak Leaf Village could be massing warriors to avenge Skinner's death; and Rockfish might return home tomorrow bearing news that his people had committed hundreds to fight an unknown people in a faraway land for a green stone called jade.

"How could you have let things get to this point?"

Her stomach cramped. She lowered a hand to rub it. One thing was certain: She could eliminate the threat from Oak Leaf Village. If she went to Sea Grass and offered her own life, she knew the old matron would accept. She'd probably be tortured for days before they killed her, but her death would pay for the loss of Skinner. The Shadow Rock Clan would have to formally condemn her and declare her Outcast to save itself, but if the alternative was their fall from power, Sora knew she could talk Wink into . . .

The guard outside said, "Good morning, Matron," and Sora recognized Feather Dancer's deep voice.

"How is she?"

"She's awake. I heard her moving, but she hasn't come out yet."

Wink called, "Sora? May I come in?"

"Yes."

Wink ducked beneath the door curtain wearing a clean tan dress decorated with red starbursts made from porcupine quills. Her graying black hair had been braided and twisted into a bun on top of her head. "How are you?"

Sora heaved a sigh. "I won't know until you tell me what's happening."

Wink came across the floor and sat down on the mat to Sora's right. A sheen of perspiration covered her narrow, hooked nose. She looked like she'd just gotten out of heated negotiations. "Sora . . . I have a question for you. I'm sorry to have to ask it so soon, but—"

"The runner returned from Oak Leaf Village, didn't he?"

"Yes, but he wasn't alone. Sea Grass and twenty warriors came with him."

Twenty was provocative. Sea Grass expected trouble.

"What price is Sea Grass asking?" Sora braced herself. Sea Grass must have come to look straight into the eyes of her son's killer before she made her decision.

"She's heartbroken and angry, Sora, but she's being cautious. She wants proof that her son was infected with Flint's shadow-soul."

"Proof? How can we prove it?"

Wink reached out and touched her hand. Her dark eyes narrowed. "She wants you to answer a question."

"What question?"

Wink was watching her with such intensity that it made dread swell inside Sora. "Sea Grass wants to know if you had received news that Flint was to marry again."

She couldn't move. It was as though her body had ceased to exist. "Wh-what?"

"Did you know Flint was getting married?"

Wink straightened and gave her a suspicious look, as though wondering why Sora hadn't answered the question. "Flint was supposed to wed a young woman named White Fawn on the first day of the Moon of Blossoms."

"How long did I sleep? I don't even know what moon it is."

Wink stared at her. "You slept for two days."

"But that means . . ." Her voice faded as the truth dawned.

"Yes, on the day Skinner died Flint was scheduled to marry a fifteen-winters-old woman. Did you know it?"

Sora anxiously twisted her hands in her lap. "No, not—not for sure. Over a moon ago, a passing Trader mentioned the possibility, but he said it was just a rumor, nothing official had been announced. At the time, I didn't believe it."

"What about later?"

They had known each other almost their entire lives. If Sora lied, Wink would see it in a heartbeat.

"I did not *know* he was going to marry," she answered. "And why would it matter to Sea Grass? What bearing could my knowledge of Flint's marriage possibly have on Skinner's death?"

The wrinkles around Wink's mouth seemed to have frozen, like lines etched in stone. "She thinks you were involved in Flint's death, as well as White Fawn's. I told her that was impossible, that you'd been negotiating with Blue Bow at the time, but she—"

"I still don't understand. Isn't the issue whether or not I killed Skinner?"

Wink looked away and toyed with the shell bracelet she wore on her left wrist. "It's more complicated than that."

"How so?"

"Apparently Flint and Skinner were not out on a scouting expedition to find barbarian Lily People. They'd gone to meet the bridal procession."

Sora's mouth went dry. "Why would Skinner have lied about that?"

"I don't know."

"Did they meet the procession?"

"No. White Fawn's distraught family entered Oak Leaf Village without ever seeing Flint or Skinner. Apparently, White Fawn had been killed and buried on the trail."

"And Sea Grass believes that I . . . what?"

Wink turned back with a steely expression. "She's not sure what to believe. But she's clearly wondering if you didn't kill Skinner because he was the only witness to Flint's death. Or maybe he knew something about White Fawn's death that you didn't want known."

Sickness rose in her throat. She suddenly needed to lie down again. "Is that what you believe, Wink?"

Wink didn't answer for several agonizing heartbeats. When she did, her voice had gone low. "I believe what the greatest holy man in the Black Falcon Nation tells me."

Sora cocked her head, not certain she understood.

Wink continued, "Teal saw Flint's shadow-soul in Skinner's eyes. He took the only action he could to make sure our people were safe. You were just the tool he used to accomplish the grisly task. So far as I'm concerned, you risked your life to help Teal protect Blackbird Town."

The loyalty in Wink's voice struck Sora like a blunt beam in the stomach. She swallowed hard. "Does Sea Grass want to speak with me?"

"She does." Wink rose to her feet and gently put a hand to Sora's forehead, testing for fever. "But Teal demanded the right to speak with her first. After she hears his story, if she still wants to talk with you, I'll make some excuse until you feel strong enough."

Sora took Wink's hand and clutched it tightly. "Is everything else all right in town? Any word from Blue Bow or Rockfish?"

"Rockfish sent a runner saying he will be home tonight, but we've heard nothing from the Loon People."

Sora let go of her hand and got to her feet. "I need to rest again. Keep me informed."

"You know I will."

Wink walked for the door. As she drew back the curtain, she said, "If you feel well enough, take a walk around your house this afternoon. It will do the villagers good to see you."

"I'll try."

Wink left.

Sora returned to her sleeping bench, where she curled into a tight ball. Confusion and guilt competed like raging bears inside her. She had to talk to someone, but it couldn't be a lifelong friend.

She needed the advice of a man or woman who did not really know her. Objective advice.

Who do I know who is utterly pragmatic . . . and trustworthy?

Her gaze drifted to the feet beneath the door curtain.

SORA SAT WITH FEATHER DANCER ON THE BENCH AT THE rear of her house, looking northward toward Wink's mound. If Wink saw them, she'd think Sora had just gone for a walk as she'd promised. Cool wind whimpered through the trees, bringing her the mingled scents of the lake and roasting fish. She felt weak, but growing stronger by the instant. She'd needed the fresh air more than she'd realized.

"Feather Dancer, I must ask your advice as my war chief."

His thick black brows pulled down over his thumblike nose. Ten winters ago the Lily People had captured and tortured him. The scars that crisscrossed his cheeks and forehead resembled thick white yarn plastered on his tanned skin.

He carefully responded, "Is this about the war chief's death and what Matron Sea Grass might do?"

"Yes."

"I, too, am concerned about that."

"I'm sure you are. Through my own fault I may have unwittingly brought a hurricane into Blackbird Town." She massaged her brow.

Wind tousled his long black hair around his massive shoulders as he stared at her. "How may I help?"

"Whatever I say must remain between us. Can I rely on that?"

He nodded once, and she knew from his stern gaze that he'd die before he would break that vow.

Sora exhaled the words, "This story begins a long time ago. I had seen fourteen winters . . ."

She told him about her courtship with Flint, leaving nothing out; then she discussed Flint's usage of Spirit Plants, his jealous rages, the men he'd killed for smiling at her. She chronicled their divorce and her subsequent despair, told him about how she'd made a fool of herself running after Flint. She wanted to make sure he understood it as clearly as she did. When she told him that Skinner had immediately claimed to be Flint and proceeded to prove it by revealing things about her that no one else in the world knew, Feather Dancer's eyes tightened. Unable to look at him any longer, she confessed their couplings in the forest, explaining that that was how she'd known beyond a doubt that she was loving Flint, not Skinner. Far more than knowing every detail of her life with Flint, he knew things about her body that no other man knew.

"Toward the end he looked startled and said, 'Who's there?' He asked me, 'Do you see him?' "

"Did you see anyone?"

"No."

Feather Dancer's arm muscles contracted, bulging through the fabric of his cape. "What happened then?"

She made a futile gesture with her hand. "He was strangling me. I tried to fight back. I lost consciousness. The next thing I recall is waking up in the temple."

Feather Dancer didn't say a word. He stared across Blackbird Town.

People walked around the base of her mound, calling greetings, waving happily to see her up and around. Sora forced herself to smile and lift a hand to them.

"Chieftess, before I respond, may I tell you what I believe?"

"Yes, of course."

His black hair blew around his scarred face. "I am a warrior. I've seen death many times. I don't believe in gods. I don't believe in an afterlife. I think a man lives and dies and that's all there is."

Her heartbeat quickened. "Then you think my reflection-soul is out wandering in the forest somewhere? Perhaps I should hire a priest to go search—"

"No." He shook his head. "I don't believe in souls either. But . . ." He let the word hang.

"But what?"

"Has it occurred to you that perhaps none of this is true?"

She shook her head as though she hadn't heard him right. "What do you mean? Some of it's true."

"Is it? There's only one thing we know for certain: War Chief Skinner is dead. We have the body. Everything else is questionable."

She held his somber gaze. "What are you talking about?"

"I have listened very carefully, Chieftess, and it seems clear to me that there's a conspiracy to force you to step down as chieftess of the Black Falcon Nation."

She couldn't even speak. She just stared at him.

"All of this—this nonsense," he said flatly, "seems to have one goal: to get you out of the way by any means necessary, and install someone else in your place."

Her entire body became a single silent scream.

"Forgive me for speaking so bluntly, Chieftess, but if you do not take action to defend yourself soon, they will succeed."

"Explain."

"All they have to do now is bully you into offering your own life to Matron Sea Grass in compensation for the death of her son. Then it's over. The thing was quite neatly done."

Why had she believed? Guilt? Longing for a man she'd loved with all her heart?

"But that doesn't explain how Skinner knew—"

"You said that at one time you suspected Skinner might be a berdache."

"Yes. He never married, and he always seemed much closer to men than women."

"Chieftess, if he and Flint were lovers he would know *exactly* how Flint loved another person."

She went still.

That's how he knew how to touch me. Flint had touched him in exactly the same way.

"I suspect, in fact," Feather Dancer continued, "that Skinner was Flint's lover long before you met him, and probably remained his lover after you married Flint."

Memories flooded her souls. Late at night, lying in her arms, Flint had often spoken about Skinner. They'd been lifelong friends. She'd thought nothing of it. But now she wondered if Flint had talked about her when he was lying in Skinner's arms. Is that how Skinner had known the most intimate details of her life?

"Dear gods, how can I stop this?"

His expression turned dark. "First, we must determine how many people are involved in the conspiracy."

She frowned in confusion. "How many do you think are involved?"

He gestured to her head wound. "Someone clubbed you in the head, probably to make sure you were unconscious while he killed Skinner; then he carefully erased his tracks. At least two, but probably many more."

. . . The satisfied smile Wink gave Skinner when he told her he just needed a few more days.

A few more days to do what? To maneuver her into a position where she would be forced to relinquish the position of chieftess? Who did they want to install in her place?

"But that doesn't make sense. If Skinner was working with someone, why would they have killed him?"

He gave her a cold smile. "With him gone, there's one less person who knows what really happened."

Long Fin walked out of Wink's house and lazily stretched his arms over his head, as though he'd just awakened from an afternoon nap. When he saw them, he waved.

Both Sora and Feather Dancer nodded in return. She prayed the youth would have the good sense to leave them alone, but as he trotted down the mound steps, she feared she wasn't going to be that lucky.

Feather Dancer said, "Let me quickly say one last thing: Whoever is playing this game isn't finished. First, he will try to get rid of you by forcing you to offer your life to Matron Sea Grass to compensate her for the loss of her son—"

"I've already considered that."

"Well, don't. That's what they want. Second, if you refuse to offer your life, they'll be forced to find some other reason you are not fit to rule. Start thinking about what they might accuse you of. . . ."

His voice faded as Long Fin trotted up the grassy mound slope toward them, smiling.

Feather Dancer whispered, "He's scared right now. He'll never be safe until everyone involved in this, except him, is dead. Anyone with a shred of knowledge represents a threat to him. Expect more people to die."

Long Fin spread his arms, as if to embrace Sora.

"Chieftess!" he said with a broad smile. "I am very happy to see you looking so well!"

He knelt at her feet and touched his forehead to her sandals in respect, *a thing he had never done in his life*.

18

LONG FIN TROTTED ALONG THE STARLIT TRAIL BY MEMORY, almost colliding with several tree trunks before he saw the Matron's Mound loom out of the foggy night. Rockfish, gasping for breath, hurried along behind him.

. When they reached the steps that led up the rear of the mound, Long Fin stopped and said, "Mother wishes to speak with you alone. Not even I am allowed to be on the mound while you two are in council."

"Tell me what's happened!" Rockfish said in panic. "Is it Sora? Is she all right? Why won't Wink let me go home before—"

"Hurry," Long Fin said, and gestured to the steps that led to the rear entrance of the Matron's House. "All of your answers are up there."

He watched Rockfish take the steps two at a time, climbing as quickly as he could. After days in a canoe, and on the trail, exhaustion seemed to weight his elderly body. His legs shook as he crested the mound and disappeared from Long Fin's view.

Long Fin folded his arms and stood guard in front of the stairs.

A PALE YELLOW GLEAM STRETCHED ACROSS THE MOUND AS Wink pulled the door hanging aside to watch Rockfish stalk toward her. His wrinkled face was coated with grime, his gray hair dirty.

"Wink?" he called. "What is it? What's wrong?"

She motioned for him to enter her house. "Thank you for coming, Rockfish."

He ducked beneath the curtain. Torches lined the long hallway, casting a burnished amber gleam over the walls. Stripping his cape from his hot body, he said, "Is Sora all right?"

"Yes," she said firmly, but even to her it sounded like a lie.

"Are you—"

"Come with me. I want to speak with you in my personal chamber."

He followed her to her chamber and ducked through behind her. His eyes scanned her belongings. Her bedding hides lay neatly folded beneath a blazing image of Mother Sun on the wall.

"Please, sit down." She gestured to the mats spread around the fire. The sweet scents of roasted corn and sunflower seeds suffused the air.

"I don't want to sit down. I want to know why your son caught me on the trail and told me that you'd ordered me to come here before I went home to my wife."

Wink rubbed her cold arms. "If you're not going to sit down, I am. I had a long, difficult day." She sank to the mat. "I ordered you to come here first because there are things we must discuss before you see Sora."

He stepped forward. "What things?"

"Something has happened, and I wanted you to hear it from me so Sora wouldn't have to tell you all the sordid details."

"Does this have something to do with the news traveling the trails?"

Her eyes narrowed. "What news?"

"Traders are saying that War Chief Skinner is dead. That Sora killed him. I didn't believe it. Are you trying to tell me it's true?"

Wink extended her hands to warm them before the flames. "There's a lot more to the story. . . ."

AS THE EVENING TURNED TOWARD MIDNIGHT, WINK HUNG her head and stared at the soot-coated hearthstones. Rain had begun to fall. The drops that made it through the smoke hole sizzled when they struck the burning logs.

"What does Teal say?" Rockfish asked in a low voice.

Wink shrugged. "He says she'll be all right. She needs time to come to terms with what she did."

"Are you certain she killed him?"

"She must have, Rockfish. I ordered Feather Dancer, the best tracker in our world, to comb the place where Skinner died. There was no one else there. Just Skinner and Sora."

"And, of course, the tracks left by Feather Dancer and Far Eye when they found them."

"Yes."

Her mouth tightened, and Rockfish noticed. He said, "Is there something you're not telling me?"

She fumbled to rearrange her blue dress over her sandaled feet.

"I must know, Wink. How can I help her if I don't—"

"I'm going to tell you," she said. "I just wanted you to know everything else first."

He waited.

Wink inhaled a deep breath to fortify herself. "How much do you love Sora?"

"For the sake of the gods, just tell me!"

"You realize that if you divorce her, she'll be removed as chieftess? Our clan will declare her Outcast. No one will take her in. She will be forever alone."

His thoughts seemed to be putting it together. He must know

that the only reason she would suggest that he might divorce Sora . . .

He squeezed his eyes closed, and anger tensed his jaw. "Blessed Ancestors, she betrayed me, didn't she?"

"You're buffalo dung for putting it that way." Wink glared at him. "The man was her husband for fourteen winters—almost five times longer than you have been."

"She coupled with Skinner."

"She coupled with *Flint*. He was evil. He seduced her." She leaned toward him with fire in her eyes and carefully said, "She had no choice. She was being manipulated by a wicked shadow-soul!"

He scoffed, "She had no choice—"

"Stop acting so righteous. If your former wife suddenly came back to life and told you that she still loved you and needed you, what would you do?"

His eyes went hollow. He hesitated for a long time before he answered, "Briar and I loved each other for forty winters. She bore me nine children. Memories of her laughter, her teasing smile, flash behind my eyes constantly . . . followed closely by images of her slow, agonizing death. Losing her tore my souls apart." He rubbed a hand over his face. "Hallowed gods, if she returned, I'd give up everything for her. Including Sora."

"Of course you would. Any one of us would do exactly what Sora did. I'm glad you realize it."

His anger seemed to drain away. He looked utterly fatigued. As he sank down to the mat, he said, "When is Sora supposed to meet with Sea Grass?"

"Tomorrow."

"I want to be there."

"To defend her, or to—"

"Of course I want to defend her!"

Wink's gaze probed his souls, seeking truth or deception. "I will not see her destroyed over this, Rockfish. Not if I can help it. Teal has already spoken with Sea Grass. He told her Sora was innocent. Teal took full responsibility for Skinner's death."

"But she didn't believe him?"

"Let's just say she wants to look into the face of her son's killer while Sora tells her what happened."

Rockfish nodded. "I can't say I'd be any different."

The wind shifted, and a cascade of raindrops blew down the smoke hole. The burning logs hissed, and sparks crackled out. Rockfish watched the glittering haze whirl upward toward the ceiling.

"You've always been her shield, Wink," he said, and smiled faintly. "Whenever she's threatened, you're there fighting for her with blind, passionate loyalty. Why?"

"I'm rarely blind, Rockfish, especially when it comes to loyalty." Wink's brows arched, daring him to contradict her. "And as to why . . . I grew up with her. I know what's she's been through."

"What has she been through? She never talks to me about her youth. I know almost nothing about her life before I married her."

Wink smoothed a hand down her long braid and gazed at the fire. "I'll tell you a few things, Rockfish. The rest, I'll leave to her."

"Tell me about her father's death. For three winters I've heard rumors."

Wink nodded. "After he died, her mother went a little mad. Yellow Cypress wandered the house at night, crying and calling her husband's name. She frequently woke the town. When Sora tried to comfort her, Yellow Cypress beat her. I don't think she meant to; she just didn't know what she was doing. Sora had seen seven winters. The only thing she understood was that her mother wanted to hurt her. She never got over it. To this day, she blames herself for things that are not her fault, like her father's death and Flint divorcing her. She even blames herself for her older sister's death."

"I thought Walks-among-the-Stars drowned in a canoe accident more than twenty winters ago."

"Twenty-two winters ago. Sora was ten. She couldn't save her sister, and she's never forgiven herself for making it to shore alive. We found her wandering alone in the forest. She couldn't even remember her own name. The water had been so cold."

Rockfish massaged his forehead. He probably felt overwhelmed. In the past hand of time, he'd learned too many things to grasp them all: shadow-souls and murder, adultery, and Sora's unpleasant childhood.

"One other thing, Rockfish. She has . . . episodes."

"Episodes?"

"Yes. Almost no one knows about them. Her mother, Yellow Cypress, tried very hard to get Sora out of sight whenever they happened."

He shifted uncomfortably. "What kind of 'episodes' are you talking about?"

"On occasion"—Wink made a lame gesture—"when Sora's under a great deal of stress, an evil Spirit wakes inside her—"

"*What?*"

"Her arms and legs jerk uncontrollably, and her jaws snap open and closed." She waved a hand before her lips. "She foams at the mouth."

Rockfish stared dumbly at her. "Why has no one ever told me of this?"

"After Walks-among-the-Stars' death, Yellow Cypress was afraid someone might suggest that the 'episodes' made Sora unfit to rule. She forbade people to speak of it."

Rockfish hung his head and heaved an exhausted breath. "I'm tired, Wink. Is there anything else?"

"Yes. What have your people decided about the jade?"

Apparently taken aback that she could think of it at this moment, he stared at her before he answered. "They're willing to commit three hundred warriors. But I think—"

"Do *not* tell Sora."

He straightened. "Why not?"

"She has enough to worry about, and it's irrelevant now. If your people decide to go after the jade, they'll have to work out an agreement with Blue Bow themselves."

The air went out of him as though his body were a punctured elk bladder. "Why?"

"I'm changing my council vote to no. Which means we won't be committing warriors."

"But, Wink, I don't understand. Why not?"

"Blackbird Town is in a fragile position. We can't afford the controversy. Nor can we spare the warriors. We might need them to protect our own people."

His hand fell to his lap. An implacable glow lit his dark eyes, as though he longed to beat her to death with a dull ax.

"I expended great effort to get my people to agree to this, Wink. I wish I'd known—"

"I didn't know myself until today. My heart has been burdened with other things."

"I'm sure, but—"

"Rockfish, try to forget your own selfish wishes for a moment." Her voice had turned to ice. "Sea Grass has asked Wood Fern to be present tomorrow."

"Wood Fern?" he said, startled. "Why would she ask the matron of Water Hickory Clan to be present?"

"Old Sea Grass may just want an audience when she tears Sora to pieces, but I'm afraid it's more than that."

"More?"

"Yes. Only clan matrons can declare war on other clans. Village matrons can't do it. Village chiefs can't do it."

"Water Hickory Clan would never declare war on Shadow Rock Clan," he said incredulously. "Over one death? The stakes aren't high enough. Shadow Rock is twice the size of Water Hickory Clan."

"I fear that neither you nor I really know what the stakes are. *That's* what frightens me."

19

THE ENORMOUS CARVING OF BLACK FALCON GLOWED IN THE light of the two torches standing on either side of the front entrance to the Chieftess' House. Rockfish dipped his head to the god, threw back the door curtain, and saw War Chief Feather Dancer standing guard before his bedchamber at the far end of the hall. Rockfish glanced into the council chamber and the temple before he headed for Feather Dancer. He had to make sure both chambers were empty. Slaves occasionally slept there. There were things he and Sora had to discuss in private. He didn't want their conversations overheard.

The war chief watched him with a curiously expressionless face as he came forward.

"Feather Dancer," Rockfish greeted. "I hope you are well."

Feather Dancer bowed. "Well enough."

"Now that I'm home," Rockfish ordered, "you may go. I wish you a pleasant night."

Feather Dancer's eyes narrowed, and his scars rippled across his cheeks. "I will leave when the chieftess orders me to go. I stand here at her request."

Rockfish blinked in dismay. Feather Dancer had never refused to obey one of his orders. In the past, he'd always treated an order from Rockfish with the same respect he would an order from Sora.

Coldly, Rockfish said, "Very well," and ducked into his bedchamber.

Sora sat cross-legged on their sleeping bench with two blankets coiled around her slender waist. A glittering wealth of long black hair spread down the front of her yellow sleep shirt. She looked stunningly beautiful.

"Sora," he said, holding the door curtain aside so that she could see Feather Dancer standing in the corridor. "Now that I'm home you may dismiss your war chief. I'll guard you."

Sora studied him with dark, unblinking eyes. "Feather Dancer?" she called. "Please stand guard at the front entrance. I'll call if I need you."

Feather Dancer nodded but gave Rockfish a piercing glance before he strode down the hall.

Rockfish stood for a moment, trying to fathom the implications, before he let the curtain fall closed. "What was that about?"

Sora leaned back against the wall with her tea cup clutched in both hands. "Hello, my husband. How was your trip?"

Her voice had a probing quality that set his teeth on edge. He'd expected a very different greeting. Contrite, perhaps, or tearful.

Rockfish hung his cape on the peg by the door and set his bow and quiver against the wall. As he slipped his pack from his shoulders, he said, "It was long and tiring."

Does she suspect that I heard something on the trail? Maybe she knows Wink told me. Maybe she asked Wink to tell me.

Walking to the large black-and-tan basket to his right, he removed the lid and began emptying the contents of his pack.

"How did your negotiations go?" Sora asked in a low voice. "Did Tenkiller agree to send warriors to get the jade?"

Rockfish stopped in the middle of placing his extra shirt in the basket. Holding it in his hands, he recalled Wink's warning. "No."

His answer didn't seem to register for several instants. Finally, she exhaled in apparent relief, but thoughts worked behind her dark eyes. What was she doing? Casting aside old conclusions and struggling to find a new explanation that fit this information? She was very clever.

"I'm sorry," she said. "I know it was important to you. Did he say why he refused?"

Rockfish placed the shirt in the basket and lowered his empty pack to the floor. Before he turned to her, he caught his image in the galena-backed mica mirror that hung on the wall. His gray brows plunged down over his fleshy nose. He hadn't bathed in days. Dirty strands of hair straggled around his wrinkled face.

He wasn't good at lying, but he didn't have to fake his upset. "Tenkiller agrees with you. He thinks it's too dangerous. So. It's over. You can stop worrying about the jade."

Rockfish marched across the room, sat down beside her, and began unlacing his black leggings.

"Is there anything you'd like to tell me?" he said as he slipped off his right legging.

She closed her eyes and took a breath. Her voice softened. "Yes. I want you to know that I love you and I never meant to harm you. I—"

"Wink told me all about it. She said she didn't want you to have to do it."

Her head snapped up. "What did she tell you?"

He let his left legging fall to the floor and pulled his dirty shirt over his head. Once he'd kicked off his sandals, he slipped naked beneath the blankets. "Everything. She told me everything."

"I doubt she told you everything, Rockfish. I—"

"Everything." He made it sound as though it were three words, instead of one.

Their gazes held for a few uneasy heartbeats.

Sora looked away. "You have the right to hate me for what I've done to you, but I hope you will try to under—"

"I don't hate you."

She blinked. "You don't?"

He ran a hand through his gray hair. He could feel the dust and sweat. "No, Sora. I love you very much."

Her head trembled before she could stop it, and that, more than anything, gave him heart. "I arrived home about three hands of time ago. I've been thinking about this for a while. I'm certain that if my dead wife returned to me, I would do exactly what you did. I would give up everything to be with her—including you."

Tears of gratitude traced silver lines down her cheeks.

Rockfish took the tea cup from her hands, set it on the floor, and wrapped his arms around her.

She hugged him hard. "Dear gods, you cannot imagine how I've prayed to hear you say that."

He gently stroked her long hair. "I can't lie. It's going to take me some time to accept it, but I will, if you'll help me."

"I'll do anything. I—"

"There's only one thing I ask of you."

She pushed away to look at him. "Yes?"

"Tell me the truth. All of it, starting with the day you met Flint. It's not that I doubt Wink's version of the story; I just want to hear yours." He gripped her chin hard to stare into her eyes. "Every detail, Sora. I don't want you to leave anything out. Do you agree?"

She nodded, but he could see the panic that clutched at her souls.

It took half the night. When she tried to skirt around the most intimate details, he knew it and demanded she tell him the truth. It hurt. But it was also a revelation. He had always known she was a woman of great passions, but until this moment, he'd never guessed the depths of her needs. Many of the things she and Flint had done to excite each other sounded brutal, almost animalistic. At one point, he was reminded of big cats coupling, the male biting the reluctant female's neck to hold her still while he roughly penetrated her. It was . . . inhuman.

When dawn's blue gleam began to lance through the smoke hole, she finished the telling.

They gazed at each other in silence.

"Thank you. For being candid," he said, and pulled her down to the bench beside him. She pillowed her head on his chest, and her hair spread over his body like a dark blanket.

As he petted her shoulder, he said, "May I ask you some questions?"

"Yes."

"Do you think that when Flint's soul realized you were being choked to death, he slipped inside you to fight Skinner?"

She twisted to look at him. True terror filled her eyes. She must be searching every corner of her souls, going from place to place, trying to discern any sign of his presence inside her. "Why would you think that?"

"That's what I would do if I were a reflection-soul. I could not sit by and watch the woman I loved die at the hands of my friend. I'd switch bodies, praying I could stop him."

"It's possible. I honestly don't remember a single moment after I lost consciousness."

"Perhaps Flint didn't want you to see what he was doing. Would you have tried to keep him from killing Skinner?"

"Probably, but that doesn't explain my head wound, does it?"

"It could. If Skinner gained the upper hand during the struggle, he might have clubbed you trying to kill Flint."

She nuzzled her cheek against his chest and frowned. "Then you think it was Flint's reflection-soul? Not his shadow-soul?"

"A shadow-soul wouldn't have fought to protect you, Sora. Shadow-souls are pure evil. They care only for themselves."

He felt her squeeze her eyes closed. Her lashes brushed his skin. "I'm so glad you're home. I desperately needed to talk to someone."

He relished the tone in her voice.

"Wink was here."

"I can't tell her the things I've just told you."

He kissed the top of her head and held her tightly. "I'm glad you told me. I can help you now."

"Help me? What do you mean?"

Rockfish hesitated. "During the meeting later today."

"What meeting?"

He gave her a confused look. "Didn't Wink tell you? Sea Grass wants to meet with you. She's asked Matron Wood Fern to be present."

Sora slowly lifted her head to look at him. Fear lit her eyes. "What time is this meeting to take place?"

"At noon."

She was wrestling with something. He could see the struggle in her changing expressions. "What is it? What's wrong?"

She seemed to come to a decision.

"Rockfish, do you think . . ."

He frowned. "Do I think what?"

"Is it possible that none of this is true?"

The pungent scent of his sweat rose when he shifted. "You mean you don't actually believe what you just told me?"

"No, I—I do believe it. Those things happened, exactly as I described them. But I've been wondering if perhaps there isn't another explanation."

"For example?"

She sat up and gave him a vulnerable look, clearly weighing whether or not she could really tell him.

"You *can* trust me, Sora."

She smoothed her hand over his chest for another twenty heartbeats before she said, "What if someone I trust, someone who knows me very well, is trying to force me to step down as chieftess of the Black Falcon Nation?"

"Sora, you are greatly loved by your people. I sincerely doubt—"

"Everyone has enemies."

Hedging, he said, "Do you have someone in mind?"

"It occurred to me that all of the things Skinner said he could have learned from . . . from . . ."

She obviously didn't want to say the name aloud.

"Who?"

". . . Flint. Or Wink."

His mouth curled in disbelief. "Wink is absolutely devoted to you. She would never betray you. Name one thing Skinner said that Flint couldn't have told him."

She seemed to be thinking about it.

Rockfish prompted, "The miscarriage, the fact that he almost killed you on the red hill, the death of the Trader, all the other things? If anyone betrayed you, it was Flint."

Pain filled her eyes, as though the realization that her beloved Flint might have been working to harm her was too much to bear.

"Tell me something?" she said. "The day of the chunkey game, did you see Grown Bear and Skinner when they entered the village? Were they together?"

"No, but they arrived within moments of each other. I saw Grown Bear first, then . . ." His mouth hung open. He murmured, *The jade*. Blessed gods! You think Water Hickory Clan is working with Blue Bow—"

"Yes." She sighed. "Wink suggested it. She asked me what made me think that Grown Bear had come to us first."

Rockfish forced a swallow down his dry throat. "But if Blue Bow already had an alliance with Sea Grass and Chief Fireberry, why would he send Grown Bear to you at all?"

"Maybe Blue Bow didn't know he had an agreement."

At the words, Rockfish jerked as if slapped. It would not be the first time that a war chief had forged an agreement without the knowledge of his clan matron or village chief. Perhaps Grown Bear had been working for himself all along. "If Water Hickory Clan could force you to step down as chieftess, it would disgrace the Shadow Rock Clan, wouldn't it?"

"Yes."

"Long Fin would not ascend to the chieftainship."

"No, he wouldn't."

"Who's next in line?"

"Short Tail."

A throbbing knot formed in his belly. "Short Tail is Water Hickory Clan." He clenched a fist at his own stupidity. "I wonder how much they paid Grown Bear to play along."

"Our share of the jade would have been enough."

As the truth began to sink into his exhausted souls, new fears emerged. He'd worked very hard to get an agreement from his people to go after the jade. In the council meeting, two of the village matrons had refused to participate. The bitter fight that ensued would be spoken of for generations. Right now, at this very moment, his people were assembling warriors. What role had he played in this debacle? Perhaps it had never occurred to Water Hickory Clan or Grown Bear that Rockfish's people might be interested? Then again, *perhaps it had.*

"Sora, I lied to you."

Her trusting eyes suddenly went dark and impenetrable. "About what?"

"My people committed three hundred warriors to go after the jade."

She rubbed her throat as though nausea tickled the back of her tongue. "Why didn't you tell me?"

"Wink said you had enough to worry about, and it was irrelevant anyway, because she was going to change her council vote to no."

The door curtain waffled, and cold, rain-scented wind blew around the chamber. As the fire leaped, shadows danced on the walls. He found himself listening intently for steps in the corridor, but heard nothing.

"What else did Wink say?"

"She said if my people wanted to go after the jade, they'd have to work out their own agreement with Blue Bow."

Sora took a deep breath and tipped her face to stare at the azure gleam streaming through the smoke hole. Her long neck shone a pale blue. "There's something missing, Rockfish—some fundamental piece to the puzzle that we haven't found yet."

"What do you mean? This all looks perfectly clear to me." But as a new picture began to form, he whispered, "Unless . . ."

"What is it?"

"I'm not sure."

"But you're frightened. Why?"

He swung his legs off the sleeping bench. Despite his exhaustion, he had the overwhelming urge to dress and head back north to his own people. "Sora, when my people learn that Shadow Rock Clan has backed out of the war party, they'll be outraged. They'll immediately start looking for new allies. It won't be long until they've forged an alliance with Blue Bow and Water Hickory Clan. When that happens . . ."

She seemed to wilt before his eyes. "Shadow Rock Clan will be doomed. But why, Rockfish? What have we done to them?"

"You've been *timid,* Sora. You blocked Water Hickory Clan when they wanted to make war on the Loon People. You blocked them when they wanted to raid the Conch Shell People to gain their oyster beds, and when they wanted to shove the Red Owl People out of their buffalo-hunting territory." He nodded soberly. "You've been in the way. And, apparently, so have I."

Her beautiful face slackened in understanding.

"Yes," she murmured, "and when Wink tells the other matrons that she's changing her council vote about the jade, she'll be in the way, too."

"We have to go to Wink right now, to warn her—"

"No, not yet." Sora held up a hand, signaling him to slow down. "There are too many things that still don't make sense. I need to think about this for a while."

He could tell she meant Flint. *That* softness filled her eyes.

"What things, Sora?"

She pulled her sleep shirt off and gestured for him to lie down again. He did. As she bent to kiss the hair below his navel, a tingle went through his tired muscles. Her mouth moved lower.

"I know you're exhausted," she whispered as she gripped his

manhood. "Just relax. Let me please you. I need to be close to you tonight."

He tried, but he couldn't help thinking that war loomed in the very near future, and to make matters worse, there was a difference in her touch; it was not as gentle as he remembered; he was fairly certain she was pretending he was Flint . . . or maybe Skinner.

When he didn't seem to be responding, she bit the tip of his manhood, hard enough to make him shudder, and started to lick, going from the root to the tip in long, lazy strokes. Her tongue seemed to know every tender, sensitive place on a man's body, and she worked each with practiced assurance.

It didn't take long before he'd relaxed enough to fall into a deep, exhausted sleep.

AS SHE HAD ON MANY OCCASIONS, SORA QUIETLY ROLLED away from him and lay staring up at the firelit ceiling. She wondered if anything he'd told her tonight was true. He'd seemed genuinely worried, and everything he'd proposed had made sense. But that didn't make it true. He could be in league with her enemies, working from inside to bring her down. When his people's three hundred warriors arrived, who was to say they wouldn't attack Blackbird Town?

Perhaps he'd just been playing his role to perfection tonight.

Tears burned her eyes. *Dear gods, don't think about it.*

She rose and dressed.

When she pulled aside the curtain at the front entrance, she found Far Eye standing there. The morning glow gave his long black hair a purple tint. Sometime in the night, he must have replaced Feather Dancer as her guard. Good. Feather Dancer needed the rest. The last time she'd seen him, he'd looked like he was ready to fall asleep on his feet.

"Chieftess," Far Eye said. "Are you well?"

His nostrils flared slightly, as though he could smell her distinctive musk.

She tugged her goose-feather cape more tightly about her. "I'm going for a walk in the forest. If my husband rises, tell him—"

"My orders are very clear, Chieftess. Feather Dancer threatened my life if I did not accompany you everywhere you went. He said you might be in danger and I was to look after you, no matter what you said."

The situation irked her. She wanted to be alone, to think straightly, but she knew Feather Dancer's instincts for danger were far more finely tuned than hers.

"Very well. But please stay a few paces behind me. I need as much privacy as possible."

"Of course, Chieftess." His elaborate tattoos flashed when he bowed.

Sora marched down the steps and took the trail that led around the lake toward the burned-out tree. Mother Sun's gleam rode the waves like an iridescent lavender blanket. As she passed the houses on the shore, she heard voices. People had started to rise. Babies cried. By the time she returned, there would be dozens standing on the bank fishing for breakfast, and each person would want to speak with her.

Far Eye followed her so unobtrusively she almost forgot he was there.

Lost in thoughts, she arrived at the fallen log long before she'd realized it. She stopped. The burned-out tree stood in front of her. Had it only been five nights ago that she'd sat here with Rockfish and listened to him talk about how much he wanted the jade? Enough to propose that she send a war party out to capture Grown Bear and torture him into telling them where to find the Scarlet Macaw People. She'd been waiting for Flint, expecting him to emerge from the forest at any moment.

"You know how it happened, don't you?" Far Eye softly asked.

"What?" She spun around.

"How Skinner died."

A numb sensation spread down her spine as fear shot through her. Far Eye had found them by the pond. Did he know something he hadn't told Feather Dancer?

"No, I don't. Do you?"

Images flitted across her souls . . . Skinner moving inside her, then his fingers around her throat, his roars . . .

Far Eye gave her a secret smile, as though he knew *exactly* what she was thinking. "You missed me, didn't you?"

Involuntarily, she recoiled a step. "What are you talking about?"

"Stop looking at me like that," he said. "You knew I was alive."

It wasn't Flint's voice, but every inflection, the way his mouth moved, *was*.

"What do you remember after we coupled?"

Mute, she shook her head.

"Nothing? Good. I didn't think you would."

Sora struggled with the sensation of horror that had started to spread through her veins like fire. How was Far Eye involved in the plan? Who had put him up to this?

"How . . . ?"

"How did I do it?"

He walked forward, slipped his arm through hers, and guided her to the log, where he pulled her down beside him. His touch made her skin crawl. The scent of the lake was particularly strong here. She forced herself to take deep breaths, trying to slow her racing heart.

"Skinner drove me out, Sora. I had no place to go, except inside you. When I took over your body I convinced Skinner to talk with me. I had always been his greatest love. I begged him to give me just a few moments. He agreed."

She stared hard at his young, handsome face, but inside she was quaking. "And then you killed him."

"Not right away." He frowned out at the lake. Ducks quacked in the distance. Their wings batted the green water, sending out bobbing silver rings. "We talked until almost dawn. We'd been laughing, sharing a pot of tea, when he thought he heard something in the forest. He turned, and I slipped the poison into his cup."

Far Eye's jaw clenched, and she could see his teeth grinding beneath the thin veneer of tattooed skin.

Could he have pieced this together from details gleaned at the pond?

Their plan is evolving. . . . Feather Dancer was right.

"When did he realize what you'd done?"

"Skinner saw dregs of the powder in the bottom of the cup. I think he could feel it taking hold by then, too."

"You fought?"

He expelled a breath. "In your body, I wasn't strong enough to fend him off. I had to do something. He managed to club you senseless. When I realized he might kill you, I slipped back into his body and *made* him stop."

She tried to add up the numbers. How many people had to be involved in the plot to make it work? At least Far Eye, Skinner, and Flint. Probably Grown Bear, Wood Fern, and Sea Grass.

In a calm, quiet voice, she asked, "Why didn't you slip back into me when he was dying?"

He gave her a small, intimate smile. "Would you have protected me?"

"Yes."

He lifted a hand and ran his fingertips down her face. She shuddered. "Do you love me that much?"

"I always have."

Teal's words floated up from the depths of her heart: *"All shadowsouls have a single goal, Chieftess: They want to find someone who will cherish having them inside. He thinks you are that person."*

If this was Flint—*Gods, stop thinking that! He's part of the plan to cause your downfall and the downfall of your clan!*—he'd had the chance to stay inside her. But he'd left. Why?

"He couldn't satisfy you tonight, could he?" Far Eye asked, his gaze deftly taking in every nuance of her expression.

"Who?"

"Your husband. I could tell the moment you stepped outside. I knew you'd needed a man and hadn't had one available."

Only Flint knew her well enough . . .

He smiled, and the coiled serpents tattooed on his cheeks seemed to writhe. "I'd forgotten how it feels to be strong and filled with wild desires." He flexed his arms. The muscles rippled.

How many people on the face of Grandmother Earth could act this well? Even if Far Eye had been schooled in Flint's mannerisms, surely he couldn't copy that distinctive tilt of the head, that smile.

For the first time, she genuinely began to think maybe the problem was not out there, not with a dozen people who were trying to trick her, *but inside her.* Had she been under enough stress that her soul had started wandering away from her body? *There are things you don't remember. . . . You had a nightmare about running through thick trees, lost, alone. . . .*

During her mother's rule, several people had lost their reflection-souls while they were alive. A priest had always gone to search for the lost soul in the forest. Sometimes he could find it and bring it back to the body. Other times, the soul wandered farther and farther away, until no one could bring it back and it couldn't find its own way home. Without the reflection-soul, the living person simply couldn't think anymore. They started stammering, couldn't remember what had happened to them five heartbeats ago, and created elaborately skewed visions of reality by stringing together facts that bore no actual relationship. Toward the end, they just sat and stared at nothing all day long until their bodies died—or their relatives generously cracked their skulls with a war club.

Is that what she was doing? Stringing together disconnected facts to make herself believe Flint had come back to her? Perhaps his death had affected her more than she realized?

Don't be an idiot. You are not the problem. They are! They've had you on the run. What will happen if you suddenly turn around and charge? How far are they willing to take this?

She did exactly what Flint would have expected. She slid her hand beneath his shirt, gripped his manhood, and ran her hand up and down his limp shaft.

Rather than being shocked, as she would have expected Far Eye to be, he took her hand and squeezed it harder.

"The past few days have been agony for me," he whispered. "In Far Eye's young body my desires have been even more overwhelming."

As he swelled in her hand, she studied his rapturous expression. He'd closed his eyes and was biting his lower lip, savoring the sensations.

"Straddle me, Sora."

"No. People have risen. There are several men standing on the bank, fishing."

"They'll never know."

"I can't risk it."

"Then use both hands. You know how I like it." He picked up her other hand and secured it around his shaft. She squeezed and massaged, pulling him in a way she knew would bring him to ecstasy quickly.

"Yes. You've forgotten nothing." He braced his hands on the log and leaned back with his face tipped to the dawn sky.

Though the clouds over the eastern horizon had begun to turn the color of ripe corn, the shore remained in shadow. Clumps of palmettos resembled still, crouching beasts.

Far Eye uttered deep-throated sounds at the height of each stroke of her hands. "Let me finish inside you? I beg you."

"No."

"Why are you tormenting me? Is it because of Skinner? I know he was your f-friend."

A moment later, he trembled violently, and warm fluid spilled over her fingers.

She pulled her hands from beneath his shirt and cleaned them in the sand.

As she rose to leave, he grabbed her wrist.

"Let me go, Far Eye. Really. I must get back."

"Not yet."

He slid off the log to the ground and forcibly dragged her down onto his lap. In the dim light, with the log shielding his back, the only thing that might be visible was Sora's upper torso.

"Do you remember this?" he asked in a teasing voice as he curled his legs around her hips and crossed his ankles over her knees. His left hand found her breast while his right hand reached beneath her dress.

When he pinched what the Black Falcon People called a woman's "little manhood," she gasped and tried to rise.

"Sora, stop fighting me."

"It will take too long. Someone will see."

"No one will see, and I plan to make it last as long as I can." He bit her neck.

In a curiously similar fashion to the way she had just pleasured him, he held her little manhood between his thumb and forefinger and gently pulled it up, then pushed it down, working it as she had, only instants ago, worked him. As his fingers rhythmically caressed her, she felt her fears draining away, being replaced by the creeping warmth.

In her ear, he murmured, "I remember the first time I did this to you. Your mother had invited my parents to a feast to celebrate our coming marriage. We were sitting outside around the fire; everyone was laughing and talking. I sat down behind you and enfolded you in my cape. People thought I was just keeping you warm. My parents kept demanding that I participate in the conversation. It wasn't easy. I could feel you quaking beneath my hand."

She stiffened. How could he know that? What a wonderful sensual spring that had been. Though they were often surrounded by people, they had pleasured each other countless times.

"I loved you so much," she cautiously said.

She leaned her head back against his shoulder, and he massaged her breast and kissed her. While his lower hand grew rougher his tongue darted in and out of her mouth.

He whispered against her lips, "I tried very hard to make you love your body, Sora."

He let go of her breast and pulled something from his belt pouch. As he smoothed his hand down her side, she wondered what it was. He tugged her dress up higher and used his fingers to probe her opening.

"You're ready." He smiled against her cheek, then touched her with the object's tip. It felt cool and silken.

"What is it?"

"You've seen it before. Soon, you'll remember. It's carved from an ancient bone."

In time with the rhythm of his right hand caressing her little manhood, he thrust the object in and out of her. The deeper he pushed it, the larger it got. It must be cone-shaped.

"You'll have to lean back more for me to get it all the way inside you."

She sank against him, letting him position her, and to her surprise, he lowered her body to the sand behind the log. She found herself lying flat on her back staring at the reflection of the water dancing over green sycamore leaves high above her.

After she had listened to Feather Dancer and Rockfish, nothing Far Eye could have said would have convinced her he truly was Flint. *But this* . . .

He shifted positions, releasing her little manhood for a time so he could work the cone. It was long and thick at the base; it took time to push it all the way inside her. When he'd finally tucked it in, he bent and took her little manhood in his mouth. As he stroked it with his tongue, he pushed on the cone. If he met resistance, he slowed down, waiting until her inner muscles gave way before he rhythmically forced it deeper. As the wave of heat rose in her body, she could feel his fingers inside her moving the cone. She moaned like she hadn't in more than three winters.

"Yes, you love this. I know you do." He bit her little manhood, and her body convulsed in throes of ecstasy. She lay on the sand thrashing senselessly, not caring who might see or hear her.

When it was over and she lay panting, staring wide-eyed up at him, he gave her a passionate kiss and untied his waist sash. "I know you have the meeting with Sea Grass at noon. I'm going to leave the cone inside you. I want you thinking of me when those old women are squawking at you."

She had barely the strength to raise herself on her elbows to watch him pass the red sash between her legs, then tie it around her waist. Her inner muscles were still periodically clenching around the cone, sending shivers through her.

"Flint?"

He looked at her.

"What are we going to do?"

He heard the fear in her voice, sank down beside her, and gathered her in his arms. "Run away with me, Sora. I asked you before. I'm asking you again. Run away with me before it's too late."

She stared into his pleading eyes and wondered what would happen next. Either he would find her somewhere alone, or she would go looking for him. Eventually the whispers would start: *"She's coupling with Far Eye now. Gods, doesn't Matron Wink care about the Shadow Rock Clan! The chieftess must be exposed and banished! Someone must tell Rockfish."*

She buried her face against his shoulder and forced herself to think.

20

SHE DID NOT ARRIVE HOME FOR ANOTHER FOUR HANDS OF time. Flint had taken her deep into the forest, where they'd talked about the coming meeting with Water Hickory Clan. He'd suggested a strategy, but she wasn't certain she could go through with it. When she did get back to her bedchamber, she had less than half a hand of time to dress and prepare for what she expected would be a barrage of unpleasant questions.

Rockfish, thankfully, was gone. She hadn't seen him when she'd crossed the plaza, but he could be anywhere, talking with Feather Dancer or Teal. Even Wink.

A few red coals glowed beneath the bed of ash in the fire pit, giving the room a soft crimson gleam. She crossed to her clothing basket and hastily stripped off her soiled dress. When she tossed it to the floor, she stared at the red sash around her waist. She considered removing it and taking out the cone . . . but she didn't. It made her feel curiously alive.

She pulled out a blue dress covered with tiny circlets of conch shell and slipped it over her head. It had an iridescent quality. As she ran her hands down over her hips, she noticed that the knot of

Flint's sash bulged at her waist. She searched her basket for her white sash and tied it right above the knot, so the trailing ends covered any sign of it.

Picking up her copper-inlaid wooden comb, she went to the mica mirror that hung on the wall over Rockfish's basket. Round, and three hands across, it gave her a good view of herself. Twigs and old leaves filled her snarled hair. She quickly combed it clean, then plaited her hair into a single braid. After she'd washed her face, she headed for Wink's house.

People filled the plaza. Dye pots bubbled around the base of Wink's mound. Sassafras made the yellow, maple twigs the black, dodder the orange, and dog-tail weed the dark red dye. Six old gray-haired women sat on cattail mats beside the pots. They lowered bundles of thread into the boiling dyes, left them for a few hands of time, then hung them to dry on pole racks behind the pots. The most important animal fiber used in fabrics was buffalo wool. But it was expensive and the supply unreliable, and opossum hair proved almost as good. Mulberry and cane fibers were also highly prized. Her people cut shoots four or five feet tall, stripped off the bark and dried them, then beat them into soft fibers that they bleached and spun into thread.

Rockfish stood at the door. His brows knit when he saw her crest the last stair. He'd pulled his gray hair away from his triangular face and tied it in back with a cord. He wore a bright yellow shirt that hung to his knees. A wealth of shell beads covered the front and encircled the hem.

"I was getting worried," he whispered. "What took you so long?"

"I went for a walk. I needed to think."

"Was Far Eye with you? When I woke and found you gone, I immediately went to Feather Dancer. He said Far Eye was—"

"Yes, he was with me. Feather Dancer threatened his life if he didn't accompany me everywhere I went."

"Good." Rockfish gave her a relieved smile and slipped his arm through hers. "Are you ready?"

Sora clutched his arm tightly. "As ready as I will ever be."

They entered the house and walked down the corridor arm in arm. Voices drifted from the council chamber. When they ducked beneath the curtain, a strange hush fell over the room. Every eye turned to stare. The room was packed. Twenty warriors stood against the walls, their expressions hard, as though waiting for their matron's signal to club someone to death.

That someone is me.

Ten torches burned in their wall holders, and the central fire blazed. Wink, Wood Fern, Sea Grass, and an unknown man sat on three of the four benches that created a square around the fire. Sora and Rockfish went to the fourth bench.

As she sat down, Sora looked straight at Sea Grass. The old woman had her white hair twisted into a bun on top of her head. Her thin face and beaked nose looked sallow, as though all the color had been leached out.

Wink passed around a conch shell filled with sacred Black Drink to consecrate the council meeting. Everyone took a sip of the bitter brew and passed it on.

When the shell had made its way back to Wink and she set it on the bench beside her, she said, "Let us begin. Chieftess Sora, as the accused, you have the right to first words."

Sora nodded. "Matron Sea Grass, forgive me. I know you must be heartbroken, as I am. Your son was one of my dearest friends. I loved him, too."

"Did you kill him?" Her dark eyes narrowed.

"I honestly don't know. He was choking me and I fainted. When I woke I was lying in the temple. But I'm sure you know that. Wink and Teal—"

"They told me my son was carrying the shadow-soul of his best friend and that it was Flint who tried to kill you." She laced her gnarled old hands in her lap. "Is that what you think happened?"

Sora squeezed Rockfish's arm and released it. It had been Skinner who'd tried to kill her, but she didn't want to tell Sea Grass that.

First of all, the old woman wouldn't believe her. But more important, it would raise questions Sora didn't want to answer. "Yes."

Sea Grass inhaled a deep breath and exhaled hard through her nose. "Why didn't you try to run away?"

"Run away? I have responsibilities. I couldn't run away."

"So you chose to stay, even though you knew a wicked shadow-soul was pursuing you. Why do you think Flint would wish to kill you?"

Sora frowned. "Pardon me?"

"Why would Flint wish to kill you?"

She made an airy gesture with her hand. "Shadow-souls are evil. They—"

"Could it be that he hated you?"

"Hated me?"

"Yes. I knew Flint well. I watched him grow up. He was a good-natured, conscientious man. He would not have taken over my son's body without a powerful reason. The only reason I can think of is that he wanted to get his hands around your throat. Why?"

Sora stared at Sea Grass. The old woman's nostrils quivered in rage. "Divorces are often difficult, Sea Grass. Perhaps he never got over—"

"He divorced you, Sora. Not the other way round. He was getting on with his life. I'd never seen him so happy. When he left Oak Leaf Village to go and meet his bride-to-be, he was as joyous as a fifteen-winters-old boy."

Rockfish subtly stiffened beside her. The hand resting on his knee tightened into a fist. Wink must not have told him about White Fawn. But of course she wouldn't have. She'd see that as an irrelevant detail.

"What are you saying, Sea Grass? That I must have done something to provoke Flint into wanting to kill me?"

"Did you?"

"I hadn't seen him in more than three winters. How could I have?"

Wink glanced back and forth between Sora and Sea Grass; then her sharp eyes went to Wood Fern. The matron of Wood Hickory Clan sat perfectly still, her nearly blind gaze fixed on Sora, but her mouth had puckered. She looked like she longed to say something.

As the tension rose, Sora could feel herself tightening around the cone. A pleasant sting began to filter through her loins. *He loved me. He* still *loves me.*

"Where were you fourteen days ago, Chieftess? I've asked around Blackbird Town. People tell me you were gone."

"Yes. I went to negotiate with Chief Blue Bow for the release of *your villagers,* Sea Grass. I had a party of thirty warriors with me. Any one of them will verify—"

"That you ordered them to camp outside Eagle Flute Village while you and Walking Bird went in to see Blue Bow alone. Yes, I've spoken to several people."

"Entering the village with heavily armed warriors would have been provocative. By leaving them outside and entering with a single guard I—"

"An act of good faith? A way of showing Blue Bow you were at his mercy?"

Softly, she answered, "Yes."

"Well," Sea Grass said curtly, "when he arrives, I will ask Chief Blue Bow about that, but in the meantime, I wish to ask you straightly if you killed White Fawn."

Skinner's frantic voice seeped from between her souls: *"How did you kill her? Did you slip something into her food? Did you hire someone to do it?"*

Rockfish turned to stare at her. She didn't look at him, but she could feel the silent accusation. Wood Fern and Wink didn't seem to be breathing. Around the room, the warriors shifted uneasily.

The cone seemed to be growing inside her, filling her like Flint's manhood did. It gave her strength. "Why would I do that? I remarried long ago. I couldn't have cared less what Flint was doing."

"Indeed?" Sea Grass' voice turned deadly. "White Fawn was very beautiful, and young. Fifteen winters. When you were married to Flint, your jealousies were well-known. Every time my son returned home from visiting Flint, he carried a new story of your wild rages."

Blood pulsed in her veins. Skinner had gone home with stories about *her* rages? Things Flint had told him? Perhaps, unknown to her, Skinner had been the most jealous of the three of them.

Her loins began to pulse as though the cone were moving inside her, swelling and shrinking in time with her heartbeat. As her arousal increased, a strange clarity possessed her; she knew what she had to do. Flint was right. There was only one way to ensure all doubts would be wiped from people's hearts.

Sora rose to her feet and, with great dignity, said, "I grieve for the loss of your son, Matron. Everyone tells me that I must have killed him, so I accept the responsibility."

She walked across the floor, knelt before Sea Grass, and touched her forehead to the matron's sandals. "In front of these witnesses, I offer my own life to you. Though I know it can never compensate you for your loss, perhaps my death will ease your pain and the pain of your clan."

Rockfish lurched to his feet. "Sora, no!"

"It is already done, my husband." She looked up into Sea Grass' wrinkled face and saw a sudden indecision enter her eyes.

With a frail old hand, Sea Grass touched Sora's head. "You would do this to keep peace between our clans?"

"I would. I assume you will give me the customary twenty-eight days to conclude my affairs."

Sea Grass hesitated for an uncomfortably long time before saying, "I must discuss this with my clan."

"Of course."

Sora glimpsed Wink's face from the corner of her eye. Her friend had gone pale enough that Sora feared she might faint.

Wink rose to her feet. "As matron of the Shadow Rock Clan, I stand behind this offering. Peace is all we have ever sought."

Wood Fern leaned sideways, cupped a hand to Sea Grass' ear,

and whispered something. Sea Grass nodded. "Matron Wink, we ask for a few days to make our final decision about this offering."

"Granted."

As Sora started to stand, Wink walked over, gripped her arm, and helped her up.

"When you are ready, send word," Wink said. "Shadow Rock Clan will help you in any way it can."

Wood Fern and Sea Grass nodded.

Wink slipped an arm around Sora's waist, as though to support her, and guided Sora into the hallway. When the curtain fell closed behind them, she stared at Sora with wide, disbelieving eyes.

"Why did you *do* that?" she hissed.

"I had to, Wink. There was no other way."

A din of hushed conversations broke out in the council chamber. Rockfish calmly said something to Sea Grass that Sora couldn't understand, but she heard Sea Grass say, "I understand that. We will take it into consideration."

A few heartbeats later, Rockfish ducked into the hall with a dire look on his face and whispered, "Let's go somewhere and talk."

21

FAR EYE STOOD OUTSIDE THE ENTRANCE TO THE MATRON'S House. When he saw the three of them step out, he searched Sora's eyes, and a small, satisfied smile curled his lips. Flint must know she had used his plan.

"Nephew," Wink said. "Please accompany us. We're going to the Chieftess' House."

"Yes, Aunt."

Wink led the way, marching down the mound stairs with determination. As they crossed the plaza, people watched them curiously. Everyone knew about the meeting, and longed to hear what had happened. Before they had finished climbing the steps up the front of Sora's mound, several of the Oak Leaf warriors who'd been in the chamber had hurried into the plaza. Hushed, incredulous voices rose as people scurried from place to place, carrying the news that their chieftess had offered her own life to Water Hickory Clan to compensate them for the loss of Skinner. Given the circumstances that she did not even recall what had happened, they would see it as either a supremely heroic act or utter stupidity.

"Stand guard at the entrance," Wink told Far Eye when they

stood below the huge carving of Black Falcon that glared down at them from near the roof peak.

"Of course." Far Eye took up his position to the left of the entry.

Wink ducked through first, followed by Sora; then Rockfish entered and led the way into the temple. The Eternal Fire blazed, filling the chamber with the fragrance of burning cypress. The sacred masks that lined the walls watched them with dark empty eye sockets and gaping mouths.

Wink swung around and growled, "Sora, have you lost your wits? What did you think you were doing!"

Sora calmly seated herself and gestured for Wink to sit beside her, which she did, but not without looking reluctant. "There's something I need to discuss with you." She looked up at Rockfish. "With both of you."

Rockfish anxiously paced in front of the fire. "I don't understand, Sora. After what we said last night, how could you—"

"I did it *because* of what we said last night."

Rockfish stopped pacing. "What do you mean?"

"I have to know what's going on. Don't you see? If Sea Grass accepts my offer, she has to give me twenty-eight days. You said it yourself. If this is about the jade, Sea Grass can't wait that long. She'll have to act quickly to get rid of me, and I—"

"What do you mean 'I' said it?" His brow furrowed.

"When we were discussing the jade," she said in surprise. "You said when your people learned that Shadow Rock Clan had backed out of the war party they would immediately try to make alliances with Water Hickory Clan and Blue Bow. When they do, we'll hear of it, and then we'll really know what's going on and we can—"

"Sora," he said a little breathlessly, "what makes you think she didn't settle this matter with Blue Bow long ago? She may have gathered enough warriors from distant Water Hickory villages to be the *only* ally he needs."

"But I—I thought—"

"Blessed gods," he said through a taut exhalation, "that was just one possibility. I never intended for you to take it as fact!"

She felt a little shaky. What if Sea Grass and Wood Fern had already sent their warriors to Blue Bow's village? What if they were, at this moment, on their way south to find the Scarlet Macaw People?

No. I would have heard about such a large movement of warriors.

Wink said, "You two had better tell me right now what you're talking about."

Rockfish roughly ran a hand through his gray hair. "Sora told me that when all this began you suggested it might be a plot by Water Hickory Clan to discredit Shadow Rock Clan."

Wink glanced at Sora, as though not certain why she'd shared that information with Rockfish, but she said, "Yes, I did. Why?"

Rockfish opened his hands. "We spent most of last night talking. I told Sora I agreed with you. It seemed to me, and still does, that if Water Hickory Clan could force Sora to step down as chieftess, it would disgrace Shadow Rock Clan and prohibit Long Fin from ascending to the position of chief."

Wink's face slackened. All of her life, she'd been grooming her son for the role of chief. "Hallowed Ancestors, what else?"

Rockfish folded his arms tightly over his chest. "I also told her that if you changed your council vote, my people would be outraged. They would immediately start looking for new allies to go after the jade, and it wouldn't be long until they forged an alliance with Blue Bow and Water Hickory Clan."

Wink bent forward as though on the verge of emptying her stomach. "Then I can't change my council vote."

"No, you can't." Sora put a hand on Wink's shoulder. "We must pretend that the council vote is still undecided. It's the only way to draw them out."

"Draw them out?"

Sora squeezed her shoulder. "Don't you see? If I can drag this out for another twenty-eight days, I'm *sure* I can discover what they're doing and why, and how many people are involved. Maybe even why they want me to believe that Flint's soul—"

"What makes you think they'll actually give you twenty-eight days?"

She sat back on the bench. "It's customary."

"Yes, which means they must officially grant you twenty-eight days. That doesn't mean they can't hire someone to kill you in secret tomorrow. I'll have to surround your house with fifty guards!"

"No. Far Eye is enough. I don't want it to look like I'm afraid."

"I don't care what you want." Wink lurched to her feet and paced back and forth before the fire. The gray hair in her long braid twinkled in the orange gleam. "I'm the matron of this clan. I will *not* allow them to assassinate you, Sora!"

"Wink, I don't think they can afford to—"

"Oh, it won't be official. Sea Grass and Wood Fern will have to scream that it was done without their knowledge, but you'll be just as dead!" Wink stabbed an angry finger at Sora. "I have to speak with Feather Dancer. But I'm not finished with you yet. I'll be back."

As she stalked toward the door, Rockfish sank down on the bench beside Sora. Sweat beaded his nose and sparkled across his wrinkled forehead.

"She's right, Sora. She has to protect you."

Sora took his hands and held them. In a soft trusting voice, she said, "Rockfish, could you go to Feather Dancer? Tell him I must speak with him as soon as he can get away."

He squeezed her fingers. "I'll have to wait until Wink has finished her business but . . . why do you wish to see him? You're not planning on countermanding Wink's orders, are you?"

"Of course not. I would never do that. I just need his advice. Something's happened."

"Can't you discuss this with me?"

A strangely suspicious tone underlay his words, as though he feared what she might say to Feather Dancer. She shook her head and smiled up at him.

"It's about town security," she lied. "I need to work out strategy with my war chief."

"Very well." He stood up. "I'll go right now. Perhaps I can catch him before he must start organizing warriors to surround our house."

"Thank you."

When he'd left the temple, she rose and headed for her bed-chamber.

22

"IT'S NOT TRUE, IS IT?" FEATHER DANCER ASKED WHEN HE arrived a short time later.

Sora handed him a cup of tea and gestured for him to sit on the mat across the fire. He took the cup and knelt. His arm muscles bulged through the thin fabric of his tan shirt.

"Yes, it's true."

"You offered your life? After what we discussed? *Why?*"

Sora dipped her own cup into the pot that sat in the ashes at the edge of the fire. After she'd entered her chamber she'd removed the cone, washed it, and tucked it away in her personal basket; but the strange carvings continued to flit behind her eyes. She remembered very well the tangles of snakes, the spirals, the enormous creatures with long tails. A strange haunted sensation had filled her. She knew that cone. It was a magical device that had belonged to Flint. He'd used it many times to bring her pleasure. Where had Far Eye gotten it?

"I need time, Feather Dancer. If I'd denied the killing, they might have ordered their warriors to attack Blackbird Town."

"I think that was a mistake." He frowned down into the pale

green liquid in his cup. "Will they give you the traditional twenty-eight days?"

"They haven't decided." Her mouth quirked. "Wink suspects they'll grant me the twenty-eight days, then secretly have me assassinated."

"Yes, she told me that part. I'll prepare for it." He clutched his cup hard. "But you could be right. If they do actually give you twenty-eight days, they may reveal their true intentions."

"I hope so."

He looked up, and his scars reflected whitely in the firelight. "Where were you this morning?"

Her breathing went shallow. She inhaled a deep breath to fortify herself. "I thought you were asleep."

"No. I saw you walk away with Far Eye."

She jerked a nod and fumbled to set her cup on one of the hearth-stones. "Far Eye is . . . acting strangely."

"In what way?"

"We walked down to the burned-out tree, and he—he forced himself upon me."

Feather Dancer's eyes narrowed with deadly intent, and she knew if she didn't quickly explain, the young warrior would be dead. Feather Dancer started to rise.

"Wait. Please, sit down."

He stared at her with blazing eyes. "Tell me quickly."

The circlets of conch shell on her blue dress flashed as she rose to face him across the fire. "I swear to you, he's not Far Eye. This may well be part of a plot, but—"

"Of course it's part of a plot! Why did you let him touch you?"

She spread her hands in a pleading gesture. "Please, tell me something. When you arrived at the pond and found Skinner and me, you said that Skinner was still alive and that Far Eye smelled his breath, then smelled the pot of poison. Isn't that right?"

"Don't tell me you believe Flint's shadow-soul slipped from Skinner to Far Eye?"

"It's possible, isn't it?"

No expression showed on his face. "I don't believe in souls, Chieftess. But I do heartily believe in human deceit. Did you tell Matron Wink or your husband about this?"

"No."

"Why not?"

She hesitated. "I don't know. I just didn't feel—"

"That was a wise decision."

"Why do you say that?"

He walked around the fire and stared down at her like a wrathful giant. "Several reasons. With you gone, Matron Wink's son will ascend to the chieftanship. Also, she won't have you around to disagree with her, which means her power will be magnified tenfold, and perhaps . . ." His gaze darted around the room, as though considering a new element.

"Perhaps what?"

He tilted his head uncertainly. "Matron Wink and your husband worked together to try to convince you to go after the jade, didn't they?"

"Yes." She felt strangely uneasy. "But they frequently agree. Why?"

"The matron saw your husband often when you were married to Flint, didn't she?"

"Well, of course she did. He was a Trader. She was the matron. She worked with him on Trade agreements."

The scars at the corners of his mouth twitched. "Did it occur to you that they might have seen the jade brooch long before you did?"

A queasy sensation taunted her belly. "No. I'm sure I saw it first."

"You couldn't have. Grown Bear spoke with Matron Wink right after the chunkey game. Rockfish was there, too. In fact, Rockfish introduced Grown Bear to Wink. I saw it."

"Yes, but I hardly think that constitutes—"

"Did Matron Wink also work out 'Trade agreements' with Skinner? As a war chief from Water Hickory Clan, he would have made a powerful ally to go after the jade. With Water Hickory Clan and Rockfish's people, she would have had only one obstacle left. You."

"Oh . . ." It was a small tortured sound. She flushed.

Grown Bear and Skinner had appeared within moments of each other. Had they walked in together?

No. No, it couldn't be true. Wink, Skinner, Grown Bear, and Rockfish?

She simply couldn't believe all of them could hate her that much.

Wink was the only person in the world that she trusted completely. If Wink told her she'd just flown to Sister Moon and returned on the wings of a dragonfly, Sora would believe it.

"This is all interesting," she said, "but it doesn't make sense to me. Why would Wink do that? How could she possibly gain personally from such an agreement?"

"If you were gone and she could obtain canoeloads of jade, it would catapult her son into a position of enormous power. Long Fin would be the preeminent chief in our world."

Impatiently, she snapped, "Yes, but none of this explains how Far Eye could know—"

"Far Eye is her brother's son! He's also Water Hickory Clan! Don't you see? He has a great deal to gain if Long Fin ascends to the chieftainship. Wealth, prestige, power. All the things that motivate young men. And if Long Fin should die, Far Eye will vie with Short Tail for the position of chief."

"He's too young. Short Tail would win."

Feather Dancer gave her a stony look. "If Short Tail is alive, yes."

Sora sank back against the mat. He was right. What was one more murder in all this? But how could Far Eye have known how to use the cone? Even if Flint had given it to him, he'd worked it exactly as Flint . . .

She felt suddenly light-headed. She turned away so he couldn't see her expression.

Far Eye had known about the first time Flint brought her ecstasy with his hand. He'd known how to use the cone and how to tie it in place.

They were all things she'd told Wink about.

She turned back and found Feather Dancer giving her a sad look, as though he felt sorry for her. "What are you thinking?"

"Everything he—he did . . . this morning . . ."

"Were things the matron knew about?"

She closed her eyes as memories flared to life. "Before I married Flint, I used to tell her everything. She was my only friend. The one person I trusted to keep my secrets."

"Was she ever jealous?"

"No."

"Are you sure?"

Sora tried to imagine how she would have felt if Wink had told her every exhilarating detail of her sexual encounters. Without Flint in her life . . . she might have been a little jealous. Or a lot.

Softly, as though to calm her down, Feather Dancer said, "You are very vulnerable right now, Chieftess. You *must* stop believing that Flint's shadow-soul exists. I promise you, it does not."

She glared at the floor. "You may go, War Chief. Please send Far Eye in."

"Why?"

"There are questions I need to ask him."

"Do you think that's prudent? Perhaps it would be better to wait."

Hotly, she ordered, "I need answers now."

"I understand, but until we know more—"

"You are dismissed, War Chief!"

Feather Dancer shifted uncomfortably, as though he wanted to say something else, but wasn't sure how it would be received.

"What is it?"

Rain began to patter on the roof and drift down the smoke hole. The fire sizzled when the drops splattered on the logs. The sweet scent of damp cypress rose.

"May I speak frankly, Chieftess?"

"Haven't you been doing that since you arrived? Go on."

"Do you still wonder if this is your former husband's reflection-soul?"

"I do."

"Then if I am not mistaken, today is the ninth day after his death."

She blinked. She had to think about it. "Yes, it is. Why?"

"Reflection-souls can only remain on earth for ten days before they must go on to the afterlife, or they become homeless, wailing ghosts. If he's still here after midnight tonight, you will know that one of two things is happening."

"What things?"

"Either you're dealing with a ravenous shadow-soul, or the people you trust most are working against you." He gave her a grave look. "I'll tell Far Eye you wish to see him."

Just before he reached the door, she softly said, "Wait."

"Yes?" He turned.

"Perhaps I should speak with Teal first."

Feather Dancer held the curtain aside for her. "If you must, but remember, no matter how much you want to, do not tell him all of our suspicions. He might feel obligated to discuss them with the matron."

"Yes, treason is serious business."

"*Deadly* business."

When she walked forward and ducked out into the hallway, she glimpsed someone stepping into the council chamber at the far end of the hall.

Feather Dancer surveyed her face. Standing there with her gaze fixed on the swinging council door curtain, she must look like she'd seen her assassin, which she hadn't, but she wasn't certain she hadn't seen the hem of his cape.

"What did you see?" he whispered as he drew his stiletto from his belt.

"A man. I think. I only caught a glimpse of someone going into the council chamber."

"Stay here."

Feather Dancer eased down the corridor, silent as Hawk's shadow. Outside the council chamber, he hesitated long enough to listen; then he threw back the curtain and peered inside.

She saw his brows knit into a single line across his forehead.

"Who is it, War Chief?" she called.

Feather Dancer gave her a knowing look and stepped aside to allow the man to exit into the corridor.

Rockfish walked out. He turned to face her, and guilt tensed his mouth.

"Rockfish? Is something wrong?"

He glanced at Feather Dancer, then tipped his chin up and answered, "I was looking for Feather Dancer. Matron Wink wishes to speak with him immediately."

Feather Dancer calmly strode back down the hall and stood directly in front of Sora, blocking her husband's view of her. He used his stiletto to point to the floor.

She looked down. Tracks scuffed the dirt.

When her gaze shot upward, Feather Dancer nodded slightly.

Rockfish was standing here—listening outside the door. As soon as he knew I was leaving, he must have tried to get away, but he only had enough time to make it to the council chamber.

She nodded to tell Feather Dancer that she understood, then walked around him and swiftly strode down the corridor. Rockfish's jaw clenched when she passed by without a word and stepped outside into the misty rain.

Far Eye stood beneath the eaves, shielded from the streamers that poured off the roof.

"Go and speak with the matron, War Chief," Sora said.

Subtly gesturing to Far Eye, he murmured, "I will return as quickly as I can."

"Thank you."

As Feather Dancer trotted away, she called, "Far Eye, please escort me to the Priest's House."

"Yes, Chieftess."

Just as the young warrior trotted up, Rockfish drew back the entry curtain, glanced at Far Eye's seductive smile, and gave Sora a look of naked fear.

23

SHE'D LEFT HER CAPE IN HER CHAMBER, AND THE RUN through the rain drenched her blue dress. By the time she neared Teal's house, her black hair stuck to her face in wet locks. She trotted beneath the overhanging eaves and called, "Teal?"

There was a lengthy pause before he answered, "Just a moment, Chieftess."

Far Eye stood beside her, his cape clinging to his broad chest. The soaked fabric outlined every muscle.

"When you are finished here," he said. "I must see you alone."

"Why?" She wrung out her hair.

"You know why."

"No, I don't."

He gazed out across the rain-stippled lake. The far trees were invisible, obscured by the swirling mist that drifted across the green surface. The cacophony of birdsong had dwindled. Only the distinctive *see-e-e-e* of a cedar waxwing carried through the downpour.

Far Eye murmured, "You told him everything, didn't you?"

"Who?"

"Feather Dancer. I could tell by the way he looked at me when he came out of your house. What did he say?"

"We discussed the situation with Water Hickory Clan. We didn't say anything that pertained to you."

His mouth pursed distastefully. "You've never been a good liar, Sora. What does he want? My destruction? Did he tell you I was evil?"

What could be taking Teal so long? She could hear him moving about inside. Was he talking to someone? Soft hisses penetrated around the door hanging.

"He didn't say anything about you, Far Eye," she repeated impatiently.

"Don't call me that. You know that's not who I am."

He flexed his hands and clenched them into tight fists. It was something she'd seen Flint do a thousand times.

Think about this! It's just a gesture. He could have learned it in five heartbeats from anyone who knew Flint!

She leaned closer to the door hanging and called, "Teal?"

"Yes, Chieftess, you may come in now."

Hastily, she tore aside the hanging and stepped into the warm orange glow. Teal stood in front of the fire with his hands out. He was shivering.

"Teal? Are you well?" she asked in concern as she crossed the floor.

"It's a small illness. Nothing more. I've been preparing the body of War Chief Skinner. I fear some of the evil spirits of corruption sneaked into me when I wasn't looking." He waved a skeletal hand. "Don't fret about it. I just need a good purging."

He looked even thinner today than he had yesterday. His knobby arms thrust out of his brown sleeves like skin-covered bones.

"What did you need?" he asked with a tremulous smile.

"Did I wake you?"

"I wasn't sleeping, just lying beneath a mound of blankets. My fever is high, I think."

Worried, Sora hurried to him and placed a hand to his forehead. "You're very hot, Teal. Perhaps I should send for a Healer."

"Don't be ridiculous. I'm the best Healer I know. I'll tend to myself." He gestured to the log bench in front of the fire. "Sit and tell me why you're here."

His bald head was shaking, reflecting the firelight like a seashell.

"You sit down," she instructed. "I'll stand."

"As you wish." He gingerly lowered himself to the bench and stared up at her with white-filmed eyes. "You met with Matron Sea Grass, didn't you?"

"Yes, but that's not why I wanted to speak with you."

He folded his hands in his lap, waiting.

Sora paced before the fire. "I wanted to talk with you about Skinner."

"His preparations are coming along fine. I suspect Sea Grass will take his cleaned bones with her when she leaves. What else is there to say?"

Feather Dancer's questions haunted her like old words that should never have been said. "I'm worried about Wink."

"In what way?"

"She seems . . . preoccupied . . . with Skinner's death."

His sparse white brows lifted. "He was a war chief. His prestige alone would be enough to disturb anyone. She still does not know what his clan intends to do—"

"I resolved that matter, Teal. I offered my own life to Sea Grass to compensate her for Skinner's death."

The fragrance of the rain soaking into the bark walls filled the chamber.

He stiffened in surprise. "Why did you do that?"

"I must have given him the entire pot of poison, Teal. You said to give him a pinch. I alone am to blame."

"Then we must now hope Sea Grass does not accept your offer.

She shouldn't. Not after what I told her about the shadow-soul malingering in her son. Is that what you came to tell me? That you had offered your life?"

"No. I wanted to ask you a question."

"I am at your disposal, of course. What did you wish to know?"

"Do you think Skinner and Wink might have been working on a secret Trade agreement?"

"An agreement to do what?"

"I don't want to say yet. Did you hear any rumors, any tidbits of conversations that aroused your suspicions?"

"When you say a 'secret' agreement, I assume you mean an agreement that you knew nothing about?"

"Yes."

He scratched his wrinkled jaw. "An agreement that, perhaps, the council knew nothing about?"

"That's what worries me the most."

He gave her a curious look. "I don't believe she would betray Shadow Rock Clan. I certainly don't think she would betray you. She loves you too much. It's possible, of course, that by keeping you out of such negotiations she might be protecting you should things go poorly. Why?"

"It may explain her preoccupation with his death. She just seems unduly concerned. Have you noticed that?"

"No, I can't say that I have." Teal appeared suddenly uneasy, or perhaps it was just his illness. He looked frail enough to collapse at any instant. "Now, please answer a question for me."

"Yes?"

"What are you feeling right now?"

"Feeling?"

"You are very agitated. This is more than worry about a secret Trade agreement. What's wrong?"

She closed her eyes for a few blessed instants and answered, "I think I'm being manipulated. I—I'm afraid that someone, or perhaps several people, is plotting—"

"I don't think that's what you're really afraid of, is it?"

She forced herself to take a deep breath. He was a canny old man, well schooled in people's expressions and fears. "No, he—he's alive, Teal."

Teal frowned, and deep furrows cut across his forehead. "Are you trying to tell me that Flint's shadow-soul slipped inside you the night Skinner died?"

"Possibly, for a short time, but . . . I don't think he's there now."

"Does that mean you believe he's moved on to someone else?"

Sora blankly watched the firelight dance on the hearthstones. She didn't want to tell him. Not yet. "I'm not sure, Teal. What I'm really afraid of . . ."

When her voice faded, his old eyes narrowed. "What are you afraid of?"

Through a long exhalation, she said, "I'm afraid all of this might be a hoax. That someone is trying to make me think Flint's shadow-soul is alive and by doing so they hope to force me to step down. I—"

"Who? Who would do that?"

She shrugged. "I can't say for certain."

His gaze darted around the chamber for twenty breaths; then he looked back at her. "You think Matron Wink would harm you because you killed her political ally and destroyed her chances of finishing a lucrative Trade agreement?"

"No, gods, that's not what I meant."

"What did you mean?"

"There are things happening that I don't understand, Teal! I've been wondering if Skinner wasn't more than a political ally. She may have been his lover. Or—or Rockfish's lover, or even . . ." It surprised her that she found it difficult to say: "Even Flint's."

Teal lowered his gaze to stare at gray flakes of ash that perched on the hearthstones. It seemed to take a long time for him to think about his question before he said, "Let me see if I understand this. You believe Matron Wink was involved with Skinner, Rockfish, and

Flint. Is that all? Or do you have other names you want to add to the list?"

Having him put it that way made it sound suddenly ludicrous. She colored.

"I'm not accusing her, Teal. I just—"

"Of course you're accusing her. The question is why?"

"I'm just trying to clarify things in my own heart."

The rain on the roof had grown stronger, pounding down like angry fists.

His white-filmed eyes closed to slits. "Don't tell me you haven't thought about the fact that if any of these 'Trade agreements' were proved to have been made without the council's knowledge Matron Wink would certainly be executed for treason. You know she would. Shadow Rock Clan would demand it."

Sora started to object, but stopped as the ramifications of her questions seeped in. "Blessed gods, if anyone ever finds out I asked you these questions—"

"It will appear that *you* are trying to cause *her* downfall. Yes, it certainly will." He paused to massage his right knee before he added, "You don't want that, do you?"

"No, of course I don't. I love her."

Then how could you ever have believed it possible?

The very fact that she'd come to Teal to ask him these questions proved she didn't love Wink. It may have been a subtle act of disloyalty, but it was disloyal nonetheless. She had just planted the seeds of rumors that might result in Wink's death.

"Teal, please do not ever mention to anyone that I suggested—"

"I won't." He cocked his head and gave her an inquiring stare. "If you will tell me who you've been talking to. Someone must have told you those things. You'd never think of them yourself. Who suggested the matron might be working on a secret Trade agreement with Water Hickory Clan?"

"I can't answer that."

She'd been treacherous enough for one day. She wasn't about to betray Feather Dancer. At this point, he was the only objective advisor she had.

Teal rose to his feet on shaking legs. "Well, whoever it was, *stop listening to him*. He's not trying to help you." He made a shooing gesture with both hands. "Now, go away. I must rest."

"Forgive me, Teal. Are you certain I can't send—"

"I think you've done quite enough for one day, Chieftess. Go home and ask yourself why you're beginning to think these thoughts. The answer to your heartache lies in that question. *Why?*"

As he hobbled toward his sleeping bench, something fell in the charnel house.

She swung around to stare at the entryway. The curtain swayed slightly, as though it had been brushed by the air of someone's passing.

"Is someone back there?" she asked in sudden terror.

Had everything she'd said been overheard? By whom?

"Mice," Teal said with a gruff sigh. "They love to gnaw on fresh bones."

A shudder went up her spine.

Sora swallowed hard and backed toward his door. "Thank you, Teal. I'll send someone over to check on you later."

24

SHE DUCKED OUT THE FRONT ENTRANCE INTO A DELUGE OF rain. The drops were so thick she could barely make out the shape of Persimmon Lake. Far Eye peered from around the north side of the house.

"Come here, Chieftess. It's mostly dry."

She stayed beneath the eaves, walking just inside the drip-line, until she could slide around the corner and stand next to him. He lifted his cape, inviting her to step beneath it with him.

Sora shook her head. "I'm fine."

The wind blew from the south, leaving a dry swath ten hands wide on this side of the house.

"What's wrong?" he asked suspiciously.

"I just don't want to."

As he let the cape down, his eyes narrowed. "Are you trying to tell me something?"

No matter what Feather Dancer said, when she looked into this man's eyes, she knew it was Flint looking back. It was more than his gestures, or the way he loved her. They had always had a special connection. In some bizarre spiritual way, their souls could touch. He *felt* like Flint.

"Sora, listen." Panic edged his voice. "Very soon there will be dozens of warriors standing guard around your house."

"Yes. So?"

"How will we meet?"

"We can't, Flint."

"Don't say that. You want to see me. I know you do."

"It's too dangerous."

He grabbed her and forced her against the wall. For a few instants, she struggled in vain to extricate herself from his powerful arms; then she sank against him.

"Flint, please, you must leave me alone for a while. I'm risking everything—"

"When didn't we risk everything to be together, Sora?" He kissed her forehead and nose. When his lips met hers, she kissed him back.

It was surreal, standing there with her body pressed hard against his. They would be in plain sight if it weren't for the wall of rain that hid them. It reminded her of the days just before he'd left. They'd rarely been more than a few paces apart.

That's because he refused to let you out of his sight.

"Oh, Sora, how am I going to get in to see you with fifty warriors blocking the way?" His hands rose to massage her breasts, and his kisses grew more insistent. "I can't stand being away from you."

He pressed against her, and she felt his hard manhood.

The growls of Thunderbirds echoed over the forest. "Why are you still here, Flint? The night Skinner died, you told me you had to leave."

"I have a little time left. Until midnight tonight. That's all. Then I really do have to go."

He reached between her legs. His fingers pressed the damp fabric of her dress inside her. It felt cool, the texture rough.

"Flint, don't. If the rain stops, people will be able to see us. I can't allow—"

"Yes, you can. You've done it before."

When she tried to get away, he roughly shoved her against the wall. Cold fear surged in her veins. It took a few awkward moments of jerking up her dress, prying her open with his fingers, and thrusting hard for him to finally get inside her, but when he did, he groaned and strained against her like a starving man finding food.

He moaned, "I can't leave you, Sora. I can't."

"You don't want to become a homeless ghost, do you? Wandering the earth, forever alone?"

His hot breath rasped against her neck. "I'll still have you."

She'd heard of homeless ghosts who fought so hard to continue "living" that they eventually drove their loved ones mad. She could imagine ten or twenty winters of seeing him looking at her from new eyes every few days, of feeling the hands of a man she barely knew on her body . . . of having a stranger pumping his warm seed inside her.

Something moved below the mound: a dark shadow drifting through the downpour. She thought for a terrifying instant that it might be a man. Tall and slender. Then it evaporated and was gone.

"Flint, you must leave. For your own good. Your relatives are waiting for you in the afterlife."

He thrust harder, pounding her body against the wall. She feared Teal might hear them and come out to see what they were doing. Not only that, the rain had begun to subside.

"Flint, I can make out Persimmon Lake, which means that people will soon duck outside—"

"Just a little longer."

He grabbed her around the waist and drove himself into her. There was something about the combination of his wild thrusts and the danger of being seen that stoked her passions. She tightened her muscles around his manhood. He moaned. It took only heartbeats for him to gasp and shudder. As he went limp, hot fluid leaked down the insides of her thighs.

The rain turned to a soft drizzle. People emerged from their houses along the shoreline and began to resume their duties.

"Sora, you must find a way to get me into your house tonight. I have to see you one last time. You need me. I know you do."

"I'll try." She stepped away from him and rearranged her blue dress.

As she started down the mound slope, he said, "Have Feather Dancer assign me to stand guard outside your bedchamber door. That way, once your husband is asleep, I can come to you."

"No, that's too risky. He might waken."

She tried to walk away, and he grabbed her arm and pulled her back. His fingers dug into her wrist with such force, they would leave bruises. "Perhaps I'll come to you anyway. I'll slit his throat and take you with him lying dead beside us."

Blessed gods, he means it.

She forced herself to say, "Be close at midnight. I'll send someone to fetch you."

He cocked his head suspiciously, as though he thought she might be lying, saying what he wanted to hear just to make him let go of her arm, but he nodded. "I'll be waiting. *Don't forget about me, or I'll have to find a way myself.*"

The threat chilled her.

If she didn't call for him at midnight, what would he do? Fight his way through fifty guards to get to her? Or maybe his soul could pass through whispers from man to man to man . . .

She hurried down the mound—with Far Eye two steps behind her—wondering if Flint had ever intended to travel the road to the afterlife.

Maybe staying with her, as she'd once begged him to, was an insane form of punishment.

Or worse.

Vengeance.

25

SHE COUNTED TEN GUARDS AROUND THE BASE OF HER mound. There must be more in the rear where she couldn't see. Feather Dancer stood at the top of the stairs wearing a bark rain cape and conical hat. His scarred face was rigid, but his gaze moved back and forth between Sora and Far Eye as they walked up the stairs to the mound top. More warriors stood at the corners of the house.

"I was growing concerned, Chieftess. What took you so long?"

"We waited for the rain to ease up." She walked past him toward her door. Before she entered, she bowed briefly to the huge carving of Black Falcon.

Behind her, Feather Dancer said, "Far Eye, I want you to guard Matron Wink's house."

"Why? You need me here. Let me stand guard outside the chieftess' bedchamber. That's where I'll be of most use."

In a gruff voice, Feather Dancer ordered, "Go to the Matron's House. I'll meet you there in a short time and we'll discuss this."

Sora turned.

Far Eye's teeth clenched, setting his jaw askew. "You just want to be close to her. That's it, isn't it?"

The other warriors glanced worriedly at each other. Feather Dancer drew himself up to his full height and glared at Far Eye with deadly intent.

"Go. Now. Before I have you escorted back to your chamber and your door barricaded."

Far Eye's mouth puckered in rage. His fists knotted as though he was considering striking his war chief. Instead, he growled, *"You leave her alone. She's mine."*

Feather Dancer looked suddenly uncertain. Perhaps he saw Flint looking out at him and was reconsidering his idea that Far Eye was part of a conspiracy to bring about her downfall.

Sora said, "War Chief, I would prefer that Far Eye stand guard around my house."

Far Eye glowered as though displeased she hadn't said "in front of my bedchamber," and Feather Dancer blinked in disbelief that she would countermand his order when she knew Far Eye was dangerous.

"Chieftess, I must protest. We need warriors around the Matron's House, and since Far Eye is her brother's son, his place is there."

"You are right, of course," she said. "But if it's possible, I would like Far Eye to stay here tonight; then tomorrow you may reassign him."

Feather Dancer seemed to be mulling her words. He had been the one who had mentioned that Flint's reflection-soul had only one more day; he must see the logic of her request.

Reluctantly, he said, "If that is what you think best, then I have no objections."

Far Eye gave Feather Dancer a smug smile. "I'll stand guard at the northeast corner."

Though he knew that was the closest corner to her bedchamber, Feather Dancer nodded. "Go on."

Far Eye glanced at Sora as he trotted away. Something sinister stared back at her. Flint had often frightened her, but never like this. For days she had been denying it was his shadow-soul that was moving from body to body. Now, she wasn't so sure.

"I've never seen him so unruly," Feather Dancer quietly said, and scrutinized Far Eye's back.

Rockfish walked around the corner of the house—*Was he out looking for me? Was he the man I saw drifting through the rain?*—and almost bumped into Far Eye. The two men stood facing each other for several anxious heartbeats; then Rockfish bowed and said, "Forgive me. I wasn't watching where I was going."

Far Eye leaned forward and hissed something in Rockfish's face. Sora couldn't hear the words. All she saw was her husband's expression. The wrinkles across his forehead deepened as his brows drew together. Far Eye trotted around the corner and was gone.

Rockfish stood rigid, as though stunned by what had just happened.

Sora whispered to Feather Dancer, "Tomorrow I'll know what to do."

"And if *he* is still here after midnight?"

Only a short while ago Feather Dancer had been convinced this was a plot to destroy her. Had Far Eye's anomalous behavior so disturbed him that he'd begun to think she was right? They were dealing with Flint's soul? That frightened her even more.

"By then I'll know."

Rockfish started toward her. He walked with his head down, frowning at the ground.

Sora said, "Feather Dancer, please send a slave to the temple chamber. I need help with dinner preparations and to keep the Eternal Fire burning through the night."

"Right away, Chieftess."

26

SORA DUCKED INTO THE BEDCHAMBER FIRST, FOLLOWED BY Rockfish, and walked directly to her personal basket. "I'm soaked," she said with a weak smile.

"As am I."

His tone was clipped. He went to his own basket and changed to a dry knee-length black shirt.

Sora tugged her wet dress over her head and reached for a plain tan dress with black stylized spirals around the hem. As she slipped it on, she caught Rockfish's stare. His gaze went over her naked body with a proprietary keenness, noting every curve, as though searching for a sign that his precious belonging had been "damaged."

"How much did you hear?" she asked.

"What do you mean?"

"When Feather Dancer and I were talking. You were standing outside the door. How much did you hear?"

Ordinarily he would have turned away in embarrassment that she'd caught him. Instead, he faced her directly. "I was searching for you. I didn't know you and Feather Dancer were alone in our bedchamber. I—"

"What are you implying? That we—"

"No, of course not! The first thing I heard was Feather Dancer asking you how often I'd seen Wink when you were married to Flint."

"Yes, and?" Sora's knees felt like boiled grass stems.

"I—"

"*Chieftess?*" a woman called from beyond the door curtain. "It's Iron Hawk. Feather Dancer said you might need help tonight."

"Yes," she responded. "Thank you, Iron Hawk. Please begin dinner preparations. You will sleep in the temple tonight to tend the fire. If I need you for other things, I'll call."

"Yes, Chieftess."

The woman's soft steps retreated down the hallway.

Rockfish gave her a contrite look. "Before we continue with our discussions, Wink wanted me to tell you that our scouts spotted Chief Blue Bow's party. He should be in late tonight. She ordered Feather Dancer to go out, meet Blue Bow, and safely escort him into Blackbird Town. Long Fin is going with Feather Dancer. He said he—"

"Did you see the jade before I did?" she boldly asked.

A hard swallow went down his throat. "Please try to understand. Grown Bear came into town a few hands of time before the chunkey game started. You were getting dressed for the game. Wink and I were both curious about what he was doing here. She asked me to fetch him, and I—"

"She asked *you* to fetch him?"

Why didn't she ask her son?

"Yes. I was at hand."

Suddenly too tired to stand, she walked over and lowered herself to one of the mats before the fire. A low blaze burned in a thick bed of red coals. She stared at them. Not at him. She couldn't bear to look at him. "Then what happened? Grown Bear showed you the jade and the three of you discussed it?"

He shifted his weight. "A little. We didn't have much time."

"Why did you hide that fact from me?"

"Wink and I decided that it would be better not to distract you before the game."

But you felt it necessary to keep it from me even after the game. You both wanted me to believe you had never seen the stone. Why?

All of the other questions Feather Dancer had asked her came crashing down. Questions about Skinner and Wink. Wink and Flint.

He spread his arms. "Who did we harm, Sora?"

"No one. I would have just liked to have known, that's all."

Rockfish came across the floor with his black shirt waffling about his legs and knelt across the fire from her. His gray hair picked up the orange tint of the flames. "Forgive me for not mentioning it. I thought you had more important things to worry about. Flint was dead. War Chief Skinner was here."

"I understand."

After a few moments, he earnestly said, "Sora, I am not working with Wink to harm you. You know that, don't you? I love you. Wink loves you."

"Yes"—she exhaled the words—"I know."

Despite her roiling gut, after her recent infidelities with Skinner and Far Eye, she had no right to treat him with anything but kindness. If he had betrayed her over the jade, she had betrayed him over other things.

"I'm tired, Rockfish. Forgive me. I think I'll sleep for a short while."

She stretched out on the mat before the fire and stared at the raindrops that glinted as they fell through the smoke hole. She felt empty. Just . . . hollow. Like a beetle-chewed old log.

Rockfish rose and came around the fire to her. As he knelt at her side, he said, "May I help you sleep?" and placed a gentle hand on her arm.

When she didn't answer, his hand shifted to her thigh. "I *do* love you, Sora," he said fiercely. "I'm sorry I was exhausted last night."

He pressed kisses on her closed eyelids, her temple, the corner of her mouth, and down her throat to her collar. Through her dress, he kissed her breasts. His breath felt warm and the movement of the fabric silken against her damp skin. He pleasured her with such exquisite slowness that her nipples ached sweetly for release from her dress.

"Are you sure, Rockfish? Perhaps later when you are—"

His teeth caught her nipple and tugged. "I must find a way to please you, Sora. To show you how much I love you."

He worked her dress up over her hips and kissed her thigh. When his tongue probed between her legs, she closed her eyes. How could he miss the scent of another man? Would he mention it? Fly into a rage? Pretend it wasn't there? Or maybe, if the gods had been good to her, the rain had washed away most of the evidence.

She was about to suggest they move to the sleeping bench when he forcefully spread her legs. "Lie still," he ordered in an authoritative tone she had never heard before.

Stunned, she did it.

He kissed the insides of her thighs and encircled her navel with his tongue. "The things you told me last night, about how roughly Flint treated you . . . I've been thinking about them all day."

"I was married to him for almost half my life, and I loved him very much. I didn't mean to hurt you."

"You didn't hurt me. Not exactly. You reminded me that my passions have grown pale. That I have grown pale as a man."

"No, you haven't. You just—"

"Don't defend me. That makes me feel worse."

He forced her to bring up her knees, and his eyes widened as she opened to him. For a long time, he just stared. "Do you know I've never really looked at you? We've been joined for three winters, and I've never just *looked* at you. You're beautiful."

He braced his chin on the mat and slipped his tongue inside her. It was a leisurely rhythm, the thrusts going a little deeper each time.

Blessed gods, couldn't he *taste* another man?

His tongue began to move hungrily, reaching for the deepest, softest parts of her.

Outside the house, a thump sounded, as though someone had slipped in the rain-slick grass and fallen against the wall.

Is Flint out there with his ear pressed to the wall, listening?

She closed her eyes and watched the firelight dance against her lids.

Rockfish's movements changed, grew more urgent, and a warm flood surged through her veins. She arched against his lips.

He let out a low groan of pleasure.

She stiffened.

His voice had a different tone. The inflection sounded just like . . .

He groaned again, deeper, and she felt him smile.

No, this can't be happening.

Sora lifted her head. When their eyes met, he laughed.

Panic surged through her. She tried to scramble away.

He leaped, and his body slammed her to the mat, pinning her.

With a thundering heart, she asked, "Rockfish? When Far Eye leaned close to speak to you, what—"

"I told you I would find a way," he hissed, and put a hand over her mouth.

She struggled against him, trying to push him away, or to scream.

His grip tightened, and she tasted blood. He glared down at her with bulging eyes. "Stop it!" he growled. "Stop fighting me!"

Despite her flailing legs, he managed to shove his manhood inside her. His thrusts were violent, like those of a careless stranger, or a lover who wanted to hurt her.

She just lay there. It was like taking a beating.

When he finally sagged on top of her, his hand fell away from her mouth, and she sucked in a breath. Her body was one huge fiery ache.

In her ear, he roughly whispered, "Don't move. I may want to take you again after I nap."

———————

FOR SEVERAL HANDS OF TIME, SHE LAY BENEATH HIM LIS-tening to his breathing. When he was finally sound asleep, she eased out from under him.

At one point he roused, but he just rolled over and went back to sleep.

Sora rose and stared down at him. Blood darkened his hand. Her blood. A faint gloating smile lingered on his lips.

With the silence of Cougar on a night hunt, she moved around the chamber, searching for the perfect weapon. If she used a bone stiletto or arrow, he would not die quickly enough. He might get his hands on her before she could escape and might breathe in her face. The war ax, or club, would be better. She would have to make certain the first blow at least stunned him. Then her second blow . . .

She reached for the ax on the wall. When she touched the smooth wooden handle, her fingers quaked. She clenched them into a fist and stood there marshaling her strength.

Rockfish inhaled a deep breath. Firelight flickered over his elderly face. He'd lived a good long life. He had loved at least two women, Traded great wealth, and helped his people.

I must make certain Blackbird Town is safe.

Quietly, she lifted the ax off the wall. As she tiptoed across the room to stand over her husband, her heart was breaking. He had been good to her. She had, in a curiously subdued way, loved him.

She lifted the ax.

For what seemed an eternity, she stood with the ax poised above his skull, studying his face. His wrinkles cast a tracery of shadows over his cheeks and forehead, giving him an ancient, haunted look.

Tears filled her eyes, and in that brief moment of sparkling blind-ness, she heard Wink's voice near the front entrance: *"Let no one pass this door, including the chieftess. Do you understand?"*

"Yes, Matron, of course, but what about her slaves? The chieftess asked that Iron Hawk sleep in the temple tonight to tend the Eternal Fire."

"Her slaves may pass in the process of carrying out their duties. That's all."

"I understand, Matron."

Sora's thoughts raced.

Her dearest friend had just ordered her imprisoned in her own house. Why?

What's happening that she doesn't want me to know about?

Wink was probably just taking extra precautions to make certain Sora was safe, but . . .

She lowered the ax and clutched it against her chest. Barely above a whisper, she said, "Hallowed gods, what am I doing? Think about this!"

She had to see Far Eye again. Before she killed Rockfish, she had to know where Flint's soul had gone.

27

AT MIDNIGHT, SORA WALKED DOWN THE DIM HALLWAY IN silence, carrying her chunkey lance. Beyond the entrance door, she heard warriors laugh softly. She did not say a word as she pulled aside the curtain to the temple and stepped into the firelit stillness.

Iron Hawk looked up from the pot she was stirring. "Chieftess! I'm happy to see you." In the gleam of the Eternal Fire, her heart-shaped face seemed chiseled from pure amber. "I was told not to disturb you, but it was getting so late I feared you would be starving." She quickly filled a bowl and held it out to Sora.

Sora leaned her chunkey lance against the wall and crossed the floor to take the bowl. "Forgive me for not coming sooner. I was occupied."

Iron Hawk wiped her hands on her brown dress. "Of course, Chieftess. There are many things happening in town. I understand."

Sora ate while she stared up at the gleaming body of Black Falcon that hung on the wall. Tonight Power radiated from him like a thousand suns. As though set loose on the wind by the gods, it flowed around and through her, turning her veins into streams of warm light.

"This is delicious, Iron Hawk. Where did you get the clams?"

The slave smiled and bowed. "Matron Wink gave them to me. She told me that you love clams. It pleases me that you enjoy the stew."

Sora stopped eating suddenly, lowered the bowl, and stared down at it. She'd eaten half the bowl and hadn't noticed any taint to the flavor. Still . . .

She handed the stew back to Iron Hawk. "I guess I'm not as hungry as I thought."

Iron Hawk's smile faded. "Would you like something else? It won't take me long to fry some fish, or—"

"No. Truly, I'm fine." Sora exhaled hard. "But there is one more thing I need you to do for me."

"Of course, Chieftess. Anything."

Sora reached out to touch the plain, coarsely woven dress that Iron Hawk wore. It smelled of wood smoke. "Give me your dress."

Iron Hawk frowned as though she didn't understand. Her gaze went over Sora's face questioningly. "My dress?"

"Yes. I need your dress," she replied as she pulled her sleep shirt over her head and handed it to Iron Hawk, "and your cape and hat."

28

FEATHER DANCER AND LONG FIN WALKED THE FOREST TRAIL
in plain sight. The rest of their party moved like ghosts through the
trees, heading toward Chief Blue Bow's party.

Blue Bow bravely marched out front, followed by War Chief
Grown Bear and twenty warriors—a pittance given the potentially
dire consequences of his visit.

"You're taller than I am, Feather Dancer. Can you see Blue Bow?"
Long Fin asked.

"Yes. Just up ahead."

Blue Bow's copper headdress and breastplate reflected the
starlight like liquid amber. He was a small, skinny old man with a
long nose and receding chin. His bald head reminded Feather Dancer
of a boiled egg.

When the party came within thirty paces, Feather Dancer
stepped in front of Long Fin and called, "Identify yourselves."

The Loon warriors immediately closed ranks around their chief,
making it impossible to see the old man, and Grown Bear shouted,
"Who are you?"

"I am Feather Dancer, war chief to Matron Wink of the Black

Falcon Nation. As a gesture of our goodwill, her son, Long Fin, is with me."

Blue Bow's brittle voice responded, "I am Chief Blue Bow, council leader of the Loon People."

"Show yourself that we may know your words are true."

Blue Bow shouldered through his warriors and stood like a small statue next to Grown Bear's burly form.

Feather Dancer said, "I recognize you, Chief. You are welcome in the Black Falcon Nation. Matron Wink asked us to escort you safely into Blackbird Town. Do not be alarmed when our warriors come out of the trees. They are here to protect you." He lifted his hand, and men filtered through the dark oak trunks to surround the Loon party.

Blue Bow's old eyes narrowed. "To protect us from whom, War Chief? If your matron welcomes us—"

Long Fin called, "Do all the Loon clans agree on political decisions, Chief?"

Blue Bow's grizzled brows lowered. "No. They do not. Which clans oppose my presence in the Black Falcon Nation? I would know so that I might prepare myself for their treachery."

Long Fin answered, "No one has openly opposed your visit, but my mother is cautious. She truly wishes to keep you from harm."

"I appreciate that," Blue Bow said, and turned to his war chief. "Grown Bear, I wish to speak with Long Fin alone. Please follow twenty paces behind us."

"But my chief!" Grown Bear objected. "That is too risky. They may be plotting—"

"I will take that chance. Do as I say."

Grown Bear murmured something unpleasant and backed away.

Blue Bow came forward and looked up at Feather Dancer with starlit eyes. "Let me walk out front with Long Fin for a time, War Chief."

"As you wish."

"But not too far out front," Long Fin said to Feather Dancer with a dip of his head.

Feather Dancer understood. He dropped three paces behind.

He heard Blue Bow say, "I would ask you some questions, Long Fin, if you do not mind."

Long Fin nodded and led the way up the trail through the towering trees. "I do not mind, if you understand that I may not be able to answer."

"That is a fair arrangement."

Blue Bow adjusted his bright copper breastplate and softly asked, "Is it true that Chieftess Sora has offered her life to Matron Sea Grass to compensate her for the loss of her son, War Chief Skinner?"

"It is."

Blue Bow shook his head. "It saddens me to hear of it. These sorts of things make political negotiations much more difficult."

"I'm sure the chieftess will put her own personal concerns aside during her time with you."

"Yes, I'm sure she'll try, but when one's life is at stake it's impossible to concentrate fully on difficult negotiations, don't you agree?"

"I am just the matron's son. Trade agreements are not my expertise. I do not even understand why this green stone is so important to possess."

Feather Dancer squinted at the lie. Over the past hand of time, Long Fin had talked of little else. He wanted the stone badly. What was the youth up to? Had he worked this out with Matron Wink?

Obviously confused, Blue Bow asked, "What green stone?"

Long Fin frowned. "The jade." When Blue Bow's expression didn't change, Long Fin said, "The jade brooch you sent to Chieftess Sora."

The warriors following twenty paces behind muttered among themselves, probably exchanging insults, as enemy warriors did. Someone chuckled, and another man growled a response.

Blue Bow's sunken face contorted. "I didn't send her any brooch. What are you talking about?"

"You sent your war chief to Chieftess Sora with a brooch—"

"It was her broken promise that forced me to send Grown Bear to your chieftess. There was no brooch."

Clearly taken aback, Long Fin said, "Explain."

If Blue Bow was involved in the plot to cause the chieftess' downfall, he might say anything.

But if he didn't give Grown Bear the brooch to bring to Chieftess Sora, who did? Who is Grown Bear's secret ally in the Black Falcon Nation?

"Explain?" Blue Bow said as though offended. "I mean that your chieftess was supposed to meet with me fourteen days ago to negotiate the release of your hostages. I never saw her! Your war party camped outside our village. She sent a man to me who promised that she would soon arrive. He said he was a willing hostage, that if she did not arrive in five days, we could kill him for insulting our people. Naturally, when the sixth day arrived, my people were outraged that she had not appeared as promised. They demanded I kill him."

A searing prickle began at the nap of Feather Dancer's neck. He stepped forward. "What man?"

"His name was Walking Bird. He said he was Water Hickory Clan."

Long Fin turned to Feather Dancer. "War Chief, do you know what he's talking about?"

"Not for certain. The chieftess ordered me to remain in camp while she and Walking Bird went into Eagle Flute Village. I didn't like the idea, but I had no choice. She is my chieftess, and I obey her orders. When she returned alone five days later, she said that when they first entered the village Walking Bird had thrown himself in front of her to take the Loon arrow meant for her heart. The renegade warrior—"

"What Loon arrow?" Blue Bow cried. "No such thing ever happened!"

Long Fin lifted a hand to silence Blue Bow. His gaze had not left Feather Dancer's face. "Finish your story, War Chief. What else did the chieftess say?"

"She said the renegade warrior had been killed by other Loon warriors and after that she'd been warmly greeted by Blue Bow himself. They'd talked of peace."

She must have instructed Walking Bird after she left camp. What had she ordered him to do? To keep them occupied while she assessed the situation more thoroughly? Had she promised that she would be there long before they killed him? Dear gods, on the sixth day Walking Bird must have been frantic.

Unless . . .

If Blue Bow was secretly involved with Water Hickory Clan, he was lying to further hurt the chieftess, and Walking Bird was alive and well. But there was something about the chief's voice that made Feather Dancer fear he was telling the truth.

"You never saw Chieftess Sora at all?" Long Fin asked.

"No. My scouts said that she left your camp with Walking Bird, but before they arrived, she walked away into the trees. They tried to track her, but she was too shrewd for them. They never saw her again. I only saw Walking Bird."

Where did she go? Both White Fawn and Flint were killed during that crucial time period.

A twig cracked behind Feather Dancer, and he heard the soft hiss of a lance cutting the air.

"Get down!" Feather Dancer shoved Long Fin aside.

Blue Bow staggered, gasped, *"No, dear gods!"* and toppled to the ground.

Warriors raced forward to surround them. Copper-studded war clubs glinted like torches as they waved in the starlight.

Feather Dancer dropped to his knees to examine Blue Bow, and hot blood spurted over his chest. Blue Bow writhed on the ground, clutching his throat, trying to clamp the artery shut.

"How bad is it?" Blue Bow screamed.

The chunkey lance had lodged below his left ear, neatly slicing the big vein in his throat. They couldn't pull the lance out or it would make things worse.

"What happened?" Grown Bear shouted.

"Chief Blue Bow has been lanced through the throat."

"*Lanced?* By whom?"

"Grown Bear?" Blue Bow called. "Am I dying? Look at my wound!"

Grown Bear knelt. Surprise and outrage slackened his face as he pretended to examine the wound. The injury was clearly mortal. His chief's life drained away onto the forest floor with stunning rapidity. Through gritted teeth Grown Bear repeated, "Who did this?"

Feather Dancer rose to his feet. "Please, let's stay calm. If we are not very prudent, this will cause war between our peoples."

Long Fin gestured to their warriors. "Follow me. We must find the chief's killer!"

His men instantly obeyed, lunging into the trees behind Long Fin, their war clubs up and ready.

Grown Bear shouted to his party, "Go with them! See that the killer is brought to me unharmed. I must question him!"

For several terrible heartbeats after their warriors left, Feather Dancer and Grown Bear stared at each other without saying a word. Blue Bow had gone still, but blood continued to pump rhythmically from his wound.

Grown Bear whispered, "Was someone out there listening to your conversation?"

"Even if there was, he should have killed me first."

A weak old man was easy to kill. A wise warrior would have killed Feather Dancer first, then Blue Bow.

Grown Bear cocked his head, and the scar that bisected his face reflected the starlight like a twisting crystalline serpent. "Yes, any of my men would have killed you, then Long Fin. Which proves the murderer wanted both of you alive. What did Blue Bow tell you?"

"Very little," he carefully answered. "He was talking about what happened in your village almost a half-moon ago."

"Why would someone kill him for that? Everyone knows your chieftess tricked us—"

Long Fin cried, *"Quickly! Someone help me!"*

A cacophony of voices and cracking twigs erupted as warriors raced to his location from every part of the forest.

Feather Dancer leaped over Blue Bow and ran. Through the weave of tree trunks, he saw Long Fin kneeling near a body that lay at the edge of a starlit meadow.

"Who is it?" Feather Dancer called. "Do you recognize him?"

Long Fin answered, "It's Far Eye!"

Feather Dancer and at least ten warriors converged on the scene at the same time. He had to shoulder through the crowd to get to the body.

Far Eye lay on his back staring up at the night sky.

A pool of blood spread around his crushed skull. It looked black and shiny in the starlight.

29

FEATHER DANCER FOLLOWED LONG FIN AS HE DUCKED BE-neath the door curtain and into the Matron's House. Only two torches, one at the front and one at the rear, lit the hallway that led to Matron Wink's bedchamber.

Long Fin strode down the corridor calling, "Mother? *Mother, wake up!*"

Just as they reached the matron's chamber, she draped the curtain back on a peg and ducked into the hall. Fully dressed in a long pale purple dress covered with seed beads, she looked regal. She'd piled her graying black hair on top of her head and secured it with a shell comb. She appeared tired, as though she'd spent the past several hands of time negotiating a difficult truce. "What is it? What's wrong?"

"We were attacked," Long Fin said. "Blue Bow is dead."

Wink's lips parted in shock. "What? How? What happened?"

Long Fin shook his head. "We don't know for certain. We found Far Eye dead in a meadow a short distance from where Blue Bow was killed. He'd been clubbed in the head."

Wink glanced into her dimly lit bedchamber, and fear welled in her eyes. Someone moved in the rear.

"*I told you,*" a man's soft voice said. "Do something now, Wink, before you have no other choice."

Long Fin frowned. "Who's in there?"

He started for the door, and Wink threw out her arm to block him. "Go find Chieftess Sora. Bring her here as soon as you can."

A shadow rose in the far corner of the bedchamber, tall, lean. He was dressed in black.

Long Fin gave Feather Dancer a questioning look. "Why? What's this about?"

Wink turned to Feather Dancer. "My son apparently refuses to obey my orders. War Chief, fetch the chieftess."

"Right away, Matron." Feather Dancer sprinted for the front entry.

Wink stared at Long Fin. "Go home. Stay there. I don't want you to leave until I summon you. I'll post six guards around your house."

"But Mother, I don't understand. Why—"

"*Do as I say!*" she shouted.

Shocked, Long Fin jerked a nod, backed up, and hurried away down the hall.

QUIETLY, FROM THE DEPTHS OF HER BEDCHAMBER, HE SAID, "I've been trying to tell you for seventeen winters, Wink. How many more must die before you believe me?"

Wink turned to stare at him. He resembled nothing more than a tall dark shadow tucked into the corner. "We don't know she killed him."

"No?" he asked in an anguished voice. "This started long ago. Didn't you ever wonder why a seven-winters-old girl ate none of the stew she prepared for her father?"

Wink bowed her head for a long while before she answered,

"Yes. I did. I also wondered about her mother's death. That's why I agreed to go along with this madness when you and Skinner first came to me after White Fawn's death. Over the long winters I've wondered about many things."

His black cape billowed as he strode toward her. He had stunning midnight eyes that seemed to glow from their own inner light. "And her older sister? Didn't you think it odd—"

"That was an accident! Many people drown in rough seas."

"What about all the Traders who looked at her 'the wrong way'? You thought I killed them?"

She felt very tired. "She said you did. It made sense. You were always so jealous you couldn't bear—"

"I was jealous. But I was not stupid. The things she believed people said to her to coax her into their arms were always so bizarre, I knew they couldn't be true. But she truly believed them. So for a time, I did, too. That was my mistake."

Wink hesitated, not sure she wanted to know the answer to the question she longed to ask. She walked into her bedchamber and leaned against the wall beside the door. "Do you think she actually *heard* people say those things? That her shadow-soul created—"

"I know she heard the words. Just as I know they were never said."

Wink struggled with herself, with her loyalty to her oldest and dearest friend in the world. "All of this sounds too plausible. I have to keep reminding myself that you could still be the culprit, that she might be completely innocent of the things you accuse her of doing."

"What about the Spirit Plants, Wink? Did you think me such a fool that I would accidentally use too many on seven different occasions? I have worked with plants all my life. I studied with old Long Lance. He taught me the exact amounts to use to Heal, to send a man on a Spirit Journey, to make him appear dead for days. I would *never* use too many."

Stunned by the hushed vehemence in his voice, she whispered, "She said you were trying to find a Spirit Helper."

He turned away and for the first time was silent.

"I was," he finally said. "The gods know that's true. I loved her desperately. I wanted to Heal her. I would have done almost anything to help her, but I did not mistreat Spirit Plants. I never have."

"Are you saying that she—"

"Yes! She tried to kill me! Several times! Especially toward the end. That's why I left. I was terrified that the next time she would succeed."

Wink's heart beat a dull staccato in her chest. Across the room, the enormous image of Birdman wavered, his wings seeming to flutter with the firelit shadows. "I must hear her side."

"Don't be ridiculous. You've heard it a dozen times. She'll tell you she remembers nothing."

Wink lifted her head. "Do you think she's lying?"

"Gods, no. I believe her. Her reflection-soul isn't there when she does it, Wink. It's lost in the forest wandering around like a child. How could she remember? If you love her, you will send her to a priest who can fix her reflection-soul in her body so it will never get lost again. I—I tried. I thought if I could make her love her body, her soul would look forward to staying home."

"You failed."

"Yes," he said in a small voice. "She needs someone far more Powerful than me to Heal her. I did everything I could, Wink. I couldn't make her remember."

"Do you have a Healer in mind? Maybe Long Lance?"

"He is one possibility, but he's very old. I'm not sure he has the strength to handle her. The only Healer I know who does is Priest Strongheart. He's young. Twenty-three winters."

Wink straightened. The man was legendary. But he was one of the Loon People, the greatest Healer in Blue Bow's village. Occasionally Traders whispered about his exploits, the people he'd miraculously Healed, the villages he'd saved from meteorite strikes and hurricanes, the people who'd tried to kill him and vanished without a trace.

"Strongheart is not one of our people, and Sora would be in danger in Blue Bow's village. After tonight, there will be many Loon People who wish her dead."

"I had a long conversation with Teal. He thinks Strongheart is her only hope." In a pleading voice, he added, "Please, Wink. She needs your help. You are her best friend."

"If I must make the choice between Long Lance and Strongheart, I choose Long Lance."

He nodded. "Very well. I will send word to him. But you might wish to send a runner to Strongheart as well, in case Long Lance refuses."

"I'll do that immediately. But if Long Lance accepts, how will we get her to his village? He lives far to the north."

He took a deep breath as though to give him the courage for his next words. "I will take her."

"You?"

"Yes. I owe her that much."

Wink studied him. Conflicting emotions danced across his handsome face. "What if she won't go with you?"

"I think she will. But if not, I know the plants to make her sleep for the entire journey."

Wink leaned against the wall while she thought. The plaster felt cool and damp. "Teal wants to try one last thing. I'll make my decision after he's had his chance."

His black cape spun when he turned to pin her with his gaze. "When?"

"Tonight."

"May I be there?" he asked with trepidation, as though she might forbid him to attend.

"*You* must be there. Teal says that without your presence, it would be utterly useless."

He breathed a sigh of relief. "Give me some time to prepare myself. I haven't looked into her eyes in a long time."

Wink studied his handsome, tormented face. Bitterly, she asked, "Are you afraid you might see how much she still loves you?"

He stared at her for a long time before he whispered, "Yes. I am."

30

FEATHER DANCER RACED PAST THE GUARDS AT THE BASE OF
the Chieftess' Mound and hurried up the steps. As he neared the
men posted on either side of the front entry, he called, "Where is
the chieftess?"

Young Speaks Low stepped forward. "She hasn't passed us, War
Chief. She must be inside."

Feather Dancer ducked beneath the door curtain. As he rushed
down the hallway, he called, "Chieftess? Forgive me for disturbing
you. It's Feather Dancer."

Before he reached her bedchamber, Rockfish threw the curtain
aside and sleepily stumbled out. "What? What's wrong?"

Feather Dancer studied his matted gray hair and said, "I must
speak with the chieftess immediately. Matron Wink needs her."

Rockfish blinked the fatigue from his eyes. "Where is she?"

"Who?"

"Sora. She's not in our chamber. I was asleep. I didn't even notice she'd left."

Feather Dancer stood there breathing hard. Black thoughts welled
inside him, twisting his belly.

Far down the hall, a soft *bang* sounded, as though someone had dropped something.

"Chieftess?" he called.

No answer.

Feather Dancer marched toward the temple and jerked back the curtain. The Eternal Fire blazed, casting a magnificent crimson aura over the sacred masks on the walls. Black Falcon hung forlornly above the altar, his head bent to the side, eyes closed serenely in death.

"*War Chief?*" a woman called.

Feather Dancer squinted into the darkness to his right and saw the woman rise up. She wore the yellow sleep shirt that he'd seen the chieftess wear when she'd been ill after Skinner's death.

"Chieftess?" he called again. "Is that you?"

"No, it's me. Iron Hawk."

He strode over to her and swiftly took in her fearful expression and huddled stance, as though she expected to be beaten.

"Where is the chieftess?"

Iron Hawk wrung her hands. "I don't know, War Chief. Truly I don't! Around midnight she came into the temple, ate a little dinner, and ordered me to exchange clothes with her. She put on my dress, cape, and hat and walked right by the guards. They never notice slaves. You know that!"

The temple suddenly went still and quiet.

Nothing moved, not even the flames in the Eternal Fire. For all Feather Dancer knew, his fears might have stopped the turning of seasons.

Rockfish called, "Feather Dancer? Did you find her?"

Feather Dancer sucked in a breath. "No," he called back. *"But I will."*

He charged by Rockfish and out into the night, shouting orders to warriors as he ran.

Men leaped to follow him.

31

THUNDERBIRDS CRACKED, AND EERIE LUMINESCENT FLASHES blasted the rainy night sky. The roar that followed seemed to shake the entire world.

Sora lunged through the downpour with branches raking her arms and face. She'd awakened alone in the dark forest with the Midnight Fox trembling her limbs. When she'd been able to rise to her feet, she'd started running wildly through the forest, trying to find her way home. Exhaustion weighted her feet like granite leggings. To her right, warriors scurried along the lake trail. Blackbird Town was in an uproar. Almost every house was lit. She kept hearing shouts.

Something dire has happened.

Feather Dancer and several warriors had raced by her about a hand of time ago. She'd called out, but with the constant growls of Thunderbirds, they hadn't heard her. To make matters worse, her woven bark cape and hat blended with the night, making her virtually invisible.

Teal's mound stood less than one hundred paces away. If she could just make it there, he would tell her everything.

His house looked dark. But he must be awake. How could he not be awake with all the noise that filled Blackbird Town?

She trotted up the mound steps in such a rush she barely noticed the line of colored sand that coiled around the house like an enormous snake. The sand broke in front of Teal's doorway, leaving a gap between the snake's head and tail.

Sora passed through the gap, calling, "Teal? It's Sora. May I speak with you?"

While she waited for him to answer, she ducked beneath the overhanging roof and gazed out at the shifting veils of rain that drenched Persimmon Lake.

The last thing she remembered was exchanging clothes with Iron Hawk so that she could go out and meet Far Eye one last time to make sure Flint's soul was not inside him. Everything after that was a blank.

She squinted up at the clouds. No stars were visible. How long had she run aimlessly through the storm? Wink must be worried sick about her. And Rockfish—*if he was Rockfish*—would be frantic, fearing the worst.

"Teal?" she called louder.

A muffled voice responded, "What? Who's there?"

"It's Sora. May I speak with you?"

Sleepily, as though he'd just woken, he said, "Just a moment."

Fabric rustled; then she heard him let out a long, tired sigh. "Please enter, Chieftess."

Sora ducked under the hanging. The fire had burned down to coals. A faint red gleam tinted the air above the fire pit. She could see a tea cup on one of the hearthstones, but the rest of the chamber was very dark.

"Teal? Where are you?"

Drenched and cold, she shivered as she searched the darkness.

Something moved straight ahead of her where the doorway to the charnel chamber stood.

A faint glow outlined the curtain.

"Teal?"

"I'll be right out. I'm conversing with the dead. They've been calling to me all night."

She tilted her head inquiringly. "Why? What's wrong?"

The curtain lifted, and a pale rectangle of light splashed across the floor. He stood like a frail skeleton in the doorway. He had a cup in his hand. When he let the curtain fall closed behind him, the house sank into darkness again.

He carefully walked across the floor. She heard his steps approach. A bitter scent rose as he lifted the cup and put it in her hand. "Drink this," he ordered. "You're shivering. It's hot tea."

Sora clutched the cup. The warmth penetrated the pottery, seeping into her hand. It felt good. "Teal, what's happening in Blackbird Town? People are running everywhere. Warriors fill the trails around the lake. Did we receive news that we're about to be attacked?"

"No, Chieftess," he answered in a gentle old voice. "Please, sit here on the mats by the fire. Drink your tea and I'll tell you everything."

Sora sat down cross-legged on the closest mat. A few coals gleamed redly beneath the white bed of ash. She sipped the tea. It had an acrid flavor, but it was warm. She took another long drink.

Teal pulled a blanket from his sleeping bench and wrapped it around his bony shoulders. "Where were you tonight? We've had people out searching for four hands of time."

"Four?" she said in surprise. "I've been gone for four hands of time?"

"As near as we can tell. Iron Hawk said you exchanged clothes with her around midnight."

"Yes, I did. I had to get past the guards, to see Far Eye. That's the last thing I remember."

The crimson glow in front of her started to eddy. Like mist touched by a cool autumn breeze, it swirled and spun into eerie shapes. "Why are people racing around Blackbird Town, Teal?"

"Feather Dancer and young Long Fin went out tonight to meet Chief Blue Bow and his party."

"Yes. I knew he was arriving tonight. What happened?"

Teal sighed. "Blue Bow was lanced through the throat. He's dead."

Scattered images flickered across her souls, things she thought she remembered, but faintly: *a shining copper breastplate . . . warriors calling insults . . . Far Eye's muted laughter.*

Teal asked, "You have a strange expression, Chieftess. Have you already heard this news?"

Such hope filled his voice that he seemed to deflate when she answered, "No. No, I haven't. Where are Blue Bow's warriors? Did we take them captive to keep them from attacking us in revenge?"

He shook his bald head. "Long Fin let them go. They are on their way home."

Sora felt suddenly sick to her stomach. Grown Bear would never just leave. He couldn't. If he arrived home and told his people that Blue Bow had been murdered and he'd done nothing, they would flay the skin from his living body and string it in the trees as decorations.

The room shifted suddenly, the colors melting, flowing into each other in a watery blur of red, black, and deep amber. She grabbed for the floor to steady herself and peered down into her tea cup. The ghostly presence of a Spirit Plant seeped through her.

"Teal? What's in this tea?"

"It's all right. Don't worry. I'm here. I'm not going to leave you."

"It tastes like a mixture of . . . nightshade seeds . . . and ground nuts." Flint had schooled her way in the flavors of Spirit Plants. "Is that what you gave me?"

My vision blurs, then . . .

I see them.

Though I know it must be the curtain to the charnel chamber, they seem to emerge from a long black corridor, a tunnel plunging into the heart of Grandmother Earth, into Spirit Worlds I have never seen and never longed to see. As they bob across the floor like swamp lights, eyes wink and glint. The hissing of their sandals uncoils like a huge lazy serpent.

"Don't be afraid," Teal says.

"What are you doing to me?"

"Nothing bad. Everyone here cares very much about you."

Sora blinked at the phantoms. Their fingers and toes seemed tipped with tiny balls of flame.

As they encircled her, a glittering swarm of sparks flitted across her vision. She almost cried out when she saw, a hand's breadth from her face, the blinding features of a man, his black eyes bulging from their sockets in fear or hatred. Beneath those eyes, full lips smiled.

"Remember me?" he asked.

"No. Who are you?"

"I am White Fawn's father. I walked at the head of the marriage procession." He knelt and spread a beautifully beaded headdress at her side: a wedding headdress.

The polished bone and shell beads shimmered.

"Why are you giving me this?"

He backed away, and Rockfish slipped from the shadows. He had his jaw clenched, as though he did not wish to participate in this charade, but had no choice. He leaned down and whispered, "I know you didn't do these things. If you were the person they imagine, you would have tried to kill me as well. No matter what you've done, I love you with all my souls."

She searched his eyes, trying to determine if it truly was Rockfish looking out at her.

He placed a copper bracelet in her lap.

She touched it. "This was my mother's. Where did you get it?"

He must have gone through my big black-and-red basket, through all of my personal things.

Rockfish sank back into the shadows, and a short burly man came forward. She knew him instantly. War Chief Grown Bear. He hadn't gone home, after all. He rested a magnificent copper breastplate at her feet. "He wanted nothing but peace, Chieftess. He'd planned to give you this himself."

The breastplate looked molten in the fire's gleam. She had vague memories of having seen it before.

As Grown Bear stepped back, Sea Grass marched from the darkness, her withered mouth pinched in hatred, and placed a bundle of cleaned human bones at Sora's feet. Skinner's bones.

"I have only just learned that my son agreed to this because he wanted to help you. He loved you, and you killed him."

As if her body were not her own, her legs trembled and jerked, and for a horrifying instant she feared the Midnight Fox had returned. Then she watched a thin crystalline serpent move up her thigh, to her belly, where a fiery tongue flicked out to taste the drops of blood on her cape.

Sea Grass pointed to the drops. "Whose blood is this, Chieftess?"

"I—I don't know," she whispered.

"Weren't you with someone tonight?"

"I was with Rockfish." She looked at his black form standing on the far side of the chamber. "He went to sleep. I sneaked past the guards to see Far Eye."

"Why did you need to see Far Eye?"

"I—I thought Flint's soul was living inside him," she cautiously answered. "I wanted to see Flint before he had to go to the Land of the Dead."

"Did you see him?"

"No. I looked. I couldn't find Far Eye."

Sea Grass glanced at Teal. The old priest just motioned for her to continue with her questions. Sea Grass said, "Then what happened?"

"I took a walk in the forest, out toward the burned-out tree. I thought he might be waiting for me there."

The strange sensation of teeth against her neck made her whirl around. In the far corner, dark eyes stared at her, wet and glistening.

"Who's there?"

He looked at her so steadily she felt as if she were gazing into the dark heart of the world.

Just above a whisper, he said, "You know who I am. I once believed you had known me before I was born, known my souls before they came to inhabit my body."

A blurry image of a tall man with long black hair formed. But she didn't need to see him to know who he was. She would recognize his deep voice a thousand winters from now in the Land of the Dead.

She stammered, "*F-Flint!* They told me you were dead!" Relief and gratitude swelled to such overpowering proportions inside her, she longed to weep.

Angrily, Sea Grass said, "I also thought he was dead."

"I drank a potion that made me appear dead, Matron."

"Why did you do that?" Sora pleaded. "I was crazy with grief!"

Flint came forward, placed Far Eye's conch shell pendant on top of the copper breastplate, then swiftly gathered her in his arms in a tight embrace. "It's all right, Sora. I'm here."

Her body relaxed in a way that it had not in three long winters. It felt so comforting to be held by him; for he knew her, inside and out, good and bad . . . and still loved her.

Teal began the sacred Song:

A long way to go,
A long way to climb,
A long way to Skyholder's arms . . .

Flint and Grown Bear picked up the words; their voices added a haunting resonance:

But no evil can enter that embrace.
Skyholder, never let our chieftess go.
Keep her close to your heart,

As we will. Always.
We will keep Chieftess Sora close to our hearts
And no evil will enter her.

Her gaze dropped to the gifts, and she sucked in a sudden breath. "You think that I . . ." The words lodged in her throat.

As though waking from a long dreadful sleep, comprehension seeped into her, and she felt more alive than she had ever felt.

Blessed gods, this is a Healing Circle.

Sora tore her eyes away from the gifts and looked at Teal. He'd bowed his head in reverence. Or perhaps shame.

"Teal, why am I here?"

"You know why."

She shook her head at the outrageous notion. "You think *I* killed these people? White Fawn and Blue Bow? Far Eye?"

"You did, Sora," Flint said tenderly.

"That's ridiculous." She tried to rise again, but he pushed her back to the floor and roughly took her face in his hands.

"You did it," he said slowly, as though speaking to a child who might not understand. "Just like you killed your father."

Her gaze darted around the chamber. Did everyone know? Had he revealed her darkest secrets to these people?

. . . As Skinner had said he would.

"It was an accident. I didn't mean to."

"What about your sister?"

"That was an accident, too! The ocean grew rough. Our canoe overturned."

"Did your mother really fall, or did you push her?"

"She stumbled! There was nothing I could do! She rolled over and over until she slammed into a tree at the bottom of the bluff. I tried to get to her in time, but her neck was broken!"

Flint stared hard into her eyes. "Please. Try to remember. You must remember, or we can't help you."

"I don't know what you're talking about!"

From the shadows, Teal asked, "Chieftess, what happened with Far Eye and Blue Bow tonight?"

"I didn't see either of them tonight! I was lost in the forest, running wildly, I . . ."

She halted. Everyone was staring at her.

"Wh-what are you saying? That it was my reflection-soul that was lost? That's why I don't remember doing these terrible things? My reflection-soul was out wandering the forest while my shadow-soul murdered two people?"

Is it possible? I often dream of being lost in the forest, of running and running.

Flint said, "Sora, always before when I found you wandering alone after someone died, you recalled bits and pieces of the event. Strange images that made no sense."

A copper breastplate . . . warriors calling insults . . . Far Eye's muted laughter.

Dear gods, is it possible? Does a murderer sleep in me?

Frightened now, really frightened, she shouted, "I don't remember anything except being lost in the forest!"

"Don't you understand?" Flint asked. "You're sick. After you killed White Fawn, I knew I had to try one more time to Heal you, but I didn't have the strength to do it myself. I truly loved her, Sora. Skinner agreed to pretend to be me. I used to be able to bring your reflection-soul home and keep it in your body for moons at a time. He was trying to bring it home so we could talk with it, maybe show it what happens when it roams the forests. But you killed him. Then my kinsman, Far Eye, agreed to try. But you killed him, too. We thought if we could bring your soul home we could convince it never to leave again, but—"

"You're insane! I've *never* murdered *anyone*!"

Teal slashed the air with his frail old hand. Everyone turned to look at him. "This is over. We know what we need to. She remembers nothing."

"That's right! I remember nothing, because I did *nothing*!"

Flint bowed his head in despair. "We think we've found a priest powerful enough to fasten your reflection-soul to your body, Sora. We're going to try one last time, before . . ."

He couldn't finish. A hard swallow went down his throat.

Before they order my death.

She looked around. There was only one person missing. The person she most trusted.

She called, "Where's my good friend, Wink? Didn't she have the courage to face me with these accusations? I demand to see our matron! Now!"

Light filled the room as the curtain to the charnel chamber was drawn aside.

Wink's dress appeared violet in the dim light. The shell comb that held her graying black hair on top of her head flashed as she hooked the curtain back on its peg.

"I'm here, Sora."

"So," she said coldly. "The traitor appears at last. What other surprises do you and Rockfish and Flint have waiting for me, Wink?"

Wink replied, "Sora, please don't say such things. We're trying very hard to help you."

"Yes, we are," Rockfish echoed.

One by one, they all stepped forward, linked hands, and knelt.

Wink said, "I love you, Sora. I would never hurt you. I want only for you to get well."

Rockfish said, "As do I."

Flint was the last. He reached out and clutched her wrists, as though to keep her from striking him. "I love you more than anyone else here, Sora. You know I do."

"You love me," she scoffed. "You're all trying to bring about my downfall! Why, Wink? So you can put your son in my place? Why don't you just kill me?"

Pain lined Wink's face. She turned to Flint, as if expecting him to answer that question.

Flint leaned very close to her ear and whispered, "Please go along with this, Sora. There is more at stake here than you can possibly realize."

Something in his expression told Sora he was straining against a weight almost too heavy to bear. "What do you mean? What's at stake?"

Flint subtly shook his head, as though he didn't want anyone else in the room to overhear them.

Wink softly ordered, "Give her the sleeping potion. Then take her to the council chamber in my house. We must prepare her for the journey."

"What journey?" Sora cried.

Teal knelt by the hearth and lifted the cup that sat on the largest hearthstone. As he brought it toward her, Grown Bear and Skinner grabbed Sora's arms. Flint cranked her mouth open.

She screamed, "No! *NO!*"

Teal poured the acrid brew down her throat, and Flint clamped her jaws shut before she could spit it out.

She struggled against them, but it did no good. There were three of them, and they were much stronger than she.

Finally, she had to swallow. The potion burned a bitter path all the way to her belly.

Flint whispered, "We're going to take you to someone who can Heal you. I give you my oath."

32

A QUEER, FRIGHTENING SENSATION POSSESSED HER AS THEY carried her limp body through the cold rainy night to Wink's house and lowered her onto a litter beside the fire. The litter, made of sapling poles and padded with a buffalohide, felt soothing against her frigid skin. Wink had obviously had the litter prepared in advance. Folded blankets rested near the hearthstones, keeping warm. She must have had this planned all along.

Teal's hoarse old voice intruded into her thoughts: "Flint tells me you have chosen Long Lance to Heal her. What if he refuses?"

Wink answered, "We must offer him so much that he cannot refuse."

"Wealth is of little concern to an old man, Matron. He will be far more worried about the consequences if he fails."

"What do you mean?"

"Well"—Teal's feet shuffled across the floor as though he was moving closer to her—"he knows he must succeed. She is the high chieftess of the Black Falcon Nation. That means he has to use every Spirit Plant and technique he knows to try to Heal her. He cannot fail. Do you understand?"

Sora's eyes fluttered open. The despair on Wink's face told her that Long Lance would have no choice but to give her more and more potions until he either Healed her, or killed her.

Wink whispered, "Yes, I understand."

As if a deathly chill had seeped into her body, Sora shivered and wept.

A hand, large but very gentle, brushed the tears from her cheeks, and Flint murmured, "Don't cry, Sora. He won't fail. I won't let him fail."

His lips pressed against her temple, and she felt herself sinking into a deep, dark sleep from which she would not awaken for days.

The last words to penetrate the blackness came from Wink. They were soft and strained:

"Dear gods, I've betrayed her. I've betrayed her."

Sora did not know whether it was the Spirit Plant leaping through her veins, or the overwhelming feeling that she was being manipulated into madness, but laughter suddenly bubbled up her throat. The mirth was followed by a rage more powerful than any emotion she had ever known.

The chamber went dark and deathly quiet.

EPILOGUE

"FORGIVE ME, I DIDN'T HEAR YOU. I WAS LOST IN MEMORIES OF things that happened over a moon ago. What did you ask?

". . . No, I had seen seven winters. I discovered him a few days after my father's death. You see, he glittered. When I looked more closely, I noticed that he resembled an animal lying curled on a dark forest floor. A midnight-colored fox, I thought. I could just make out his shape, but I was entranced by his sheer size. How could an animal that big live behind my eyes?

"In time I learned that he was not merely darkness.

"He was a darkness that saw. That spoke.

"And he was just a baby.

"He would grow.

"As I would.

". . . No, don't touch me, Priest. I'm all right. I just can't help shaking when I remember.

". . . Yes, of course, Flint tried. He thought he could kill the Fox. Then one night he woke to find the Fox staring down at him from my eyes. I was very happy. I knew that he must finally understand."

The ache inside me becomes too much, and I drop my face into my hands.

"... But it's perfectly clear. How can you not understand?"

I massage my temples while I listen to his soft voice.

"... Yes, I agree that killing is a kind of mourning, but I killed no one. If murder was done, it was done by the Fox."

I lift my head to peer at him.

"... Who am I mourning? I'm not mourning, I ..."

The words die in my throat.

I sit back on the buffalohide and stare up at the Star People who spread across the night sky like a great dark blanket covered with sunlit seashells.

... Am I?

NONFICTION AFTERWORD

Four miles north of Tallahassee, Florida, in the lush oak and gum forests, sits the Lake Jackson Mounds State Archaeological Site. During the fifteenth century this site was the heart of one of the most powerful political entities in North America. Part of the grand "Mississippian Culture" that spanned the eastern half of the continent, the Lake Jackson site consists of seven earthen mounds. Six of these are pyramidal, flat-topped mounds. One is round. The largest mound, Mound 2 (the Chieftess' Mound in this book), measures 270 feet by 300 feet along its rectangular base and stands 36 feet (11 meters) high. The other mounds vary from 3 to 16 feet in height. Radiocarbon dates taken during the excavation of Mound 3 indicate the cultural florescence of the town occurred between A.D. 1250 and A.D. 1500, but the site was inhabited as early as A.D. 1050.

The total polity population—that is, the number of people who lived at Lake Jackson phase sites (called the Black Falcon Nation here)—was probably around twenty thousand. Most of these people lived in dispersed villages, hamlets, and farmsteads that stretched from the Ochlockonee River on the west, to the Aucilla River on the east, and north to just across the Georgia border.

They were an agricultural society, primarily raising corn, beans, and sunflowers; but they also relied heavily on hunting, fishing, and collecting foods like hickory nuts, acorns, persimmons, maypop, wild cherry, plums, saw palmetto and cabbage palm seeds, and chinquapin. The bones of deer, turkey, squirrel, various birds, and a wide variety of fish, turtles, and shellfish are common to Lake Jackson phase sites.

We know little about their houses, except that some were circular, others rectangular. They probably had winter and summer houses. The winter homes may have been made of wood and thatch. The summer homes were probably little more than ramadas, upright poles set in the ground and roofed. Though wattle and daub impressions were found at the Lake Jackson site, these were associated with an elite building. There's no evidence to indicate that ordinary villagers went to the trouble of "plastering" their homes.

The Lake Jackson site acted as the capital, the locus of governmental and ceremonial activities for the people it served. We also know it was the residence of the high chief or chieftess, his or her family, and political associates.

High chiefs like the ruler of the Lake Jackson site governed the surrounding villages and controlled the redistribution of goods. The chief received "tribute," a sort of tax, from outlying villagers in the form of raw goods: shells, pearls, tool stone, rabbits, venison, feather cloaks, buffalohides, etc. In return, the high chiefs gave village chiefs protection when their villages were in danger and food when they were hungry.

The status of elite individuals was reflected in the way they were buried. The higher one's rank in the society, the more prestige goods were included in the grave. A person of high nobility was buried in a tomb dug into the floor of a building erected on one of the pyramidal mounds and was covered with opulent goods like an engraved copper breastplate, hundreds of pearls and marine shell beads, a headdress and cape of rare feathers. The array of objects is extraordinary: arrow points, T-shaped steatite pipes, limestone bowls, elbow pipes, lizard effigy pipes, pottery vessels, paint palettes stained with red ochre, lumps of yellow ochre and graphite, stone axes, a galena-backed mica mirror, a shark jaw knife, and numerous stone "discoidals." Discoidals are stone discs, concave on both sides, that we believe were used in a game called "chunkey," which was played by historical southeastern tribes. The chunkey stone was rolled across the field and a spear thrown at it. Whoever hit the stone, or came closest, earned a point.

Some floors had more than one burial. Mound 3 contained twenty-four floor burials. A dog was also found in a floor tomb, probably a beloved pet.

Other high-ranking individuals may have had their bones cleaned, then stored in charnel houses on the mounds, overseen by priests and priestesses.

Commoners were buried in cemeteries, two of which have been excavated and that contained about one hundred people each. The bodies were either in flexed or extended positions, or grouped in mass graves. Burials have also been found in trash middens or fire pits. A few burial mounds are known in the region—that is, mounds dedicated to the dead, rather than pyramidal mounds with burials—but they are not common.

Many of the burial goods were fashioned from materials not native to Florida: copper, lead, mica, anthracite, graphite, steatite, greenstone. This is not surprising. One of the most important ways Mississippian chieftains maintained their status was through an elaborate trade network that crisscrossed the continent. The artifacts that distinguish these elite goods at the Lake Jackson site include copper, shell, and stone items. Several are weapons, elaborate headdresses, carved shell gorgets, and copper plates. They also exchanged practical items: shell cups, ceramic beakers and bottles, and pipes and pins decorated with the images of crested birds, among other things. In receipt for these elite goods, the Mississippian rulers at the Lake Jackson site probably traded marine shell beads, pearls, shark's teeth, and holly leaves (*Ilex vomitoria*), used to make sacred "Black Drink," a high-caffeine drink used in religious ceremonies.

We know that for some reason their trade routes were disrupted at around A.D. 1400—the number and type of prestige goods drops suddenly. Was it warfare?

In the sixteenth century, the chiefdom was respected and feared. Ethno-historical documentation exists that demonstrates violent factional competition between members of the nobility—which means the answer is probably yes. Warfare is well documented across the Mississippian world, as those of you who read *People of the River* know.

The artwork tells us a great deal about what they wore, believed, made, and what kind of activities they engaged in. A number of copper plates were recovered during the Mound 3 excavations. Four were found lying on the chests of elite individuals. Each was made from copper nuggets, cold-hammered into thin sheets, riveted together, then embossed by the hand of a master artist. One plate, measuring ten by twenty inches, shows a dancing Birdman in profile. Birdman—a half-human, half-bird figure—is common in the Mississippian world. In this particular plate he holds a ceremonial baton in one hand and a severed human head in the other. A waist pouch is suspended from his belt. He wears a feather cape and headdress, earspools, a busycon shell pendant, beaded anklets, bracelets, and has shoulder tattoos. Another copper plate, 6 inches wide by 21 inches high, shows Birdman from a full frontal view. This is a curious figure because he appears to be in a state of decomposition. Part of the face is fleshed, the other part skull. He wears a feathered headdress and cloak, but the cloak seems to be wrapped around him, in the same way cloaks were in burials. Another elite individual found in Mound 3 had five cutout copper plates with him, each depicting falcon figures. Peregrine Falcon and his forked eye motif fill Mississippian religious art.

From the study of historical southeastern tribes we suspect the chieftainship was a hereditary position. They were matrilineal, meaning they traced descent through the female only, but generally passed on leadership positions to sons. However, if there were no sons, daughters ascended to the position of chieftess. Daughters remained in the villages where they were born. Sons, except for those who would become chiefs, went to live in their wives' villages. In the case of divorce, women generally retained the house, land, and custody of the children. Adultery was frowned upon. Especially among the elite, couples were expected to be faithful. If caught in adultery, the man or woman was likely to be beaten by his or her spouse's relatives and mutilated with a knife, or declared Outcast and banished.

Marriage negotiations were handled strictly between women. Fathers, not being blood relatives, were not formally consulted, though they might be told about marriage considerations out of politeness.

The cosmos of southeastern peoples consisted of three worlds: an Upper World in the sky, This World on the surface of the earth, and an Under World beneath the surface. The Upper World was a place of purity and grandeur; it represented order. The Under World was chaotic. This World vacillated between the two. It was the duty of human beings to strive for harmony and balance. As with Birdman, historical southeastern tribes had a variety of sacred creatures that combined elements of all three worlds: serpents with human faces and wings, deer with talons and snakeskin, cougars with fishlike tails and falcon eyes. These creatures seem to have been able to traverse all three worlds to speak with the sacred beings that lived there.

The southeastern tribes had interesting concepts of justice, particularly relating to what we would call "murder." In the strictest sense, they did not believe in murder. Intent was not a consideration. If one person caused the death of another, whether it was accidental or intentional, he was liable for that death. The offended clan had the right to take the life of the killer in retaliation, or one of his relatives could be killed in his place. Killing a member of your own clan was the worst crime a person could commit. The killer was generally put to death, but if his clan decided they needed the person, he or she could be forgiven, or another person killed in his place to satisfy the family. A mother had the right to kill her own child until it was a month old. But if the father, being from a different clan, killed that same child he would be held responsible for that death under the law of retaliation, and he or one of his relatives might be put to death (Hudson, p. 231).

It Sleeps in Me is set at about A.D. 1400, the peak of power for the

Lake Jackson rulers, and explores a subject I've barely touched in my previous novels: the sexual side of healing rituals among pre-historic societies. These rituals are fabulously colorful and fascinating. One of the most spectacular was the *andacwander* among the Huron tribe. During this ceremony the unmarried young people of the village assembled in the sick person's house and, while two priests shook rattles and sang, engaged in sexual intercourse while the sick person watched. Oftentimes, the patient joined the ritual. When Jesuit missionaries arrived in the seventeenth century they were so appalled by this healing ritual they were loath even to mention it (Trigger, p. 83).

What the Jesuits failed to understand was that to the Huron illness was largely caused by unfulfilled desires of the soul, which if left unattended could result in death. The *andacwander,* and similar soul-curing rituals that went against the basic moral teachings of the tribe, demonstrated the extent to which the Huron would go to heal their sick relatives.

While many people in modern western cultures look at this idea with a jaundiced eye, you must understand that to the Huron, our sexuality, our fruitfulness, indeed our very creativity itself were the heart of a truly spiritual life.

Of course sexual energy had healing powers.

In the next book in this series, *It Wakes in Me,* we'll explore this subject more thoroughly.

SELECTED BIBLIOGRAPHY

Davis, Dave D., *Perspectives on Gulf Coast Prehistory*. Gainesville: University Press of Florida/Florida State Museum, 1984.

Gilliland, Marion Spjut, *The Material Culture of Key Marco, Florida*. Port Salerno: Florida Classics Library, 1989.

Hudson, Charles, *The Southeastern Indians*. Knoxville: University of Tennessee Press, 1989.

Kilpatrick, Jack Frederick, and Kilpatrick, Anna Gritts, *Walk in Your Soul: Love Incantations of the Oklahoma Cherokees*. Dallas: Southern Methodist University, 1965.

———, *Run Toward the Nightland. Magic of the Oklahoma Cherokees*. Dallas: Southern Methodist University, 1967.

———, *Notebook of a Cherokee Shaman*. Smithsonian Contributions to Anthropology, Vol. 2, Number 6. Washington, D.C.: Smithsonian Institution Press, 1970.

Lewis, Barry, and Stout, Charles, eds., *Mississippian Towns and Sacred Spaces: Searching for an Architectural Grammar*. Tuscaloosa: University of Alabama Press, 1998.

McEwan, Bonnie G., *Indians of the Greater Southeast: Historical Archaeology and Ethnohistory*. Gainesville: University Press of Florida, 2000.

Milanich, Jerald T., *McKeithen Weeden Island: The Culture of Northern Florida, A.D. 200–900*. New York: Academic Press, 1984.

———, *Archaeology of Precolumbian Florida*. Gainesville: University Press of Florida, 1994.

——— *Florida Indians and the Invasion from Europe*. Gainesville: University Press of Florida, 1995.

——— *The Timucua*. Oxford: Blackwell Publishers, 1996.

Milanich, Jerald T., and Hudson, Charles, *Hernando de Soto and the Indians of Florida*. Gainesville: University Press of Florida, 1993.

Neitzel, Jill E., *Great Towns and Regional Polities in the Prehistoric American Southwest and Southeast*. Albuquerque: University of New Mexico Press, 1999.

Purdy, Barbara, A., *The Art and Archaeology of Florida's Wetlands*. Boca Raton: CRC Press, 1991.

Sears, William H., *Fort Center: An Archaeological Site in the Lake Okeechobee Basin*. Gainesville: University of Florida Press, 1994.

Swanton, John R., *The Indians of the Southeastern United States*. Washington, D.C.: Smithsonian Institution Press, 1987.

Trigger, Bruce G., *The Children of Aataentsic. A History of the Huron People to 1660*. Kingston: McGill-Queen's University Press, 1987.

Walthall, John A. *Prehistoric Indians of the Southeast: Archaeology of Alabama and the Middle South*. Tuscaloosa: University of Alabama Press, 1990.

Willey, Gordon R., *Archaeology of the Florida Gulf Coast*. Gainesville: University of Florida Press, 1949.